The Accidental Sheriff

Also by Ron Schwab

The Accidental Sheriff

Ron Schwab

Uplands Press

OMAHA, NEBRASKA

Uplands Press
1401 S 64th Avenue
Omaha, NE 68106
www.uplandspress.com

Publisher's Note: This is a work of fiction. Names, characters, places, and incidents are a product of the author's imagination. Locales and public names are sometimes used for atmospheric purposes. Any resemblance to actual people, living or dead, or to businesses, companies, events, institutions, or locales is completely coincidental.

Ordering Information:
Quantity sales. Special discounts are available on quantity purchases by corporations, associations, and others. For details, contact the "Special Sales Department" at the address above.

Uplands Press / Ron Schwab -- 1st ed.

ISBN 978-1-943421-60-2

Preface

THE JOHNNY REB who faced me with bayonet fixed would not have been older than my own eighteen years. I could nail a target with my Sharps rifle better than any man in the company, and Sergeant Locke generally called on me first for sniper duties. I liked that, didn't like close-up killing where you could see the man's eyes and knew this was a human with a mother, maybe a wife and children, you were trying to put down.

I would have killed him if I could, but my cartridges and fixings were used up and my own bayonet was lying somewhere in the dirt downslope on Cemetery Ridge. I had converted my rifle to a club as we continued to hold our spot on the hill. Sarge must have killed a dozen men with his own bayonet and that many more with a dead Confederate officer's sword he picked up. He was crazed, a madman, as we fought off the attackers swarming the hill. There had been thirty from our company when we dug in to defend the ridge, but Captain Dawson had gone down early on, and Sergeant Locke took over. We were down to four of us now, and I expected to die that day.

Strangely, I did not fear death at that moment. It was the knife coming for me that had me swinging that rifle, causing my blood to run cold. *A lead slug in the brain, please,* I prayed. That would do fine. Nobody was listening, and the Reb dodged my rifle swing and plunged the bayonet into the flesh just below my collar bone. The pain was excruciating when he twisted the blade some and pushed harder until the blade was stopped abruptly by my shoulder blade. I fell backward, and the bayonet slid out, but the soldier stood above me now raising the rifle for a fatal thrust. I tried to scream but my voice refused to come forth. Then my adversary was struck across the neck, nearly decapitated by Sergeant Locke's sweeping sword before he fell away, and a black curtain fell over my eyes.

I awakened then and sat up in bed, my undershorts and sheets drenched with sweat. I hoped I had not awakened occupants of other rooms with my moaning. The nightmare had taken a furlough for a few weeks, but it had been a reliable visitor for over twenty-one years now. This was March of 1885. I would turn forty May 15th, and the twenty-second anniversary of the Battle of Gettysburg would occur the first several days of July.

I rubbed the knotted scar below the front of my left shoulder, faded some by time, but ever-present to remind me of that afternoon. Four of the Eighth Ohio Infantry soldiers assigned to Cemetery Ridge that day survived, three wounded sufficiently to warrant discharge. All were decorated, but Sergeant Ian Locke, who saved my life and incurred not the slightest scratch, was awarded the Medal of Honor. He was only three or four years older than I, but there is no man I have admired more. He fought until after the surrender agreement was signed by Grant and Lee at Appomattox on April 9, 1865. Ian Locke was a brevet major when the war ended.

It was still dark, but I sensed that sunrise was not far away, so I lit the kerosene lamp and looked at my timepiece on the lamp table and confirmed that light would appear in a half hour or less. I swung my legs out of bed, got dressed and went downstairs to claim an early entrance to one of the outdoor privies. Afterward, I used the bowl and pitcher of water in the bedroom to shave and wash up. Baths were available in a room to the rear of the boarding house but only after five o'clock. Fortunately, I had finagled one of the tubs the previous night.

This would be my last night at the boarding house in Portsmouth, Ohio. I had spent more than a year during my most recent visit here in the town at the confluence of the Ohio and Scioto rivers where I had been raised and my sister Alice lived with her family. I was departing on the noon train headed to an undetermined destination west, but first a stop in the southeastern Nebraska town of Borderview, where my former sergeant, Ian Locke, practiced law with his wife.

However, first, I must face Alice. The things that mattered to me were already collected in two trunks, which I delivered to the train station yesterday. I notified my landlord two weeks earlier that I would be vacating my room, and I would settle with her after breakfast downstairs. Alice's home was an easy walk from the boarding house, and I chastised myself now for the terrible coward I had been for not telling Alice of my plans. What was there to say when a man floats his boat without a rudder? But I would be starting a new decade in another few months, time for a man with my checkered history to start a new chapter.

Grant Coolidge, also known as P.J. Bowie and Jake West, must try again to outrun his past, including the two former wives who still resided in Portsmouth.

Chapter 1

ALICE COOLIDGE BOND, at age forty-five was a striking woman who shared Grant's chestnut-brown hair and hazel eyes. Grant loved his sister, but she was a bossy sort and sometimes treated him as a child. Of course, he conceded that his behavior sometimes had not reflected much maturity. She eyed him suspiciously from the other side of the tea table as he sipped dutifully at his tea.

"This is a strange time of day for you to show up," Alice said. "What are you up to?"

He sighed. "I am leaving Portsmouth. Today."

Her brow furrowed. "Where are you going?"

"West."

"West. That leaves a bit of territory, I should say."

"I won't know till I get there. I will write and let you know where I am at. With the transcontinental railroad

{5}

system, nothing is all that far away these days. I can return for visits. You could even come visit me. Bring Arthur and the kids."

"You need to think about this."

"I have been. I've decided."

"What about your books?"

"I can write those from anyplace. I wrote to Erastus Beadle about my plans, and he replied and said he thought it was a wonderful idea, that I could possibly add some authenticity to my stories. Beadle saw it as an opportunity to dig up something new. He wants a P.J. Bowie novel every other month and a Jake West on the alternate months."

His West novels featured historical characters such as Buffalo Bill Cody, Wild Bill Hickock, Kit Carson, Davy Crockett and many others, written with no particular concern for historical accuracy. The Bowie books' protagonists were his own creation, the most popular featuring U.S. Marshal Buck Tyree, who had an obligatory, chaste romance in every novel and gunned down at least a half dozen outlaws per book.

"You have never been west of the Mississippi as near as I know," Alice said. "There are savages out there, and a crude, uncivilized people occupy that country."

"Peace has been made with the tribes, and most folks out west have roots in the east. There is no reason they should be that much different. Who knows? They might even be better people," he said, doubting those words. "Anyway, I served in the war, Alice, and I grew up here and rode and walked a lot of the rugged country south across the Ohio River into Kentucky."

Alice said, "And some woman is bound to set her cap for you, and you will add another failed marriage to your list—or catch some disease. Worse yet, you will take up drinking again like that Ned Buntline."

"I haven't had a drink in almost ten years. As for Ned Buntline, he is one of the two or three best-selling dime novelists of all time and has six wives to his credit. I've got some catching up to do. Maybe it's an occupational hazard. Ned's made a good amount of money, and I wouldn't have got in the business without his encouragement. I have told you, haven't I, that Ned's real name is Edward Zane Carroll Judson?"

"Yes. Sometimes, I wish you had not met that man. He has been a bad influence on you."

"He got me on the way to writing almost forty books and making a decent living at it. And Beadle and Company will send me a new contract when I get settled in someplace. Erastus has cleared it with his brother, Irwin, and promises to increase payments over what I'm making now. I will not come close to matching your husband's income, but I won't go hungry. And I have set aside some money at the Portsmouth State Bank to tide me over a spell and get me resettled someplace. I don't intend to be a wanderer once I sink roots."

"I'm hurt and angry you didn't tell me you were thinking of doing this. I just don't see why you can't buy a little house and do your work in Portsmouth."

"I have had two homes here. Suzette and Phoebe each have one. Phoebe's new husband shares hers, and Suzette doesn't have many lonely nights, I am betting."

"That's a terrible thing to say. Suzette is sweet. I liked her better than Phoebe."

"You didn't live with her. I didn't do right by Phoebe, and I hope she's happy. She deserves it."

"She is with child, you know. She should have had your child."

"I know she is with child. This is at least the fourth time you have told me. And both she and the phantom child you speak of are fortunate I did not become a father." He stood up to leave. "Give Arthur my regards and tell the kids I'm sorry I couldn't see them. I spoke with Junior a few days ago, but with James and Sarah being away at school, it wasn't possible, obviously."

Arthur Bond, Jr., at twenty-three worked with his father in the family shipping firm. Grant was not certain what the business did, since it owned no boats, but it earned enough money for Alice to occupy one of the finest homes in town and to send seventeen-year-old James and fifteen-year-old Sarah to private schools in Massachusetts. Junior had earned a degree from Harvard, although to what purpose beyond prestige Grant was unaware.

He placed his cup on the table and stood to leave, and Alice rose to accompany him to the door.

"You do promise to let me know where you are at?" Alice said.

"I promise."

"I know I annoy you sometimes, but I do just want the best for you."

He stepped forward and hugged her. "I know you do, Sis, and I am grateful for all you have done for me." The tears streaming down her cheeks made him hesitate a moment, but no, he had to do this.

Chapter 2

GRANT COULD NOW claim to have travelled west of the Mississippi River. Ten minutes earlier, the train crossed the railroad trestle that spanned the river, and he had not been especially impressed, having grown up along the Ohio. The Mississippi formed Iowa's eastern border, and the only difference he noted in crossing the farmlands of that state was the thinning out of villages along the route that would take him to Omaha, Nebraska. He planned to spend the night there before picking up another train that would take him the hundred miles to Borderview, Nebraska, where he would meet up with his former sergeant, Ian Locke.

Grant had dozed most of the previous day, lulled by the clickety-clack of steel against steel as his train followed the Ohio River from Portsmouth to Cincinnati before heading northwesterly across Indiana to Springfield, Illinois, where he stayed the night in a boarding house near the station. Yesterday, however, he had enjoyed the luxury of a journey without a seatmate. He was a loner who enjoyed solitude and generally found his own company quite sufficient.

Today, he found himself next to a window, sitting near the rear of the passenger car and sharing the stuffed bench-style seat with a hefty man wearing a top hat and a pickle-green business suit that fit him like a second skin. The stressed jacket threatened to burst off the sole button that held it about the man's watermelon-like belly. The jowly face of Grant's unwelcome companion was dominated by a black handlebar moustache. After lighting a cigar and exhaling its eye-burning smoke, the man said, "Hope you don't mind if I enjoy a cigar. I've got another, if you would like one."

Grant said, "No, thanks." He did not especially enjoy the smoke, but it was not his nature to fuss about such things.

"My name is Percival Garth. Most call me 'Percy.'" He plucked a card from his inside coat pocket and handed it to Grant.

"Grant Coolidge." Grant perused the business card. Garth was president of Garth Publications. An Omaha address appeared on the card. He thought he might have heard of the company but could not place it. There were hundreds of small publishing firms springing up across the country these days. Many produced garbage, but who was he to look down his nose at the products? His own work was not the stuff of Hawthorne, Kipling or Twain.

"As you can see, Mister Coolidge, I am in the publishing business."

"Yes, I see that."

"May I ask what you do?"

"I write some."

"May I ask what you write?"

He hesitated a moment. He did not want to discuss his writing efforts with a stranger and was a bit embarrassed about being a dime novelist. Some in the industry were quite snobbish about the genre, although few writers could make a living off their books, and many of the dimers did.

Finally, he said, "I write for Beadle and Company."

"Dime novels? You don't say? And Erastus Beadle. I knew that scoundrel when he lived in Omaha in the late fifties. He came here seeking his fortune in the west. I was in my early twenties then. He tried selling real estate for a spell, investing in larger tracts and selling off lots that were just stepped off without survey. Sometimes, he sold the same lot to two or three different folks—not intentional, mind you. He just lost track, I think. Anyhow, he lost every nickel he had settling with unhappy buyers."

Grant said, "So what happened then?"

"Well, I went to work with him in starting a medicine wagon to sell patent medicines. He talked me into loaning him money to buy a wagon and mule, and he promised to provide the medicines, which he concocted in his one-room cabin. I was to get a ten percent commission on all sales if I rode around with him to sell the stuff. He found a printer to make labels and got bottles from the dumps, some with other company names engraved in the bottles. I only saw the inside of his cabin once, and it was filled with barrels. The main ingredient was alcohol I learned later, and I don't know what the hell else he added."

"So you were a business partner?"

"For a business that lasted about three months. Omaha had roughly two thousand people at that time—grew to almost twenty thousand a dozen years later. We sold no more than five dollars of the medicines a day, leaving me with fifty cents for all I had invested and my day's labor. Then one day, he was gone, left me a note giving me the mule—which I had been feeding and caring for—and wagon. Of course, he hadn't paid the loan, so he was giving me what I had paid for in the first place. Went back to his wife and kids in New York. They refused to come out here. Can't say that I blame them. Omaha was no place for families in those days. Dirty and dangerous, but those who held on have done well enough, and the town's got a future, being on the Missouri River and getting to be something of a railroad hub."

Grant said, "You say you are a publisher. What do you publish?"

"We do five magazines right now, but I'm looking to get into books. One's the *Omaha Gossip*. It's a weekly and riles up some folks, but it's my little gold mine. Sells out every issue. Can't print enough. The others are monthlies. Profits are less, but they're growing. Most popular is *Western Yarns*. Features fiction stories set in the west. Sales have doubled the past year, and I'm looking to triple this next. You wouldn't be interested in a submission, would you? I'm not familiar with your work."

"I publish under P. J. Bowie and Jake West."

Garth's eyes widened and he tossed his cigar in the cuspidor made available for tobacco spitters. "I am impressed. I have read both. Bowie is my favorite, and his character, Marshal Buck Tyree. Are you under contract to Beadle?"

"Not technically, but he recently made an offer, and I am waiting for the contract proposal. It would be a one-

or two-year agreement for my novels. Beadle gave me a start in the business, so I feel obligated to give the company first chance to come to terms. I haven't been hard to deal with."

"May I ask if he pays you royalties on your work?"

"No. I sell him all rights to the book for a set fee."

Garth said, "He's stealing from you. Talk to a lawyer before you sign. Your books will be earning money for Beadle twenty years from now. Like I said, I've been wanting to get into book publishing. If you and Beadle don't make a deal, contact me. At least get Beadle to agree to royalties. More writers are getting an advance guaranteed payment these days, and after the book earns the payment back for the publisher, the writer receives a royalty of ten or fifteen percent of sales. You will be surprised to learn how much money P.J. Bowie is making for Beadle with Buck Tyree."

Grant was not certain how much truth came from Percy Garth's mouth, but he was aware that some writers made serious money from their book sales. On the other hand, others made a little of nothing and relied upon other employment to survive or support families. He had been grateful to earn a bit more than a subsistence income from telling stories, which many did not consider respectable work. "I appreciate your thoughts, and I will certainly take them into consideration when I receive Erastus Beadle's contract to look over."

"And reserve the right to publish for others under other pseudonyms or your own name. Think about doing some short stories under another name for *Western Yarns*. We pay a one-time fee for a single printing, and you keep the rights to future publication. Ten dollars per thousand words. We like the stories between three thousand and seven thousand words. It's also a way to get your name or another pseudonym familiar to other readers."

"You've given me a lot to think about. I thank you for that." Then he saw the disheveled, whiskered man shuffling up the aisle toward them. His wild eyes were fixed on Garth. That would not have been so troubling were it not for the pistol in his hand that was leveled at the publisher.

Percival Garth's face was turned toward Grant, and he was obviously unaware of the approaching visitor. "Mister Garth," Grant said. "Don't move suddenly. There is a man with a gun moving this way."

Garth turned his head slowly toward the slightly built man who was dressed in a ragged shirt and denims and a tattered straw hat. His face turned white at the sight of the unwelcome visitor. "Hello, Mister Jeffords. What can I do for you today?"

"You can die. And I'm here to help."

"Oh, come now, Jeffords. Do you really want to hang? Why don't we talk this out?" Grant thought the publisher was remaining surprisingly calm.

"What's to talk about? That story you put out in the *Omaha Gossip* cost me my business and my wife. And the witch will poison the kids' minds against me."

Grant noted that the pistol was shaking in the man's hand. He obviously was not a practiced gunman, but that did not make him less a threat, especially with the pistol barrel not more than five feet from Percival Garth's head.

Garth said, "Mister Jeffords, you should have been tending to business at your livery instead of bedding that girl in the straw. Lucinda was not yet sixteen during those weeks you took advantage of her kind nature."

"Advantage? Kind nature? It was business. I paid her a dollar a poke for fifteen minutes. She couldn't make that in a day doing real work."

"She came to the *Gossip* because you didn't pay her and threatened to kill her if she said anything. The sheriff just laughed at her."

"Blackmailing me. Wanted double or she was going to tell my wife. I didn't have that much, and if I scratched up the money, she'd have been back for more. She's a wily little bitch, and your story didn't mention she was a whore."

"She is a child, Jeffords. You should have kept your pizzle in your britches. Your youngest daughter isn't much older than Lucinda."

The man's eyes narrowed, and the gun steadied in his hand. Grant sensed Jeffords was going to squeeze the trigger, and he stood up. "Don't do it, Mister. You are under arrest."

Jeffords shifted his aim to Grant's midsection. "Under arrest? Who the hell are you?"

"I am U.S. Marshal Buck Tyree. Now give me your gun."

"Heard of you someplace. Don't see no badge."

"It's clipped to my belt—right side. Rest easy, and I'll get it." With his left hand, he reached under his coat, closing his fingers on the grip of the derringer that was holstered there, but facing his frontside. Garth commenced coughing, distracting Jeffords, who swung his weapon back to the publisher, and Grant readied the derringer and drew it, aiming at Jeffords's chest. "Give me your gun," Grant said. "Now. Don't make me squeeze this trigger."

Jeffords froze, and his eyes darted back and forth between the two men. He clearly did not like being on the other side of a gun's sights. He lowered the pistol and handed it to Grant. Applause broke out in the car, and

Grant saw that the passengers at the front had turned and watched the drama play out. None of the men had seen fit to intervene, however. Jeffords just stood there, slumped and head down, evidently waiting to be handcuffed.

Grant turned to Garth. "What shall I do with him?"

"Let him go. If we turn him over to the sheriff at the next town, I'd have to come back to testify. I think if the man thinks about this, he won't be bothering me again, especially after his name appears in the next issue of the *Omaha Gossip*."

"You are certain?"

Garth spoke to Jeffords. "I know you've been following me, Jeffords. I caught sight of you in Springfield, but I didn't think you would be foolish enough to do something like this. Your travel money would have been better spent turning your life another direction. My guess is that you are a bit short of fifty. You could have some good years ahead, but you won't find them in Omaha. I strongly urge you to leave the city within five days after we return. That's when the next issue of the *Gossip* comes out."

Jeffords nodded. "I'll be leaving. Don't want no more trouble." He turned and trudged back to his seat, trying to ignore curious eyes.

No sooner had he left than Grant tensed for more trouble, when a man carrying a holstered pistol on his hip and attired in boots and what he judged to be cowboy garb walked in their direction. He stopped beside their seat and held out a dime novel with a picture of a tall man astride a white horse on the cover. "Tyree's Revenge" was emblazoned on the cover. P.J. Bowie's name appeared in smaller letters at the bottom.

"Marshal Tyree, I ain't got nothing but a pencil, but I'd be honored if you would sign this book inside the cover."

"I would be delighted," Grant said, happy that the man was not going to be drawing his sidearm. "What's your name?"

"Hank Wassom, sir."

Grant accepted the book and proffered pencil, opened the novel and in blank space on the title page wrote "To my good friend, Hank Wassom, with kind regards. Buck Tyree. U.S. Marshal." He passed the book and pen back to the fan.

When Wassom read the inscription, he beamed. "I thank you, Marshal. I can't wait to get back to the ranch and show this to the fellas. Ain't gonna believe I met up with the live Marshal Buck Tyree." He wheeled and strutted away like a proud rooster.

"You sure made that fella happy," Garth said. "It doesn't bother you that you're not Buck Tyree?"

"I'm as much Buck Tyree as I am P.J. Bowie."

"I guess that's true enough."

"And I don't like to get into long explanations with folks. I also don't want Grant Coolidge's name in the *Omaha Gossip*."

Garth chuckled. "I won't argue with the man who stepped up and saved my life. As far as I'm concerned, the benefactor who likely saved my life was a man who identified himself as U.S. Marshal Buck Tyree. That will send the tongues of dime novel readers flapping, sell magazines. And Grant, I don't think you have any idea of how many of your novels Beadle is selling. I suggest you find out. Also, please let me know where I can find you once you get settled."

Chapter 3

GRANT HAD WRITTEN Ian Locke of his plans to stop at Borderview on his journey to an unknown destination west, and his former sergeant had responded with an invitation to stay over at the Locke ranch home for as long as he liked. The residence, located a few miles from town, was a single-story, clapboard and part stone structure with a recent addition, comfortable but not pretentious.

Grant envied the apparent stable and contented life enjoyed by his former sergeant, who was the senior partner of a law firm practicing under the name of McGlaun, Locke and Heasty. He had been married to his law partner, Casey McGlaun, for less than a year. Grant guessed the welcoming woman to be a dozen or more years younger than her husband. Tonight, she was ensconced in the home study that she shared with Ian, likely with the intent of giving the war comrades some time to chat alone.

Casey was a stunning, auburn-haired woman who would likely fall short of five feet in height without her shoes. A trial lawyer and one of the few female lawyers in Nebraska, she handled cases statewide and was occasionally absent for several days or a week when a trial was in progress. Ian joked that he had been forced to surrender first place on the firm name to convince Casey to move from Omaha to Borderview, a town of fewer than fifteen hundred inhabitants. Grant doubted that but knew Ian was a modest man who did not struggle with his ego.

The two men sat in the parlor in leather-covered chairs in front of the fireplace, savoring a fire just large enough to remove the chill from the nippy night air. Spring was scheduled to arrive in a few days, but the weather had chosen to disregard the calendar. Both men nursed steaming mugs of black coffee quietly, a relief to Grant who was still uncomfortable declining a social whiskey or beer. He had learned the day before that demon alcohol was a part of Ian's past as well, so they shared more than the war experience.

Ian's twelve-year-old daughter Mandy entered the room. Long golden hair and translucent, blue eyes, she was a lanky girl already several inches taller than her stepmother. She would be a beauty in two years, Grant thought. She was followed by a pretty Indian girl, Mandy's schoolmate, who was staying the weekend. Shorter with haunting dark eyes, he had already met Rosemary and found her soft-spoken and shy but sensed that a very intelligent girl was hidden behind the reserve. Those eyes were always moving and taking in everything around her.

"Dad," Mandy said, "can we take your chessboard set to my room? I want to teach Rosemary to play chess."

"Go ahead, everything's in the cupboard next to the fireplace. After she's had some experience, we'll have a tournament."

"She will be whipping us both, Dad. You know she will."

"We'll see. I'm not conceding anything."

After the girls left, Ian said, "Rosemary Washington has been a blessing to this family. As I told you, Mandy's mother and I had a difficult divorce. Mandy had been raised in Omaha, and I saw little of her after I moved to Borderview. My former wife's new husband did not want the girl in their lives, and when he and Mandy's mother took a European trip, Mandy was turned over to me, at first temporarily, but now it appears it will be a permanent arrangement. Anyhow, Rosemary is a quiet, shy girl who needed a friend, and the two connected instantly. I wish you could have met her father, but he is in Lincoln where the legislature is in session."

"He is a representative?"

"A senator as a matter of fact. Represents our three-county district in the state senate. He is a full-blood Pawnee, and his name is George Washington."

"You are serious?"

"Yeah. And he lives at Mount Vernon."

"Now, I know you're joshing me."

"No. George owns over five thousand acres of land in this county and resides in a Southern-style manor with three wives and twelve children. His number one wife's name is Martha. He is involved in a half dozen enterprises, all successes. His two eldest sons are running day to day operations since George became a politician last fall. He is a dear friend."

Grant chuckled. "This man is going to be a character in one of my novels. If I put him in a different location, I can probably get by with it. How old is he?"

"Just hit his sixtieth birthday last fall. He was educated in a Quaker school, learned about George Washington and opted for the white man's ways and borrowed the first president's name. A lot of Pawnees didn't go to the Indian Territory reservation when the tribe was moved. Those that had already made a place in the white communities stayed behind. Nobody cared so long as they weren't wielding a scalping knife at the wrong place."

"But there are laws against polygamy."

"Again, who cares if the wives don't? Oh, there are a few tongues spitting venom about town, but if a man can get the votes to be state senator, you can see most folks aren't too much bothered—men anyhow."

Grant said, "Already, I'm starting to see I am venturing into a different culture as I move west."

"Yes, I suppose. I was mostly raised in the east until my father brought the family west to settle in Manhattan, Kansas with the Free Staters. He was a staunch abolitionist. The town is quite civilized now, but it was a wild place when we arrived in the late fifties. I went off to law school at Yale, and my twin brother Cam headed for the University of Virginia to study the law there. Then the war came and interrupted things, and I ended up wearing blue, and Cam chose gray. But we don't need to get into all that. You said you are leaving tomorrow. Have you decided where you're going yet?"

Both men had danced around discussion of their war experiences beyond the current whereabouts and activities of men they had served with. It was as if that chapter of their lives had been torn out of the book and burned, but, of course, it was still buried in memory. Grant answered Ian's question. "I'm going to connect with a train that follows the Platte River across Nebraska, stay over in North Platte or Ogallala a bit farther west."

Ian said, "That's Sandhills country. Way more cows than people out that way. You will start to get that flavor of the real west that you have been wanting to taste. But I've been thinking. I've got a seed to plant. Not much farther beyond is Wyoming."

"Yep, that's what the map tells me."

"There's a town called Lockwood, Wyoming in a valley out in the middle of the mountains some miles north of Cheyenne. There's a new railroad spur from Cheyenne to the town built because of coal discovery there, but there is a good cow market out that way, too, I'm told. By and large, it's ranch country, though. Last I knew about a thousand folks live there, but it's growing and likely taking on some of the troubles that come with that. You could find some seclusion for your work there and fodder for your yarn spinning."

"Have you been there?"

"Well, no. My little sister Hannah lives there."

"I knew you had the twin brother. He practices law in Manhattan, Kansas with your father."

"Hannah's a lawyer, too. It's something of a Locke family disease. She is also a twin, has a brother who is a trained physician but makes his living as a veterinary surgeon in the Flint Hills near Manhattan. My oldest brother, Franklin, is a Methodist preacher headquartered at North Platte, but he rides the circuit to small towns scattered about the Sandhills. Hannah is my half-sister, and I don't know her all that well. You see, my mother died, and my father remarried a younger woman eventually. She died giving birth to the twins on July 4th. It would have been 1855 as I recollect."

"So she would be considerably younger than you."

"Yes. Fourteen years. And she was raised in a different household. Their mother's sister and her husband were early Flint Hills settlers and ranched nearby, and they took in the twin babies. Dad had all he could handle to deal with me and my brothers. He saw the twins frequently, had them in town to stay over, and by the time they reached high school, they spent the school week in town."

"Sounds like things worked out."

"Fine, I thought, but when she finished high school, she accosted my father and chewed his ear for abandoning her and her twin Thaddeus. The next day she took the train to Denver and hasn't returned since. I'll give her credit, though, she's never asked family for money. She worked as a researcher in a Denver law office, took up a clerkship with a Cheyenne lawyer, passed the bar and ended up as a partner in a Lockwood firm, 'Ramsey and Locke.'"

"Sounds like she's on the stubborn side."

"Yes, and she always did have a temper. Probably why she's an old maid. Now that there is a rail connection, Dad claims he is going to make a surprise visit to try to patch things up. He writes to her, and she replies, but the letters are brief and terse. Most of what the family learns about her comes from letters to Thad and the aunt and uncle who raised her. Thad plans to accompany Dad when he decides to visit, thinking he can be a buffer of sorts. He and his twin remain close, but they haven't seen each other for some years either."

"I will ponder Lockwood. I always thought I might end up in the Southwest. Santa Fe, maybe."

"I've never been there, but it's rich with history, of course. A mix of cultures. I write wills and contracts. I have no idea what it takes to inspire a novelist."

"I get the inspiration in my head. It doesn't matter so much where I'm at, but I would like to have a better feel for what I'm writing about. I'm grateful I can make a living telling stories that show up in my imagination, but the past few years I've been thinking I would like to write a story of the west that goes beyond a dime novel. Not now, but someday."

"I'm betting you will, Grant. But let me know where you end up. We should stay in touch."

Chapter 4

GRANT STOOD ON the planked railroad platform installed by the Union Pacific at its new station in Lockwood, Wyoming. His two trunks had been unloaded from a cart at the platform's edge next to the dirt road that appeared to connect to the town's main street. His decision to make the journey to Lockwood had been impulsive. Ian Locke planted the seed, and it just seemed to take root. The train that was transporting him to North Platte was continuing to Cheyenne, so he had arranged with the conductor to purchase a ticket that would take him to that destination. There, he stayed overnight in a hotel near the station and caught an early morning train north to Lockwood.

Noon was approaching and he was hungry, but his priority was to move his trunks to a place to lodge until he decided how long his stay in the town might be. He reserved the option to head back to Cheyenne the next day. The scenery as the train rolled into the vast North Laramie River valley had been breathtaking. There were miles of greening meadows split by clear streams snaking toward the river. Cattle grazed with antelope and white tail deer on what appeared to be open rangeland, all framed by majestic snow-capped mountains in the distance. He looked skyward now and caught sight of several bald eagles drifting overhead.

He would hold off judgment on the town. From where he stood it seemed to be what he had read—and written—cowboys called son-of-a-bitch stew, contrived without planning and put together with whatever ingredient was handy. There were some nice, new buildings like the station and what appeared to be a bank down the street, but other structures were unpainted with warped boards and leaning one direction or another. The streets were nice enough now, but he saw nothing but dirt outside the intermittent boardwalks, and he could only imagine what a rain or thawing snow would do to the roadway.

A buckboard pulled by a team of mules pulled up beside the depot platform. A young man attired in a well-worn buckskin jacket and dusty, low-crowned hat offered a welcoming grin. "Howdy, mister," he said. "My name's

Trouble Yates. Appears you might need some transportation."

As Grant edged closer to the wagon, he saw that the
driver was more boy than man. He displayed blond fuzz
above his lips to match the longish hair that crawled from
beneath his hat crown, a futile effort at a moustache,
Grant suspected. He could sense the boy's greenish-blue
eyes sizing up the stranger. "My name is Grant Coolidge.
I do need transportation and a lot of information."

"Wagon costs two dollars to anyplace in town. I will
help carry the trunks to your room. Information is free—
to a point."

Aha. A budding capitalist. The price was twice what
he would pay back in Ohio, but he was in no position to
quibble. "My problem is I don't know where I am going
with these things. Is there a decent boarding house here
where I can rent by the week, take meals?"

"We got four such places and the Lockwood Hotel. The
hotel's nice enough and has a dining room where you pay
by the meal. Cost you three dollars a night, though, just
for a sleeping room. The Tipi's got a vacant room. Breakfast and supper included for just two dollars a day. Bright
Moon can make a special deal for weeklies, do even better
for a monthly. Separate privies for gentlemen and ladies.
Decent tub bath available nights. Got to set up a time. No

sharing the wash-up room. She and her daughter will do your laundry for extra."

The kid made the place sound like a vacation haven. Grant would bet a gold eagle that Trouble Yates got a commission for the folks he brought to the place. "I'll look at it," he said. "It's not really a tipi, is it?"

Trouble laughed. "Nope. Bright Moon is half Sioux and liked the sound of the name, I guess."

He got out of the wagon, and he and Grant hoisted the trunks onto the wagon. They were not heavy, but the bulk made two men necessary. Grant was surprised to find that the lanky boy was taller than himself by an inch or two. The tautness of the shoulders of the old buckskin jacket suggested serious muscle beneath.

They climbed onto the wagon seat. Trouble said, "The Tipi is west of here at the far end of town. We'll go down main street, and I'll show you where most things are at. You here on some kind of business?"

Grant wasn't ready to talk about his business. "You could say that."

Trouble evidently took the hint because he did not press. When they reached the street that connected to the trail that led to the railroad station, Trouble pointed to a large frame building at the northwest corner of the intersection that was identified with a large sign across the front: Fletcher's Livery. "That's where this wagon and mule team is from. I work for Enos Fletcher off and on. Right now, I'm working for myself and pay rent for the critters and wagon. Won't be doing that much longer. I'm buying the place from Enos next month when I turn sixteen."

Grant was incredulous. "Seems like a big undertaking for a young man."

"Not so much. I've been working and putting away money since I was a kid. Besides, Enos will carry the note for five years, and I'll make the last payment when I'm twenty-one and can take title. He will stay on and work for me till the note's paid, if he lives that long. He's older than the mountains hereabouts. You'll meet Enos. He knows everything about everybody in case you're some kind of Pinkerton or something."

Trouble was still fishing. "I'm not a Pinkerton."

They continued down the dusty street, the mules plodding at a walk. Trouble said, "Off to the right is the Salty Dog. You can get good beer and whiskey there, decent meals, too, if your tastes aren't too fancy. Just across the street is Dead Man's Paradise. It's more of an uppity place—drinks only, no eats. It's owned by George Caldwell, the undertaker next door. I should mention

The Chowdown. Best food, I'd say, but no liquor. Owner's a reformed drunk."

Grant supposed that's what he was: a reformed drunk. That was another reason he had pulled stakes in Ohio. In the west he would decide how much of his past trailed him. "It's nice to know about these things."

"We missed the biggest drinking place. The Doll House is across Main Street from the livery but opens off a side street. Big as a barn. Doesn't look like much on the outside but all fixed up nice inside, big chandeliers and such. Liquor at all prices, depending on whether you mind rotgut or not. Women available on the second floor at different prices, too. Depends on the man's hankering and cash in his pocket, I guess. Never been upstairs."

They continued down the street, and Trouble pointed out other establishments, some on side streets branching off Main Street. Grant learned there were two banks, the Lockwood State and the Gaines Bank, which his guide recommended. There were three law offices, including one for the firm of Ramsey and Locke. There were other bed and board establishments, one called Sally's Bed and Board which looked especially inviting. He was told again that a small side street restaurant called The Chowdown was the best eating place in town.

Grant noticed the Oaks General Store, an enterprise that appeared to take up what was formerly three separate store fronts. "Is that where a man would pick up some clothes?" Grant asked.

"Yep, and anything else you might need. If they ain't got it, nobody's got it. Likely ain't been invented. Jeb Oaks and his wife, She Bear, own and run the place. Across the street is the new sheriff's office and jail. The old one burned down."

They came to a large house with a sign beside the front entryway that read: 'Weintraub Hospital, Henry Weintraub, M. D.' Trouble said, "That's Doc Weintraub's. He has his hospital and offices downstairs, and family lives upstairs."

By the time the wagon reached The Tipi, which sat west of the last town building a good half block, Grant decided that Lockwood was more town than he had anticipated. He perused the exterior of the boarding house. No, it was not a tipi. It was a block-shaped, two-story building, very simple in design and appeared solidly constructed, freshly whitewashed. A covered porch ran across the house's front. He saw a new stable off to one side, large enough to quarter guest mounts, it appeared. There were a few pine trees in the yard, but otherwise the land around the house was bare save for a scattering of small stones.

The two swung off their respective sides of the wagon, and Trouble said, "I'll run into the house and tell Bright Moon she's got a guest." He started up the stone path that led to the front porch and then stopped abruptly when he heard screams coming from the house.

Grant brushed past him. "That's not a mouse scare. Somebody's taking a beating." As he reached the porch, he heard a male voice yelling above the shrieks of pain.

"You go to the sheriff, you squaw bitch, and I'll be back and show you what a real beating looks like."

Grant heard a thump against a wall and another scream as he burst through the doorway with Trouble close behind. He entered the parlor and passed on through when he heard the commotion in the room ahead. He entered the kitchen and saw a tawny-skinned woman, blood spurting from her nose and dripping from the corner of an eye, on her knees struggling to get to her feet. A hulking, black-bearded man was at the kitchen counter emptying coins and paper money from a small metal box, obviously readying to fill his pockets.

"Put the box and money down, mister," Grant said speaking evenly and softly.

The big man turned and faced the source of the voice. "And who the hell are you?"

"Just do what I say," Grant said. "Trouble, would you see to the lady?"

"Uh, yes, sir, I can do that." He moved around Grant and knelt on the floor beside the woman.

"Get out of my way, mister." The man grabbed a butcher knife from the counter and moved toward Grant. The sight of the blade froze him for an instant, but when the man charged, he deftly stepped aside, slammed his foot across the attacker's ankle and dropped him to the floor with a crash, knocking over a counter stool. The thief groaned and fought to get up. Grant again put his foot to work and drove it down like a sledge on the middle of the man's back, flattening him on the floor. Grant went to his knees, clutched the wrist of the hand that still held the butcher knife and twisted sharply with all the force he could muster. The wrist popped like a firecracker. The man screamed and his fingers released the knife.

The knife was now in Grant's hand, and knee pressed between his foe's shoulder blades, he clasped the man's long hair, yanked his head back and pressed the knife blade to his throat. "Now, before I let you up, we are going to have an understanding. I am going to tie your good arm to the wagon bed, and you will remain seated there while Mister Yates delivers you to the sheriff's office. He will be holding another rope anchored to your injured wrist. You cause any trouble, and he gives it a pull. You won't like that, I promise."

Grant stood and watched as the man clumsily got to his feet. He was obviously in agony and would not be up to another scuffle. Surprisingly, he carried no sidearm, so he was no longer a threat. He turned to Trouble and the woman, who was now seated at a small kitchen table, her head leaning back while Trouble pressed a rag to her nose. The swollen face indicated she had taken three or four blows. Her left eye would be closed tomorrow. She was a trim, attractive woman that he guessed to be in her mid to late forties, but it was hard to say. He had expected to meet a woman wearing moccasins and doeskin dress, but she wore a light blue cotton dress and high-lows or ankle boots. She was what Ned Buntline meant when he said dime novelists are guilty of writing stereotypes. Of course, that was what many readers demanded.

Trouble said, "This here's Bright Moon, Mister Coolidge." Then he spoke to the woman. "This feller is Grant Coolidge, and he wants to see about renting a room."

"Certainly," she said, "I will show you a room and explain terms as soon as I am presentable. I thank you for your assistance." She glared at her attacker, who had righted the stool and was sitting at the counter moaning and cradling his injured wrist. "That pig has been here three days and was to leave this morning. I was out back spading up ground for my spring garden and he found my money box in the cupboard. It contained two weeks' rents that I planned to take to the bank later this afternoon. I think he rented a room just to scout the place and steal my money. He signed in as John Goodson, but I doubt if that is his name."

Another stereotype demolished. This woman spoke better English than most whites back east did. He assumed she would not be typical and that there was an explanation for her language abilities. He supposed that many Indian children were receiving some formal education now. He reminded himself, however, that most of his stories were set ten or more years earlier. On the other hand, Bright Moon was likely born in the late 1830s or early 40s.

"I think the bleeding's stopped, Moon," Trouble said. "If you want to get cleaned up, I'll help Mister Coolidge tie this jasper to the wagon. I'm wondering, though, if you shouldn't see Doc about stitching up that gash above the eye."

"I'll check it in the mirror. If it needs something, I can stitch it myself. Doc would charge me at least a dollar."

Trouble turned to Grant. "If we get this feller anchored in the wagon, I've got my gun belt and an old Navy Colt under the seat, and I'll see him to the sheriff. Jim Tolliver, the sheriff, is my step-pa. I'll tell him what happened here. This no-good won't be turned out anytime soon, I promise. He's likely got paper on him someplace. If there's a reward on it, how about a three-way split?"

This kid was always on top of a dollar. Grant said, "A reward seems farfetched, and I doubt anybody sees a nickel, but we will talk about a split if we see some money. This guy seems like just a no-account thug to me, not one that would have a price on his head."

"Never know, unless we check, and I'll be pushing Jim to find out. You can count on that."

Chapter 5

BEFORE TROUBLE YATES left with his prisoner, he helped Grant carry the trunks upstairs to the vacant room at the far end of the hallway. Grant liked the location. There would be no foot traffic past the room, and he had been informed that the room across the hall was occupied by an older male teacher who taught English and literature at the Pennock School. Bright Moon, or "Moon" as she preferred to be called, had informed him that the school was founded by Quakers for Indian pupils some years earlier but now served the entire community and had established a high school several years earlier. Much of the funding came from an organization called the Lame Buffalo Association, the balance from private tuition from those who could afford it. Not quite half the pupils were Brule Sioux or carried a significant percentage of the tribe's blood.

Obviously, civilization was arriving at this isolated community, yet he sensed that it was of a different brand than the familiar sort he found in the eastern states, and he found himself increasingly curious about this land and the people who occupied it. He decided he would not depart Lockwood till the curiosity was sated.

He sat on a straight-back chair, studying his room, surveying his new habitat. He was to meet Moon downstairs in the kitchen at three o'clock which was only fifteen minutes away. The double bed was neatly made, firm and comfortable, he decided after testing. A night table with an oil lamp sat adjacent to the bed. There was a small closet where he could place one trunk and still hang clothes above it. A chest of drawers sat against the wall across from the foot of the bed. He had little to put in it now and would need to remedy that soon.

He focused on a bare spot adjacent to the room's only window. It opened to the west, so he should have light later in the day. That suited him, since he was not an early riser. The vacant space adjacent to the window would work perfectly for a desk, which he considered more important than a bed. He would require an extra lamp there.

All in all, the room met his approval, and he got up and went downstairs. He entered the kitchen and found

Moon already at the table with papers and pen and ink-well within reach.

She smiled despite her swollen lip and nose. He saw that she had indeed stitched the wound above her eye. Tough lady. She got up and retrieved a coffee pot and mugs and placed them on the table, and then she brought him a plate with a sandwich and slice of pie and placed it in front of him. She sat back down and said, "You must have come here immediately after the noon train came in. You could not have eaten. Perhaps this will tide you over till supper. I hope you don't mind a ham sandwich and apple pie."

"I love both. You are very kind."

"It's the least I can do for coming to my aid. Go ahead and eat while I explain The Tipi's rules."

He said, "I'm listening." He took his first bite from the sandwich. Delicious.

Moon said, "Rates are two dollars a night. That includes breakfast and supper. Weekly charge is twelve dollars. A full month would be forty dollars. Breakfast is served from six in the morning to eight o'clock. Same for supper, six to eight in the evening. That makes it easy to remember. We like to know if you will not be here to eat, but no credits or refunds if you choose to eat elsewhere."

Grant said, "I would like to start with a month. It could be longer, but I will know within a few weeks."

Moon continued. "The parlor is available to any residents and their guests but no reservations. No liquor there. You can have alcohol in your room and drink there, but no guests, male or female."

"I understand."

"We change the bed weekly and wash the sheets without additional charge. If a resident uses the chamber pot under the bed, he is responsible for emptying it in the privy and washing it at the outside pump. We have powdered lye just inside the rear door. Laundry services are available at rates posted on the door to the bathtubs. Baths are one dollar. Tub room is open from seven to ten o'clock evenings. You should reserve a half hour if you want to count on availability. We will fill the tub with warm water. It drains to a gully outside. There are two tubs with a curtain between them. There is a mirror, sink and handpump in the room if you choose to wash up and shave there. No extra charge. Otherwise, there will be a basin and water pitcher in your room. You will have to fill it. Questions?"

He finished his sandwich and picked up a fork for attacking the pie. "No questions now. I have two double eagles in my pocket for a month's rent." He could tell that the eagles pleased her. Most folks would take greenbacks or a draft on a local bank but preferred gold. This reminded him that he would need to set up an account at one of the banks.

She handed him the papers. "I have already signed. I will require two signatures from you, so we will each have a copy. Look them over while you eat. I have ink and pen, and you can sign and settle after you finish your pie."

This woman was all business and somewhat guarded, notwithstanding his intervention in her dilemma. He liked her, though, and figured she had reasons for caution. "I should tell you," Grant said, "after I get settled in, I will be in my room a lot. I am a writer. That's why I will need a desk."

She looked dubious. "I don't care how much time you spend in your room if you do not have someone else with you and don't make a racket that disturbs the other roomers. You should be aware that I have my daughter living with me here. She is fifteen and helps me when she is not in school or studying. Her name is Jasmine. We share a last name—Dupree. I am a widow. She is very responsible, so you may tell her if you are having problems with the living arrangements."

He finished his pie. "Thank you, Moon. This was delicious, and I must admit I was starving. Now I am ready to sign." He dug the two double eagles out of his pocket and placed them on the table. She passed him the pen and ink. As he signed, he was struck by the perfect hand printing that set out the rent terms on the paper, a great deal of work for someone. He had never encountered a written agreement for a room before. "The form printing is beautiful. Yours?"

"Jasmine's. She is an aspiring artist. Not very practical, I fear."

"Neither is being a dime novelist, but I make a living."

"Dime novelist. I've seen those books in the general store. I've never read one, though."

"Mostly men readers, my publisher says, but I have had a few women confess to picking up the things."

She was studying his face now as if she were searching for truth. "I must find one of your books."

"Don't look. I have a fair number in one of the trunks upstairs. I will give you one. I write under pseudonyms. For now, however, I would prefer folks didn't know who I am. It's not that I am famous, but when people learn you are a writer, they want to tell you their ideas for the book you should write."

She smiled through her swollen lips. "Your secret is safe. I'm not certain yet I want anyone to know I am lodging such a person."

Chapter 6

"YOU SHOULD HAVE seen it, Enos. This guy flattened that thief like he does it every day. I don't know what to make of the feller. Dressed like some eastern dude. Claimed he wasn't a Pinkerton, but I ain't so sure."

Enos Fletcher sat on the rickety bench just outside the stable door, eyes half-closed and nodding off occasionally with a wad of chewing tobacco nestled in his cheek. The portion of his face that was not covered by a scraggly, brown-stained beard was a landscape of crisscrossed arroyos and gullies. Nobody knew his age, but he had slipped once and let it be known he had been a rancher in Texas when he fought in the Texas Revolution some fifty years earlier. Trouble guessed him to be something over eighty, but how much was anybody's guess. Beyond that, Enos's life was a closed book before his arrival as one of the first five or six settlers who set up an outpost named for a man who financed a trading post in the middle of Sioux and Cheyenne country.

"Trouble, it don't matter who he is if he ain't here to harm nobody. Sounds like he started off with a good turn. Just leave it at that."

Trouble was confident he had planted a seed in the old codger's head. Enos was curious as a cat, always collecting information with the notion it might be useful sometime. The old devil wasn't above selling his knowledge to the right folks either. It wasn't that he had a loose tongue or gossiped; he just stored things that might come in handy later. Sometimes, it seemed to Trouble that the livery owner was deafer than a post, and most who knew him casually would think that, but Enos did not miss anything worth hearing. Trouble was careful about what he said around the man.

Trouble said, "I've got to be heading home. I've got some cattle on the Morris place I need to check out. We've got a few more weeks of calving, and I need to be sure none of the mamas aren't having problems."

"How many head are you running these days?"

"I got twenty-five cows now. That's about all I can handle on the quarter section I rent from Ma and eighty-some not planted to crop on the Morris land. I'm hoping to get some more land this summer. I've got a decent down payment, and the Gaines Bank will loan me the rest if the seller won't carry the loan."

"You're still buying the livery in a few weeks, ain't you?"

"Yep. Time to talk to Miss Locke about the paperwork. I've got that down payment set aside in a separate account."

"You see to that—and pay for it. I ain't paying no law wrangler fees."

"Figured as much." Cheap old fart. Still, he had to admit that Enos was treating him fair enough on price and terms. Trouble just wanted everything nailed down tight. If Enos died, he did not want some lost heir to show up and claim the business. Matt Gaines had educated him about such things. The owner and president of the Gaines Bank had mentored him on business and economics for some years before they both learned a few years earlier that the banker was his biological father, a secret so far kept from the community and Enos Fletcher.

"You going to move to town when you take over the livery?"

"Don't plan to. You're going to keep your room in back of the stable, ain't you?"

"That was part of the deal."

"Well, I'm not buying or renting a house in town so long as I can live in the Morris house. It's just across the river from Ma and Jim, and it comes with the land I rent. Besides, I won't be here all the time. I'll be hiring some extra help."

"You never told me that."

"No reason. When I take over, I'm responsible, but I got a lot of irons in the fire. You know that."

"Too many. Especially for a kid. Do you ever show up for school?"

"When I can, once or twice a week for a spell. I got books. Teachers say if I do the work and pass the tests, they'll overlook my absences. If they won't, I'll just quit going. They get money from the association for every enrolled student, though, so they don't hassle me anymore."

"Never seen the likes of you. But your money is good as any man's, so the deal's still on."

Trouble knew that Enos would give his right arm, or for that matter, his life for him and did not take the old timer's grumping seriously. "I arranged for Polecat Smith to work from six o'clock till noon tomorrow, so I won't be here till early afternoon just before the train comes in. Polecat will get the mules hitched for me."

"You going to school tomorrow?"

"You could say that. Me and Charlie Hoffman are whitewashing the grade school building. The Pennock School pays for the paint, and I agreed to do the work for seventy-five dollars. I hired Charlie to help. Paying him two-bits an hour—decent wages. He'll keep working after I leave, and I can trust him to give me my money's worth."

"I guess you're treating him fair enough."

"You say so because that's what you pay me."

"Yep. Of course, I let you run your little side schemes out of here, too."

"You're a generous man, Enos. I've never said otherwise to another soul." But he had sure as the devil thought it.

Trouble turned away and started down the alleyway between the stalls to retrieve Tag, his big sorrel gelding that was corralled in the pen at the rear of the building. "I'm going to get Tag saddled and head out," he said.

"I'm betting you got an interesting day ahead of you yet, young feller."

Trouble called back, "Now what the hell does that mean?"

"You'll find out soon enough."

Chapter 7

TROUBLE WAS SURPRISED when he arrived home and saw the dapple-gray mare hitched to the rail in front of the house. The horse was one of a dozen owned by the livery and rented out on a per-day basis. He did not see the rider anyplace, so he dismounted and led Tag to the stable, unsaddled the mount and brushed him down before treating his friend to a bit of grain and turning him out onto the twenty acres of fenced off new grass with the other five horses. He would toss some hay in the feeding rack along the fence line outside the stable door after supper. He did not want the early grass to get gnawed down to dirt.

He strolled to the house, casting his eyes about for the mare's rider. He had locked the house, so there was no access there. That's what he thought until he stepped onto the porch, pulled the key to the front door from his pocket and found that the door was already unlocked. He was not carrying a sidearm and he had left his holstered Winchester in the stable with his saddle and tack. He considered returning to the stable to retrieve the rifle before entering but decided that someone who meant him harm would not have left the horse tied where he could see it.

Slowly he opened the door and stepped inside, pausing to allow his eyes to get accustomed to the dusky room before he went farther. He started when he saw someone facing him from the rocking chair across the room. The visitor's low crowned hat was tugged down on his forehead, and Trouble could not make out the wearer's face. "Hello," he said. "I wasn't expecting company."

"Hello, Brady. It's been almost three years."

A female voice. Brady? Nobody called him Brady but his mother and the banker Matt Gaines, his blood father, not even his new stepfather, Jim Tolliver. There had been one other: Samantha Morris. It couldn't be. "Sammy? Is that you?"

The visitor stood and walked to him, slender and long-legged, wearing snug denims and boots and making no effort to conceal a sleek, womanly figure. She stopped and looked. "The last time I saw you, Brady, I was taller than you. Now I've got to look up. I'm five feet, nine inches. You must be a good six feet two inches tall now."

She stepped forward and gave him a quick hug, almost knocking him off his feet, and then backed away.

"I'll be danged," Trouble said. "Sammy. It is you. I can't believe it. Uh, good to see you."

"You always did have a way with words."

He caught her sarcasm. "I'm sorry. I didn't expect you. I don't know what to say. You've turned my tongue to wood."

"We could go into the kitchen where there is some light. I've got some coffee brewing. I know where everything is at. We left almost all the furnishings, pots and pans and everything behind. You haven't changed anything."

He tried to collect his wits while Sammy retrieved mugs and poured the coffee. When they were seated across the small table from each other with the light from the adjacent window casting a glow on her face, he found himself wondering if the girl who had been his best friend when they were both thirteen had been that stunning three years back. He knew he did not give the notice to females then that he did these days. The long sable hair tied back in a ponytail, coffee-brown eyes and flawless, olive-tinted skin, all hinting that she was quarter-blood Sioux.

Sammy said, "You could ask me what I am doing here."

"Uh, sure. What are you doing here?"

"We are moving back to Wyoming to the house we are sitting in."

"You are?"

"You knew my father died a year ago?"

"Yeah. Mom told me. I'm really sorry. He was a good man."

"I would have written, but you quit answering my letters, so I stopped."

He was embarrassed. "I meant to. I just had so many things going on. I'm sorry."

"I told you when we left that you would quit writing, that you'd be too busy with what you called your 'enterprises.' To your credit, you lasted almost a year before you forgot who I was."

"I never forgot. We were best friends. I think about you a lot. Wonder what you're doing, if we'd ever see each other again."

"Well, we did."

"Yeah. That's good. I'm glad." He noticed she was staring at something on his face.

"What's that above your lip? A caterpillar or a moustache?"

He could feel the crimson spreading over his face, but he was more annoyed than discomfited. Sammy had always tended to blurt out whatever she was thinking, never reluctant to test his sense of humor. Today he was lacking and bristled.

"Ain't your concern."

"I was teasing. I didn't mean to make you mad. Am I still going to have to remind you that 'ain't' isn't a word?"

The grammar teacher had returned, but he had not minded in the past. Today he did. He suddenly realized the friendship was not going to pick up where it left off.

"I never write it, but I say it sometimes."

"Maybe that's because you never write."

"You're really upset about my not writing, aren't you?"

"I won't deny that I was hurt. I missed you a lot. It took me a good spell to get over you, but I did. So let's just get down to business."

"What business have we got?"

"I told you we were moving back. I came early. My mother will be arriving with my little brothers in another month. Several cousins from Mother's Sioux side of the family have left the reservation and moved back to Lockwood. Their husbands are going to work in the coal mines. We know nothing of her father's side, and she wanted to live near family. Besides, we're mountain people. We never wanted to leave. Dad was not making a living here and was needed on Grandpa's Iowa farm. And now they're both gone, so we're coming home."

Trouble said, "Well, we seem to be off to a bad start, but I'm glad you're back."

"Thank you for saying that, anyhow. You don't have to move for a month. I am staying with your mom and Sheriff Tolliver until my family arrives. I was going to find a boarding house, but when I rode out to look over the place and stopped by to visit your mom, she insisted I stay with her. I'll be using your old room. She says you can have it back when I move out. We'll just trade places. Oh, I forgot to tell you that your mom gave me the extra key. That's how I got in here. I hope that doesn't upset you."

"No, I guess it's more your house than mine. But I won't be moving back across the river. I'll find a place in town. Most of my businesses are there anyhow. I'll be taking over Fletcher's Livery in a month or so."

Her brow furrowed. "You're serious?"

"I am. I've got the arrangements all worked out."

"You're not quitting school?"

"No. I plan to graduate high school in another year. I've got an arrangement that lets me tend to my work."

"You never did show up much. You always were too smart for your own good. I'll graduate in another year, too, of course. I'm going to see about getting enrolled to-morrow."

"You were always a better student than me."

"But I never missed a school day, hardly ever." She switched the subject abruptly again and caught him off guard. "I suppose you've got a girlfriend?"

"Uh, why would you ask that?"

"So you do. Who is it? Anybody I know?"

He did not consider Jasmine Dupree a girlfriend as such. It wasn't like they went to dances together or anything, but they had danced together a few times when they met up at the town hall or barn dances. She was the only reason he showed up for such things. They talked sometimes and he admitted liking the sweet gal and thought she had eyes for him. He thought about her a lot, imagined her naked and in his bed. Yeah, Jasmine was in his mind but damned if he was going to talk to Sammy about such things. It suddenly occurred to him that the return of Samantha Morris was going to bring new complications to his life. "I don't have a girlfriend," he said, "and I *ain't* going to talk about it."

Chapter 8

WHEN GRANT COOLIDGE appeared for supper promptly at six o'clock, he found that his only companions were the across-the-hall neighbor, Milton Lockhart, and Moon Dupree and her daughter, Jasmine. Moon explained that most guests ate at a later hour, so she and Jasmine took their meals early. Jasmine was a pretty, petite girl with lightly bronzed skin suggesting her Sioux blood. Given the last name, Grant assumed that the late husband-father might have been French.

Before she sat down to join the diners, Jasmine placed platters of roast beef, fried potatoes, beans and fresh-baked bread rolls on the table, promising that apple cobbler was warming in the woodstove oven for dessert. There was an uncomfortable silence at the meal's beginning. Lockhart, a short, bald man Grant guessed to be in his early fifties seemed quite shy but not an unfriendly sort. Moon with her swollen face and closed eye looked like she belonged in bed. On the reserved side himself, Grant was often uneasy with casual conversation. A bubbly Jasmine broke the ice.

She directed her words to Grant. "Thank you for helping Mama, Mister Coolidge. You and Trouble got here just in time."

"I'm glad we could help some."

"Mama said you made it look easy. Are you a lawman? Or a Pinkerton or something?"

Moon broke in. "Jasmine. It's none of our business."

This is silly, Grant thought. He was going to attract more attention with his foolish attempt at secrecy than he would by openness. People were curious when a stranger showed up in a small town, and it was not like he was a famous writer who would attract a parade of admirers when he strolled down the boardwalks. If he decided to sink roots in this mountain community, it might be best to start with honesty. "It's okay, Moon," he said, and turned to Jasmine. "I am a writer."

"Like a newspaper reporter?"

He smiled. "No, I make up stuff—well, some reporters have been accused of that, too, I guess—but I'm a yarn spinner. I write books." He noticed that Lockhart paused the fork delivering a chunk of roast to his mouth and looked at him with interest.

Jasmine continued, "Like Mark Twain and Louisa May Alcott?"

"Hardly. The only thing I have in common with Twain is that we both use pen names."

"I know. His real name is Samuel Clemens. What is your pen name?"

Moon cautioned again, "Jasmine, please . . ."

Grant said, "P.J. Bowie and Jake West."

Jasmine said, "I've heard of Bowie and West. They're dime novelists. Trouble reads those books. Talks about them all the time. He's tight as a wood tick in a dog's tail and doesn't buy them, but Mister Gaines at the bank passes them on to him. Trouble reads a lot at night when it's too dark to work. I don't think he sleeps."

Grant sensed a hint of admiration in her voice when she spoke of Trouble Yates. Lockhart returned to his meal, signaling that he had no interest in the works of dime novelists, whom most scholars saw as the dregs of the literary world. Grant sometimes envied Twain, Henry James, Jules Verne and others whose books were four or five times the length of his novels, bound in hard covers and found their ways to the more affluent households and libraries. He doubted that P.J. Bowie's book *Gun-*

fight at Wildcat Creek had ever been introduced to a school classroom.

After supper, as Jasmine cleared the table and prepared for guests who would trickle in to eat later, Moon caught up with Grant before he went upstairs. "I'm sorry about Jasmine's questions. Your secret didn't last very long, I fear."

"Don't worry about it. I think it turned out to be a good thing. It made me realize the foolishness of trying to live a secret life. It is best I start out in Lockwood with the sordid truth about my occupation."

"It's hardly sordid. I am impressed and honored to have a published author residing in our establishment, and we will try to protect your privacy here."

"I will sort through the books in my trunk this evening and try to pick a few that you might not find too outlandish and bring them down at breakfast. They will be yours with my compliments."

"You will autograph them, I hope."

Chapter 9

THE NEXT MORNING following breakfast, Grant walked east on the boardwalk along Lockwood's Main Street. He had presented Moon with two dime novels, one written by his alter ego Bowie and the other by West, signing his own name to each and placing the pseudonym in parenthesis below. To his surprise, Moon seemed genuinely thrilled. He hoped she was not disappointed with the books. He suspected she might be a reader of some sophistication and admitted to himself that he was insecure about his work.

He had a long list of stops today, tasks to dispose of before he got back to his work. He planned to try his luck at The Chowdown at noon, although Moon had informed him she unofficially made a simple lunch for her guests who found it inconvenient to take a noon meal elsewhere. A sandwich, fruit and a few cookies were the standard fare. He told her that he might take advantage of the opportunity when he started his writing routine.

His first stop was the local Post Office where a thin, white-haired, bespectacled man named Dayton Roberts filled out a form for his signature. "You just have your mail sent to your name, U.S. Post Office, Lockwood, Wyoming. You won't be notified of any arrivals, so you should stop by once a week to see if you've got mail, more often if you are expecting something. If you got a letter or package to send out, the rates are posted there." He pointed to a hand-printed sign on the wall adjacent to the counter.

"Can you tell me where the Western Union office is located? I need to send a few telegrams."

"Next door east."

He left the post office and went to a narrow-fronted building with a Western Union sign hanging in the window. He entered and was puzzled when he encountered Dayton Roberts, the postmaster, seated at a desk with the telegraph equipment behind the counter and now wearing a visor cap.

Grant said, "Hello again. You are the postmaster, aren't you—the man I just spoke with."

"Very astute," Roberts said.

Grant was not certain whether he was the recipient of sarcasm or if the man was joking.

"So, I guess you are both postmaster and telegrapher."

Roberts surrendered a sheepish smile. "Yep." He nodded toward a closed door that separated the two offices. "Keeps me running some days, but generally the visits aren't that many. A man would starve with the contract for one of the jobs in this little town, so I went after both. I got a lady in the general store across the street that can cover if need be. It works. Post office department says I got to have a separate office for government business, so I bought the building and split it. Not so bad. I get two rents." He paused and looked up at Grant over the wire-rimmed glasses that perched on the end of his nose. "Now you know all about Dayton Roberts, and I don't know a damn thing about you."

Not again. The old devil was wanting to trade information. "I'm sorry. I don't have time to tell my life's story, but I'm looking at this town with the thought of living here. I'm staying at The Tipi for now. I'm a single man, and I am a writer. I'll be glad to tell you more sometime, but I've got business to tend to today and need to get some telegrams off."

"I understand. If you're looking for a real job where you don't get your hands blistered and your clothes dirty, talk to Jeb Oaks over at Oaks General Store. He's looking for a clerk and a delivery man. Can you drive a mule team and cipher?"

"As a matter of fact, I can, but now I need to send those telegrams." He plucked a folded sheet of paper from his jacket pocket, opened it and handed it to Roberts. "Same message to the three listed people. Just my name and mailing address for Erastus Beadle and Percival Garth. Same for Alice Bond but add: 'Okay. Will write. Love.'"

"Got a lady in Ohio, huh?"

"Sister." It seemed like folks in Lockwood never quit trying to pull information out of a stranger.

Finally, the telegrams were sent, and Grant paid the telegraph agent-postmaster and started to leave when Roberts spoke. "I've got a boy who stops by twice a day to see if I got telegrams to deliver. Customer has got to pay him. Do you want me to send him with any replies? Otherwise, I just hold them till you stop by."

"It would be fine to send him to The Tipi. I'll leave money with Missus Dupree to pay him if I'm not there. How much?"

"Two-bits would be generous."

Next stop. The Gaines Bank. Moon Dupree had recommended the bank and its owner, Matthew Gaines, for Grant's banking business. Gaines served as the town's mayor and was apparently widely respected. He entered the stone structure that housed the bank and found a traditional layout that included a low wooden railing that separated several desks from the lobby on one side and a counter with a cage-like barrier with three teller stations on the other. To the rear, behind an extension of the railing, he saw an open door that he assumed led to a private office and adjacent to that, a huge walk-in vault with the entryway currently sealed.

A young man, obviously a junior officer, puzzled over a stack of papers on his desk. Two tellers, an older man and a youngish woman were at teller's slots today. The male teller appeared to be working on a project and his frown was not welcoming, so he stepped up to the woman's station. The teller, who had seemingly gold-spun hair that cascaded over her shoulders, greeted him with sparkling blue eyes and a smile that reduced him to instant putty.

"I am Virginia Culper," she said, "but everybody calls me 'Katy.' You're new here. May I help you?"

"My name is Grant Coolidge," he said. "I am new in town and need to open an account and arrange transfer of funds from my bank in Ohio."

"I can certainly help with that but let me check with Mister Gaines. If he's available, he likes to meet new customers." She turned and hurried along the walk space behind the counter. He watched as she entered the office door. She emerged a few minutes later and returned to her station.

"Mister Gaines will be out in a moment, but he said I should get the information for the paperwork. How much would you like to deposit today?"

"One thousand dollars cash. Then I want to transfer my entire balance from the Portsmouth State Bank of Portsmouth, Ohio. That should be roughly sixteen hundred dollars." He opened the small canvas gripsack that he used for carrying documents, manuscripts and the like and plucked out ten one hundred-dollar bills and a sheet of paper, which he placed on the counter.

He counted out the money in front of a wide-eyed Katy and handed her the sheet. "The name of the Portsmouth bank president and the bank's address are written out here as well my name and current information. You will see that I am staying at The Tipi, and, of course, I will notify you if my residence changes."

"Thank you, I will complete the paperwork. I see Mister Gaines coming this way. Just stop by here before you leave. I will have some papers for you to sign and will give you some blank drafts, so you will be able to draw on your account."

Grant turned and saw a trim man with salt and pepper hair walking his way. As Gaines approached, he judged the banker to be only slightly shorter than his own six feet and the man's age somewhere in his mid-forties. Gaines tendered a friendly smile as he came up to Grant and extended his hand.

The men exchanged firm grips, and Gaines said, "I'm Matt Gaines, Mister Coolidge. If you can spare a few minutes, why don't you join me in my office, and we can get acquainted a bit?"

Grant was just starting to learn that he had been naïve if not negligent about tending to business matters, but he did know that a man always made the time to give his banker as much time as he wanted. "Certainly, it would be my pleasure."

He followed Gaines to his office and was seated at a small round-topped table in a corner to the right of the banker's desk, which was stacked with files and papers, obviously a working desk. Gaines took one of the three remaining chairs, and no sooner was he seated than Katy Culper appeared with two mugs and a coffee pot. She filled the mugs and left the pot behind, patting Grant on the shoulder before she departed the room. If he did not know better, he would have thought there was a hint of flirtation in the gesture.

"Katy likes you," Gaines said. "The coffee is not a mandatory task. She decides on the coffee." He chuckled.

"Remarkable young woman. Brings a parade of eligible bachelors to the bank, and they stand in line at her station even if old Phil doesn't have a customer at his spot."

"She appears very efficient, certainly has a welcoming way about her."

"She's a good one. Katy's been with me four years now. Came to the bank when she was seventeen, right out of high school. She knows more about the day-to-day operations of the bank than I do. I hate to take her away from the teller's desk, but I'm going to give her a vice-president's job soon. It will chafe the men some, but she's earned it, and I don't want to lose her." He blew on his coffee and took a sip. "But let's talk about you. I gather you are planning to stay a spell."

"Yes. I guess you could say indefinitely. I might sink roots if everything works out."

"Do you plan to start a business here, Mister Coolidge?"

"Please, call me Grant."

"And I'm Matt."

Grant said, "To answer your question, I am bringing my existing business with me. You see, I earn my living as a writer." He braced for the questions that would follow.

"That's interesting. I can't say I've ever known a writer outside the local newspaper. Do you write magazine articles?"

"No, I write dime novels, currently for Beadle."

"Do you write under your name?"

"No, I write under two pen names, P.J. Bowie and Jake West."

"You write the Marshal Tyree books?"

"I do."

"I have all of those and most of your Jake West novels. You are very gifted."

"Somehow I didn't see a banker as one of my readers."

"You might be surprised to learn who reads your novels. I read a wide range of books, but sometimes I just want to relax and escape to another world and not be tied up to a book that takes me a month to read. That's when I call on my dime novels. I'm not alone. Jeb Oaks over at the general store tries to stock all the dime novels, but he says he can't keep his shelves filled. He lets me know when a shipment comes in by rail and gives me first chance."

"A businessman needs to get along with his banker," Grant said.

"Well, Jeb doesn't have to worry about his credit. He's a good man. You must meet him soon."

"I'm looking to buy some clothes, and I was told Oaks General Store is the place to go, so that's on my list of stops today."

Gaines said, "See Jeb's wife, She Bear. She will give you more help than Jeb when it comes to buying clothes. They have a nice inventory. She picks all my suits. Since you are wearing a suit, I assume that is what you will be looking for."

"No, as a matter of fact I expect to retire this suit and wear it only for special occasions, and I hope it is rarely put into service."

"I understand. Unfortunately, as a banker my customers expect to see me in a suit."

A soft rapping on the door grabbed their attention. "Come in," Gaines said.

Katy stepped into the room. The seemingly perpetual smile had disappeared from her face. "Matt, Ozzie from the county sheriff's office says Jim Tolliver needs to meet with you right away. Ozzie seemed beside himself, said something awful has happened."

"I'll head right over." He turned to Grant. "Ozzie White is the sheriff's deputy and also holds the town marshal title. I will have to excuse myself, Grant. Just stay put. Katy will bring your paperwork, and you can finish your business here. We will continue our conversation another time. It has been a pleasure meeting you."

The men shook hands, and Gaines hurried out the office door. Katy remained but was flushed and teary-eyed. Grant slid his chair back and stood. "Katy, are you okay?"

"I don't have much of the story, and Ozzie said he wasn't supposed to say anything, but the body of a girl has been found near the Pennock School. Her throat was cut, and it appears she was debauched." She started sobbing, and Grant stepped forward and wrapped his arms about her, holding her till she was cried out.

Chapter 10

AFTER GRANT COMPLETED his business at the bank, he decided that his next stop would be the livery. Moon had told him that Enos Fletcher was something of a horse broker, holding others' horses for sale on commission and that he would be the first to contact if he wished to purchase a horse. "Watch out for the wily devil, though," she warned. "He will skin you if he can."

His feet would not take him everyplace he would wish to travel in the days ahead, and he preferred not to rent a horse by the day. Besides, a mount available in a stall in The Tipi's stable would be much more convenient. A dollar per day rent for a stall included hay to supplement or replace pasture off-season and a few daily servings of grain. The owner was responsible for care and feedings, but Grant had no objection to that. He preferred looking after his own critter. It was a chance to become better acquainted with the animal.

As he approached the livery, Grant saw a man slouched on a bench beside the entryway, chin resting against his chest. He was either dead or napping. As he neared, he confirmed the rise and fall of the man's chest that signaled he was alive. The sleeper had a tattered hat pulled down on his forehead to block the rays of a near blinding sunshine. The spiderweb of wrinkles above an obviously self-trimmed ragged, white beard told Grant that the man's youth was just a memory. When he was about ten feet distant, he paused, not wanting to startle the old man and unsure how to approach him.

"State your name and business, mister," came a gravelly voice from the figure that still did not move or open his eyes.

"Grant Coolidge. I'm looking to buy a horse if you've got a critter that isn't crow bait or a knot-head."

The old man straightened and glared at Grant, revealing sea-blue eyes that challenged his visitor. "I don't sell nothing but good horse flesh, not that I couldn't to a damn tenderfoot."

Enos Fletcher was obviously lacking in sense of humor. Best to back off and make peace. "I was just joshing you. I'm guessing you are Enos Fletcher. If so, you come highly recommended. I was told that you offer quality horses for sale and won't try to take advantage of a man," he lied.

Enos stiffly pushed himself up from the bench. His stooped posture made him almost a foot shorter than Grant, but he would not have been a tall man in his prime. "Yeah, I'm Enos Fletcher. You can call me Enos till I tell you otherwise." He offered a gnarled hand, and Grant found the grip surprisingly firm, reminding him that Moon had warned him not to underestimate the man.

"Can I look at your horses?" Grant asked.

"I got a half dozen geldings and two mares in the corral out back if you want to see what I got. If there ain't nothing to suit you, I got a feller from a small horse outfit bringing a few more animals in tomorrow."

Grant followed the grizzled man down the alleyway. Fletcher limped noticeably as he walked. There was likely a story there, but it would be ill-mannered to inquire. It was a writer's failing to create a back story for every incident and person he encountered. He had wondered earlier about Katy when he held her at the bank while she regained her composure. The tragic event the law was investigating sounded horrible, but her reaction seemed extreme. Was there something in her history that triggered her response? And he felt a bit of guilt at the pleasure he felt at holding a pretty woman under such circumstances. He had been living like a monk for such a long time that the memories of such times had dulled.

"Here we be," Enos said. "Tell me if you think there's a bad horse in the bunch."

Grant studied the horses that milled about the large corral, stirred to action by the visitors. He could sense Enos watching him, probably trying to guess which mounts were catching Grant's eye, so he could play tough on the price. Horses were expensive, often costing ten times the cost of a brood cow or heifer. "There might be a horse or two I'd consider. I'd want to ride the critter, see how it responds to a rider and reins."

"They're broke. All of them. Broke good, I guarantee it. But some is more spirited than others. I wouldn't deny it. If you're looking for something on the quiet side, you might want to try that sorrel mare. She's calm as water in a horse trough. That calico gelding is as fancy as anything you'll find and on the gentle side, too. Did you ride much back east, or was you more of a buggy sort?"

It was interesting how folks from different sections of the country viewed each other through stereotypical eyes. The horse was transportation coast to coast, but he noticed some westerners had the notions that a man from the east knew little about horses. It did not matter. He had learned that being underestimated often provided a helpful edge in dealing with his fellow humans. "I rode horses on occasion," Grant said. He had his eye on a grayish-blue gelding that did not share the curiosity of some of the horses that came up close to the board fence. The critter did not appear spooked, just disinterested. It was an eye-catching horse with a dark mane and tail and dorsal stripe, a rare color back home, and he had not seen another since arriving in Lockwood. But what caught his attention was the gelding's size and muscling. It was a deep-chested horse with powerful-looking hind quarters.

He rubbed his chin thoughtfully. Did he need a horse like that for his purposes? Of course not. He said, "I'd like to ride the gray gelding."

"The grulla?"

"Is that what you call a horse with that strange color?"

"Yep. Comes from the Mexicans they say."

"Groo-yuh. How do you spell that?"

"How the hell would I know? Why would I care? Feller said the color's named after a damn bird—a crane of all things."

Grant had English and Spanish dictionaries in the trunk. He liked to track new words and would know how to spell the horse's color by nightfall. "Well, I'd like to ride the critter. Do you have a saddle and bridle I can use?"

"Didn't expect you'd ride bareback."

The mount turned a little spooky when they tried to catch it in the corral, but fortunately the gelding was haltered and did not resist once Grant clutched the leather straps. The horse accepted bit and bridle and did not fight the saddle, verifying Enos Fletcher's claim that it had been broken. "I would like to take him out for an hour if that would be alright."

"Finish saddling. I'll open the north gate," Enos said.

Grant stepped into the stirrup and swung into the saddle. The instant he settled in, the horse started bucking and almost catapulted the rider from the saddle, but Grant refused to panic and reined the animal to the open gate. The gelding broke for the opening, and Grant let it run, easing the mount toward a trail that appeared to lead toward the foothills.

The horse did not fight him after that and seemed to be enjoying a good run. The grulla responded to the rein signals but obviously liked to be on the move. It should be ridden frequently, but Moon Dupree's pasture would give it ample exercise space when the horse was struck by the urge to trot or gallop. As they rode into the foothills and he was able to shift his focus from the mount, Grant surveyed the panorama about him, the vast green valley and its branches, the winding North Laramie River that twisted through the grass-carpeted floor and the snow-capped mountain peaks to the west. He thought of the artist Albert Bierstadt and his breathtaking landscapes of the West, and it occurred to him that he had been given the opportunity to make his home in such a place if he could carve out a niche here.

When he returned to the livery, he found Enos waiting near the corral gate. When he dismounted, the geezer hobbled over. "What do you think?"

Grant said, "I'd like to take him in the stable and brush him down after I get his saddle off. We can talk while I do that. He had a decent drink from the stream that borders the town, but maybe he could be treated to a bit of grain."

"I can have a boy do that later."

"I'd like to, if you don't mind."

"What suits you. Don't matter none to me."

While Grant tended to the horse, Enos watched, obviously waiting for Grant's verdict, reluctant to seem too eager to sell. Grant admitted to himself that he was handicapped when it came to dickering about things, he had little patience. Many enjoyed the little game of haggling over a price. He hated it. He wanted to own this horse in the worst way and figured he was destined to lose this game. The question was by how much.

Grant said, "How old is this critter?"

"Three years this spring. You'd be taking on a young-ster what could last you the rest of your riding years."

"Two years could do that."

"True enough, but a man's got to have optimism about such things. I ain't made no plans for dying yet."

"What's the owner want for this horse?"

"Four hundred dollars."

Grant bristled. He expected to pay more than he should, but this was robbery. "You cannot be serious. I could buy a decent gelding back in Ohio for a hundred fifty."

"This ain't Ohio, and this ain't just any gelding. I'm thinking you ain't as dumb as some would guess and that you know that."

That was a dubious compliment. He supposed that the horse market was higher in the west, especially for good mounts. He always put Marshall Tyree and his other fictional heroes on top horseflesh. They tended toward stallions, though. "Let's quit wasting time. Tell me what the owner will sell for. He doesn't expect four hundred dollars."

"He is she. The lady won't take less than three hundred fifty dollars. You'd best be on your way than offer less. I've only had this horse two days. He won't be here two more, I'm betting."

Well, it would not be the first stupid thing he had done and not likely the last. "Okay. I'll go the three-fifty. Do you want my check today?"

"Nope, you pay the owner direct, and she will take care of the commission."

"Where do I find this owner?"

"Here's how it works. I'll let the owner know this afternoon, and she will make up a bill of sale. You pay her tomorrow and come back and show me the bill of sale, and you can take that grulla gelding with you."

"Where do I find this woman?"

"You go down to the law offices of Ramsey and Locke on Main Street. Her name is Hannah Locke. If she's busy, her clerk will take care of things."

"Hannah Locke?"

"Yep. You know her?"

"Uh, no. I've heard the name."

"Her and her partner, Ethan Ramsey are the best law wranglers in the territory. Now, you'll need a saddle and other tack. I got a fair inventory of used tack here. I can cheapen the cost of the horse if you don't got to have new."

"I'll see what you've got and let you know when I come in tomorrow." He was sure as hell going to see what new tack cost at the general store before he dealt with the old crook for the used stuff.

Chapter 11

I T WAS WELL past noon when Grant walked away from the livery, and he was starving. Perhaps it was the mountain air, but he could not recall the last time his stomach had growled so forcefully in protest. He asked a cowboy dismounting in front of the stable about the location of The Chowdown.

"About four blocks west, keep your eye on the side streets, and you'll see it about a block north of Main," he was informed.

Strolling along the boardwalk, he passed the general store and was again amazed at the enormity of it. It appeared that during expansions, the owner had acquired one adjacent building after another until he had collected a good half block of structures and connected them by punching doorways. Peering through the windows, Grant could see that the store was sectioned off by merchandise categories, food supplies in one part nearest the center entry, hardware in another area. Men's clothing and ladies' garments were allotted separate rooms, and there was a section for saddles, ropes and livestock items. These were along the boardwalk frontage, and who knew what treasures were hidden deeper in the store. He had seen such things in New York City, but he had not expected such an enterprise in the primitive west he wrote about in his novels, perhaps a secret best kept from readers.

When he arrived at The Chowdown, he had second thoughts about entering. The paint on the small building was peeling, the sign above the door was faded to bare readability and the window was so filthy that he could not see any customers dining inside. Several men in business suits exited the restaurant, seemingly in good spirits, so he opened the door and stepped into a room packed with diners of all types—cowhands, matronly ladies, clerks and working men dirtier than the restaurant's window. There were several vacant chairs, but they were at tables otherwise occupied.

The incessant chatter and laughter from the patrons were deafening. He turned and started to exit when he heard a voice behind him say, "Hey, Coolidge, over here."

He turned and saw a man sitting at a two-chair table next to the window. He was pointing at the table's vacant chair, waving him over. Grant had no desire to dine with a stranger, let alone with one that looked like this one. The man who proposed to host him was a stocky man with a black scraggly beard displaying white stripes off the corners of his mouth that dropped past each side of his chin, making it appear that he carried a skunk on his face. He was barrel-chested with hams for shoulders.

Grant sighed, removed his hat and walked toward the table, unable to think of a way to gracefully decline the invitation. Besides, he was curious about this man knowing his name. When he reached the table, the man stood, revealing he was taller than Grant would have guessed, almost his own six feet, but likely fifty to sixty pounds heavier. The stranger's own dusty hat remained perched on the man's head. The stranger offered a big smile that revealed a missing front tooth, and extended his hand, gripping Grant's like a vice. When his host released the hand, Grant hoped the had not suffered any broken fingers.

"My name's Bushwa Sparks—baptized name is Obadiah, but nobody's called me that since Mama died twenty years back."

They sat down. "I guess you know my name," Grant said. "Have we met?"

Sparks let loose a throaty laugh. "Nope, we ain't met. Stranger in town, staying at The Tipi. Word gets around."

"The postmaster."

Sparks laughed again. "Nope. Not this time. Trouble Yates. He was painting over at the Quaker school when I went by. He told me about you taking down that outlaw. The kid thinks you're a Pinkerton. Are you?"

"No. I hate to disappoint Trouble, but I swear I am not a Pinkerton."

Before Bushwa Sparks could pursue the subject, a hefty blonde waitress appeared at the table. "Need your orders. You can choose between the roasted beef dinner or the roasted beef dinner."

Sparks said, "Two roasted beef dinners, both on my ticket, Rosie."

She said, "Seems fair if this poor man has got to put up eating with you. We're running behind some. You will have a fifteen-minute wait."

"It's not necessary for you to buy my dinner," Grant said.

"It ain't, but it's my pleasure. Trouble judges you'll be a good man to have around Lockwood once you get seasoned to things here."

"I hope so."

"I live southwest of town a few miles up in the higher foothills just below where the steep mountains start. I rent, buy and sell properties."

"I see." Grant would not have guessed it.

"Yep. Come here after the war some twenty years back. South Carolina is home. Fought for the Confederacy, as you might guess. You was likely a mite young for that."

Bushwa's southern accent lingered, but it had doubtless faded. "I fought with the blue. Ohio's home to me." He had no interest in talking about Gettysburg or his injury.

"Cavalry?"

"Infantry."

"Me too. Still got a numb foot from all that walking. Never walk when I can ride."

Grant shifted the conversation. "Do you deal in mostly town properties."

"All kinds. Buy run-down houses and cabins. Fix them up. Sell when I can. Rent out till I do. Got some grazing lands, too, but I ain't in the cow business. Are you here for a spell?"

"Hope so. I may sink roots if things work out."

"You're outfitted like some kind of law wrangler or something. Are you one of them?"

There was no way out, and Bushwa was obviously going to hear soon enough. Better it came from the horse's mouth. "I write novels."

"What's novels?"

"Books. I make up stuff and write stories for folks to read."

"A man can get paid for that?"

"Yes. I've made a living at it for nearly ten years now."

"I'll be damned. Never read a whole book. Ain't had no formal schooling. Mama taught me a little, but she never went to school either. Pa could barely write his name out. If I study it, I can read what's on a deed. The important legal stuff I leave to Hannah Locke. She does my lawyering. Trust her with my life, I would. I'm hellish good with numbers, though, if I say so myself. Mama got me started good, and I just took off from there. Anyhow, I admire somebody that can read good. And writing a whole damned book, now that's something I got to look up to. Are you famous or something?"

"No, I'm not famous."

He was rescued by the waitress who returned with two heaping plates of roasted beef, fried potatoes drenched in gravy, and beans. She set the plates on the table and said, "I'll be back with coffee and cherry pie."

Grant said, "I would have been fine with half this much."

"You're too skinny. We're going to fatten you up out here in God's country."

Grant attacked the plate of food and concluded quickly that the meal was every bit as good as it looked and smelled. The eating environment was far less than pristine, but he could see why the establishment carried a reputation for excellent cuisine. He was certain this would not be his last visit, but the evening meal at The Tipi promised to be every bit as good, and his waistline would not tolerate two such meals daily without his belt surrendering a notch or two.

"So, you're going to make up your yarns right here in Lockwood?" Bushwa asked.

"I'm going to try it for a time and see how things work out."

"If you decide to stay on permanent-like, talk to me. I got some places I'd sell cheap."

Grant suspected he was dealing with Enos Fletcher's twin. "We'll see. I won't be in a hurry. I'm staying at The Tipi and think I will be content there for the time being."

"Oh, you've got Moon Dupree looking after you. She's a fine woman. Now that she's a widow, I'd come courting if I was looking to have a woman share my bed. Pretty thing. Smart. Favorable disposition. But I turned sixty a few months back and never took on a real wife. Kept company with a few squaws when I first got here, so I got nothing against Injuns, but I ain't inclined to change my ways. I find company when I got the itch at The Doll House. You do know about the Doll House?"

Grant really did not want to talk about Bushwa's intimacies. "I've been told about The Doll House."

"Too bad about Moon's husband, but he was a no-account half-breed what showed up here about the same time as me some twenty years back. You'd thought she'd have knowed better since her first man was a breed Frenchman, too. They wasn't married legal-like, I'm told, and she wouldn't leave Lockwood when he wanted to move on. He didn't leave her with any whelps, but somebody told me they had a stillborn. She had the girl and a boy by Dupree. Boy died of the diphtheria when he was a little feller."

"What happened to Moon's husband?"

"He done a rope dance at a neck-tie party."

"I don't understand."

"Some ranchers strung him up for rustling cattle about five years back."

"Hanged him?"

"Yep. Big ruckus over it. Sheriff arrested the two ranchers who put on the party. County Attorney charged them with murder, and the jury found them not guilty. Most folks around here ain't going to fault somebody for stringing up a cattle rustler. Besides, Pierre Dupree had made his way stealing one thing or another all the years he'd been here. Poor Moon was always bailing him out of trouble, and he did three or four six-months stays in the county jail for one thing or another. She was always a hard worker and made her own way. Never let him near the business she started up. By that time, they wasn't living together no more."

"Divorced?"

"No, nothing official like that I know of. And she must have still cared for him, because she took it hard when he died. Saw to the burial of the corpse and got him planted up on Sunrise Hill. She's better off without him, but I ain't sure she knows it."

The crowd was starting to thin out of the restaurant, so the men enjoyed a second cup of coffee to wash down the pie, and Grant found himself enjoying the company of this rough-cut man, thinking that Obadiah "Bushwa" Sparks would make a great character for a novel. For that matter, it seemed that he was already collecting a troupe of characters and a basket of ideas for future novels.

Finally, Grant said, "I've got other visits to make this afternoon, Bushwa. I thank you for dinner and good conversation. I hope we meet up again soon."

"You can bet on that, Grant. Maybe you will put me in one of them books."

"You can bet on that."

Chapter 12

GRANT FELT A twinge of guilt when he returned to The Tipi late afternoon with several sacks of clothes, and Moon Dupree insisted on laundering two pairs of Levi's and three new cotton shirts and a week's worth of undershorts and socks. Moon said, "It won't take long. They aren't dirty. You just want to get the newness and stiffness out. Folks will notice if you don't wash them, and they will be more comfortable."

"But you can wait till tomorrow. They will need to dry."

"This dry mountain air will do the job by sundown. If not, we can hang them in the house to finish."

"I do appreciate it. I was hoping to wear some of them tomorrow."

"And you can't walk around town in those clothes another day. Folks will think you are a dude. They certainly scream 'tenderfoot.' You still have unpacking to do. Go work on that. Come down for supper at seven o'clock. That will be the tail end of the diners, and we can talk some afterward if you like while we wait for the laundry to dry."

"I would like that."

"By the way, I like your taste in the purchases you made. Simple shirts in solid colors without all the swirls and spangles that some newcomers would buy. You are wearing a working cowhand's boots, and the buffalo hide jacket is perfect, has a worn look but will block the wind even better than cowhide."

He rolled his eyes. "I have a confession to make. I didn't make the selections. Carissa Oaks made the suggestions, and I followed them."

"I'm not surprised. That was She-Bear, a renowned Sioux warrior. She and her husband, Jeb, were fierce fighters in their day. Jeb is a former buffalo soldier. It took him some years to convince She-Bear to use what he considers a more civilized name for business purposes. She finally gave in, but the name did not gain her any social status, as if she cares a whit. Full bloods are not welcome in some circles, but half-bloods are accepted by necessity because of their large numbers. Of course, it likely does not help that She-Bear is married to a colored man."

"That's a problem here?"

"Not with most. They are respected merchants, and I am not aware of any overt hostility toward either. Their business is needed desperately, and they have prospered. Those things have a way of destroying barriers, I think."

Grant thought that Moon Dupree was an intelligent, thoughtful woman, and as the swelling in her face melted away, a quite lovely one was being unveiled.

Later that evening, he helped Moon clear the table and dry dishes while Jasmine tended to the laundry.

"It seems very strange having a man help with this task," Moon said. "I have lived alone for some years. Of course, I never experienced a man lowering himself to do this chore."

"I'm used to it and don't mind."

"I read one of your books today when I should have been working."

"Seriously?"

"The P. J. Bowie novel, *Sioux Sundown*. I loved the story and the happy ending to the romance between the young Sioux woman and the soldier. You write realistic dialogue."

He sensed that she was holding back, "But . . ."

She shrugged. "I couldn't begin to write a novel, but a few things troubled me. The setting was not identified, but Sioux were not likely to be encamped near desert and cactuses, and I don't think chiefs would have been wearing full headdresses during a buffalo hunt, that sort of thing. I know the story is the important thing, and I am probably the only Sioux who has read the book. I'm sorry, I don't mean to criticize."

At first, he was stung by her comments. The author craves praise no matter how undeserving. The book is his or her child and the first impulse is to defend. But to defend the indefensible? "I do virtually no research. I make up stuff as quickly as possible to meet my publisher's deadline, so he will send the next draft for payment. I sell words like you rent rooms, or the Oaks sell food and clothing."

"You are offended, and I did not intend to do that. I truly admire and envy what you do, but I suspect you could do so much more if you chose. I see you like a craftsman who can build a serviceable cabin but possesses the skills to build a magnificent mansion. You have an untapped talent. I truly believe that."

He finished putting plates and cups in the cupboard, while she put bowls and pans away. "I came west because I thought I could make my work more authentic if I saw some of the places I write about and, more importantly, came to know and understand the people who live here. I must confess that I dream of writing something beyond the dime novels. Saying that, I would never look down my nose at those of my brethren who make a meager living at such work. They are entertaining their readers and that is their purpose, and I console myself with that thought."

"And you rightfully should," Moon said. "We can sit at the kitchen table in here if you like and if you have time. I keep no spirits in the house. Have you tried peppermint tea?"

"I have been running from the demon alcohol for some years now. I do not recall drinking peppermint tea, but I would love to try it. And I have nothing but time this evening."

They sat on opposite sides of the tiny table that had no room for a third person, and Grant, sipping at his tea, discovered a new delight. "I could make a habit of this. I may have to give up coffee."

"I enjoy my morning coffee," Moon said, "but the remainder of the day, I prefer to drink one tea or the other. I grow most of the plants for my teas. Tell me about your day. What do you think of Lockwood?"

"An interesting town. I am rapidly changing my image of the west. My impression is that there is a different culture here that I have not captured yet, but it is not a country of backward simpletons as some in the east tend to portray it, and that I fear my own writing has sometimes implied. When it comes to fools, I suspect the proportions on both sides of the Mississippi will be about the same."

She laughed. "I have never been far east, so I cannot say."

"I met some interesting people, Enos Fletcher and Bushwa Sparks to name a few."

She laughed again, and he noticed the flash of perfect white teeth. It occurred to him that he had not seen her smile much before tonight. He guessed he had not been Mister Good Cheer since his arrival either, but it had been a good while since he had felt so at ease with a woman, or any person for that matter.

"Interesting? That is a kind way to put it. I love them both, but neither is universally loved, I assure you."

"I am not surprised. Fletcher got the best of me on a horse purchase. I will be bringing a grulla gelding back to occupy a stall in your stable tomorrow after I settle with the owner. New saddles are expensive at the Oaks store. I hope I can deal with Fletcher for used tack. I suspect he skinned me on the horse's price."

"I doubt if anyone ever got the best of Enos on a horse trade. You will have a lot of company. May I ask who the horse's seller is?"

"Hannah Locke, one of your local lawyers. I happen to know her brother. I am to settle at her office tomorrow. I don't know if I will meet her."

"You know her brother? What are the chances of that happening?"

"Well, it's not all coincidence. We served together in the war. He was a hero. I was not. He is a lawyer, too, in southeast Nebraska. I stopped to see him on my way west, and he mentioned a sister in Lockwood, Wyoming. I had no destination in mind and by the time my train hit North Platte, I thought, why not? I certainly didn't antici-pate I would be buying a horse from Ian Locke's sister."

Moon said, "Hannah is my personal lawyer—and best friend."

"Seems like everybody knows Hannah Locke."

"If you get to know her, you will come to like her."

"If I get to know her? What does that mean?"

"She is not very trusting of men and can seem a bit brusque at first."

"I hope she is busy and that I can deal with her clerk tomorrow. The horse is a fine animal. How does she hap-pen to be in the horse business?"

"She has a small ranch outside of town, not more than a thousand acres—that is next to nothing in these parts. She runs about ten mares and raises foals. She breaks

Ron Schwab

and trains the colts and fillies except for some she sells as foals or yearlings to ranchers who want to do their own breaking and training. Most she sells as three-year olds, so she will have thirty to forty critters on her place at a given time. She hires parttime help when she needs it— especially winters when the grass won't feed the stock. Trouble Yates helps her break the horses."

"Is there anything Trouble doesn't do?"

"If there is, I haven't discovered it."

Chapter 13

"I HAVE APPOINTMENTS after eleven o'clock for the remainder of the day," Hannah Locke told Hamilton Fish, the firm's young law clerk. "If this Coolidge shows up to settle on the horse before ten-thirty, I would like to speak with him." It was shortly after nine o'clock, and she had just given Fish the signed bill of sale so he could collect the purchase price and settle with the buyer.

She turned back to the will she was revising on her desk. It was written in longhand, one of the first documents she had prepared when she joined Ethan Ramsey in his law practice. After she penned in her changes, Ham would type a new document on the firm's Remington typewriter, producing an impressive, printed exhibit for the client but not more valid.

She tended toward skepticism about the worth of such things, and her partner, Ethan Ramsey, who was some ten years older than she, occasionally teased her about her resistance to change. What new contraption would they think of next? Ethan predicted that within ten years telephone service would arrive in Lockwood. He was rarely wrong about such things. She thought of the instrument as another annoyance.

She was pleased about sale of the grulla gelding. He was a magnificent creature, and it was always hard for her to part with her special babies. She hoped to procure some reassurance from the new owner that Blue was being placed with someone who would appreciate and care for him properly. The money was arriving at a convenient time since her bank account balance was on the verge of striking zero. The horse business had been sucking up all her law firm earnings lately, and the ranch mortgage payment was due in a few weeks.

She finished the will revisions a few moments before the law clerk gave his usual single tap on her office door. "Come in, Ham."

When he entered, she handed him the revised will. "Ready for your magic, Ham. I think Mister Rafferty is planning to stop by later this afternoon to sign."

"I can get right on it. I wanted to tell you that Mister Coolidge is here to settle for the horse. Did you still wish to meet him?"

"Yes. You can show him in and bring the bill of sale back to me. I will collect the payment." She rolled her chair back from the desk and stood. Habitually, she swept her fingers across her forehead to brush a few wild strands of her shoulder-length, copper-colored hair away from her forehead.

Shortly, Ham escorted a clean-shaven man with neatly trimmed, chestnut hair into her office. He was taller than the average man but not a towering figure, she noted. He was wearing Levis and a pale green shirt that nearly matched his hazel eyes. The garments could have been tailored for his lean frame. He was too handsome for his own good, she thought. Thankfully, she had removed herself from the market as far as males were concerned. Appearances were far too deceptive.

Ham dropped the bill of sale on her desk and slipped away, and Hannah stepped around the desk and extended her hand. "A pleasure to meet you, Mister Coolidge. Please be seated." They shook hands and sat down, Coolidge taking one of the chairs in front of her desk.

"It's nice meeting you, Miss Locke. I'm excited about buying your gelding. He's a fine animal. Enos Fletcher drives a hard bargain, though."

She would not tell Coolidge that she had informed Enos she would sell for sixty dollars less than the man was paying.

"He earns his commissions." Enos claimed a ten percent commission but he more than earned it. He sold all her horses unless somebody came out to the ranch to make a deal. "Blue is a bit spirited but once he comes to trust you, I don't think you will have any regrets about the purchase."

"Blue? That's his name? Blue. I like that. It fits. I won't change the name."

She was happy to hear that. "Where will you be taking him, if I may ask?"

"Not far. Within an easy walk from here. I'm staying at The Tipi indefinitely, and I have arranged to put him up in the stable there. I will spoil him, I assure you. And I'm sure you will see him on occasion. Moon says that you and she are friends."

"Yes. We are friends." Enough of this idle chatter, she decided. He came to pay for a horse, and she had other business to tend to. "I assume you are prepared to pay for the horse?"

"Yes, of course. I have made out a draft payable to you at the Gaines Bank if that is satisfactory." He handed her the draft, and she gave it a quick glance before pushing the bill of sale across the desk. "If you show this to Enos Fletcher, he will release Blue to your care."

Coolidge picked up the bill of sale. "Thank you, Miss Locke. I will be going directly to the livery from here."

"I believe that is all the business we have then, Mister Coolidge. Thank you, and I will be disappointed if things do not work out well between you and Blue."

Coolidge started to say something, and then seemed to think better of it and was half out of his chair before he sat back down. "Can you spare a few more minutes, Miss Locke?"

She was not inclined to waste any more time with the man, but he had been pleasant enough and she was not that pressed. "Well, yes, I suppose. What is it?"

"First, I had planned to stop by sometime and tell you that I had a recent conversation with your brother."

"Thad?"

"I'm sorry. I know you have four brothers."

"Thad is my twin. The others are half-brothers and much older. I barely know them."

"Ian. He and I served in the war together. I visited him at Borderview, Nebraska on my journey to Lockwood. I would not have come to Lockwood if he had not mentioned that he had a sister here."

She hoped this man was not a perverted stalker of women. She thought of the Indian girl who had been raped and murdered not far from the Pennock School yesterday. How long had Grant Coolidge been in town? "You came because I was here?"

"No. No. I just did not have a destination in mind at the time. I still didn't know when I arrived in North Platte and Lockwood jumped into my mind."

"I see." But she did not. "Well, except for my twin, I have little contact with my family. I hope Ian is doing well. I know he was a war hero and all that but because of age differences and separate households, the half-brothers are mere acquaintances as far as I am concerned. Now if that is all . . ."

"Well, Miss Locke, I did have some possible legal business to discuss, but I guess I should be on my way."

After Grant Coolidge departed, she chided herself for her abruptness. She could not imagine that this stranger could have any legal matters that would be worth her time, but certainly he had not caused the estrangement from her father. She owed him an apology, she supposed, but not till she learned more about him. She hoped the sheriff was aware of the stranger in town. She worried about Moon with this man in her house. She assumed her friend still kept the shotgun and derringer in her bedroom. Perhaps they would have an opportunity to talk soon.

Chapter 14

TROUBLE YATES WAS cleaning stalls at the livery when Grant entered the stable to claim his horse. When he saw Grant walking down the alleyway, Trouble leaned the pitchfork against a wall and waved.

"Ready to pick up that gelding?" Trouble said when they met up.

"That's what I'm here for, but I want to see what you've got for tack first. If you don't have anything for the right price, I may need to make a visit to the general store. I'm not much for bareback riding."

"You don't want to pay those prices. We've got something that will do fine. Enos is out for his annual bath, haircut and beard trim at the barber shop. He won't be back before noon, but I can deal with you for the tack. In fact, I've already picked out a saddle, bit and bridle

I think you'll like, and I'll toss in saddlebags at no extra charge."

"Are you going to skin me like Enos did?"

Trouble chuckled. "There won't be any dickering. I'll give you the bottom dollar price, and you can take it or leave it."

Grant was skeptical, "I'll look at it."

Trouble led him to a stall that was crammed with saddles and other tack. "We've got all kinds at lower prices here, and I can go cheap if you want, but this outfit is like new." He nodded toward a saddle with bags and bit and bridle resting on a bench along the stall partition.

Grant stepped over, lifted the saddle and examined it. Nary a scratch on the leather. It was like new and top-grade. It would cost over a hundred dollars at Oaks General Store without the other gear. "Okay, what would this cost me?"

"Fifty dollars for the works, and you can pick one of the saddle blankets draped over the side panel. Like I said, take it or leave it."

"I'll take it."

Trouble said, "Enos is going to bitch and moan for a week. He was hoping for seventy-five, but he told me what he got for the grulla. I think a newcomer ought to be treated better, and he's still got a good profit. He got a horse and this tack from a man that got himself killed in a gunfight so never showed up to claim his property. Nobody knew who the fella was or where he came from, so he's buried in the potter's field outside of town. He had enough gold coin in his pocket for George Caldwell to fix him and charge for his most expensive coffin, which likely wasn't the one he was buried in. County sheriff took the rest for his contingency fund, and everybody was happy—especially Enos."

"Well, I've got enough gold coin to pay you with an eagle and two doubles." He plucked the bill of sale from his coat pocket and presented it. "Here's the bill of sale. Maybe you would help me get the horse and saddle up, and I'll be out of your way."

Trouble said, "Did you meet Hannah?"

"I did."

"What did you think of her?"

This was getting into dangerous territory the way words travelled in this town. He was not about to say he found her cold and distant and on the brink of rude. "She was very businesslike. I'm sure she's a good lawyer."

"She's the best. Well, probably not any better than her partner, Ethan Ramsey. But he's been lawyering longer." Trouble leaped to another subject. "You really aren't a Pinkerton, are you?"

"No, of course not."

"I talked to Bushwa Sparks. He said he ate with you yesterday at The Chowdown."

"Yes, he's an interesting man."

"Me and him work together lots. Do you know what 'bushwa' means?"

"Never thought about it."

"Buffalo shit. Some say bullshit. Means the same. Stories that ain't more than half truths. Bushwa earned his name, so I can't be sure what he's telling me is true."

As a novelist, Grant supposed he wrote a lot of bushwa. "What are you getting at, Trouble?"

"Bushwa said you write books, and I'm starting to hear whispers other places."

"Yes, I write dime novels."

"I'll be darned. I read those all the time. I buy a few at the general store, but Matt Gaines gives me most. He loans me other kinds, too, more serious stuff. He's like a library. I don't recollect reading any with your name on them."

Grant took his comment as a challenge to his claim to be an author, and his own vanity forced him to respond. "P.J. Bowie?"

"Sure, I've read all his novels. I like them better than Ned Buntline's stuff, especially those with Marshal Buck Tyree."

"I am P.J. Bowie."

"You're joshing me."

"Jake West?"

"Not as good as Bowie, but I think I've read most of his, too."

"I am Jake West."

Trouble turned silent, cocked his head to one side and studied Grant's face, evidently looking for a lie there, Grant thought.

"I'm starting to think you're telling me the truth. Kind of like Samuel Clemens being Mark Twain, something like that?"

"Something like that, they're called pseudonyms or pen names."

Trouble grinned, "This is an honor—meeting P.J. Bowie in person. Say, are you going to write about the killing?"

"I don't know anything about the killing. I only heard that a young woman was killed, but no other details."

"This might be something to put in your books. Tell you what. We'll get your horse, and you meet me over at The Chowdown's at noon and feed me, and then I'll take you over to meet my step-pa Sheriff Tolliver. Maybe he'll let go of some information. He used to be a U.S. Marshal before he married my Ma. He's somebody you ought to get acquainted with anyhow. Your books are a bit off kilter on how things are in the west sometimes. No criticism intended."

Grant winced. He took it as criticism and had to remind himself that his purpose for coming west was to discover authenticity for his stories. And, yes, it would be good to become acquainted with the sheriff. He could be a rich source to be mined for information.

"Okay, I'll meet you later. You've got a free meal this noon."

Chapter 15

DINING WITH TROUBLE told Grant that he had stumbled onto a virtual encyclopedia about the inhabitants, geography and history of Lockwood and Big River County. Trouble seemed to know everybody and had journeyed over every inch of the county. He was amazingly well read, chattering one minute about a P.J. Bowie dime novel and the next quoting the economic philosopher and writer Adam Smith. It was clear that he was one of Smith's disciples for a free market unfettered by the whims of government and its bureaucrats. This was not surprising given his tenacious work ethic and creativity. It was also obvious that banker Matthew Gaines was a hero and mentor to the enterprising young man.

Nearing the end of their meals, Grant decided to press Trouble on the murder. "Tell me about the girl who was killed, Trouble. Where did it take place? How was she killed?"

"Her name was Abigail Doe Eyes. She was fifteen, a year younger than me. Pretty, tiny thing. Lived with her grandma. Mother is dead and father drunk and wandering most of the time. Found her by Fox Creek not far from where it joins up with the North Laramie River. The three buildings that make up the Pennock School are within maybe a hundred yards." He lowered his voice to a near whisper. "She was naked, and somebody slit her throat ear to ear. Doc Weintraub acts as county coroner when such things come up. He had the body at his hospital yesterday. He ain't given a report last I knew, but between you and me, Jim—that's my step-pa—thinks Abigail was . . . ravaged, maybe by more than one person. There were hoofprints in the soft ground along the creek, three critters it looked like. Jim knows sign. If he says three, you can bet that's the number."

"Any suspects?"

"None that I know of, but old Jim's pretty close-mouthed about such things."

When they finished, Grant and Trouble led their horses down the dusty road back to Main Street and turned west to where the sheriff's office sat midway down the block. Grant had often passed the building, a new brick structure which also quartered the county jail.

They hitched the mounts to the rail in front of the office. Trouble said, "I'll introduce you to Jim and then I've got to be heading out to the Pennock School. I've got a painting contract out there that I'm working with some fellas on. I need to get it finished up tomorrow because I'm working half days at the sawmill for a week after that. Hoping to buy the darn thing in a few years if I can keep Old Man Brown happy. He's not close to satisfying the market, and he'll have competition coming in if he can't get production up."

Trouble Yates was making his head spin, and he was starting to feel like a lazy oaf. Time to edit his novels, so he would have something ready when the Beadle contracts showed up. Next stop would be Lockwood Furniture & Funerals where he hoped to find a used desk. Blue's cost was forcing him to economize before he spent up his saved funds. Money from the next books would be several months distant, and he would need to draw on his accounts to meet rents and living expenses.

Trouble led him through a creaky, heavy oak door into the sheriff's office which had barred windows on each side of the doorway. Just inside was a large, scratched and pocked desk with two captain's chairs in front of it.

Behind the desk stood a tall, sturdily built man wearing a leather vest with sheriff's gold badge pinned to it. His face was largely hidden behind a short-cropped black beard. He had obviously been standing in front of the window and seen the visitors coming.

He turned toward them, displaying friendly brown eyes. "Howdy, Trouble. Saw you coming," the sheriff said. "I don't have any paying work for you today, so I'm surprised to see you here."

"I have to be on my way to a job, but I want you to meet my new friend, Grant Coolidge. He's the author folks are talking about."

Sheriff Tolliver stepped around the desk, and the men shook hands. "And the man who took down one of the jail tenants. I've been wanting to talk to you anyhow."

Tolliver pointed to a string bean of a man sitting at a rolltop desk pushed against the wall on the opposite side of the room. "That's Ozzie White, town marshal and chief deputy. Say 'howdy,' Ozzie". The man turned and offered a quick wave and a shy smile and said, "Howdy." He immediately swung back to his desk. Ozzie had unruly wheat-colored hair, a protruding Adam's apple showing above his shirt collar and obviously was not one for conversing with strangers.

"Sit down, Mister Coolidge. Maybe we can talk a bit."

"I'm gone," Trouble said and headed for the door.

Grant sat down, and the sheriff eased into his chair. He judged the sheriff to be about his age, maybe a few years older, and wondered if he had seen any war service. There was a hint of a Southern accent in his soft, mellow voice, so he probably would have been a Confederate.

"I heard about the poor Sioux girl," Grant said. "A tragedy. This must be preying on your mind night and day."

"Yeah. I didn't go home last night. So far, everything is a dead end."

"Well, I won't take up your time. You said you wanted to talk to me about your prisoner."

"Yeah. The prosecutor is going to be in this afternoon to talk about the incident at The Tipi. She will decide what, if any, charges to file."

"If any?"

Tolliver opened a desk drawer and pulled out a wanted poster, pushing it across the desktop for Grant to see. The face pictured on the poster was clearly that of the thief he encountered at The Tipi. "Hubert Grainger. Bank robbery in Denver. He's your guest, all right."

The sheriff said, "Moon told me he was registered as John Goodson at her place."

"Goodson? A sense of humor maybe."

"I doubt it, but there is a five-hundred-dollar reward listed on that poster. I'd say it's yours."

"I don't want a reward. I just happened to be there when the no-good was going to make off with the money. I'm not a bounty hunter. I just write about them."

"Seems to me like you've got a story about an accidental bounty hunter."

The sheriff had a point. Lord Byron had written in *Don Juan* that "Truth is stranger than fiction." Perhaps he should be searching for truth and converting it to his fictional stories. He supposed that notion hidden in the back of his head was what had pushed him westward in the first place. "I guess I will claim the reward and share it. I am thinking that Moon, Trouble, the sheriff's contingency fund and I will divide it equally."

"The sheriff's contingency fund? Now that's mighty generous."

Inclusion of the contingency fund had been an impulsive decision, and Grant admitted to himself that he had ulterior motives. He liked the sheriff and until proven otherwise judged him an honest man. But a former U.S. Marshal could be a trove of useful information for a writer whose most revered character was a U.S. Marshal. "I don't even know what it's used for, Sheriff, but I heard there was such a fund, and I assumed it serves a public purpose for a department strapped for taxpayer funds."

"It does. We use it to house itinerants in the jail temporarily, to buy a meal for a down-on-his-luck cowhand passing through, helping folks when their house has burned down—that sort of thing. Sometimes the fund provides a small reward for information. Anyhow, when Hannah Locke drops by—she's acting county prosecutor, she's going to ask my opinion about whether to file charges here or to just contact the Denver law and have them come and take him into custody. If we tell Denver to come and get him, we would have him out of here in a week, and the charges there are a hell of a lot more serious. Does that make sense to you?"

"Yeah, but why even ask me?"

"You're a writer. We don't want you putting out a story that we're not enforcing the law here."

"I'm not a newspaper reporter. The thought wouldn't have crossed my mind. I write dime novels. I make stuff up."

"You're serious? I read a few of those once. Ned Buntline books. Don't take offense, but I gave up on them. Just too farfetched. I was a marshal then, and his stories had so many inaccuracies, I couldn't read another."

"I know Ned. His real name is Edward Judson. I write under P.J. Bowie and Jake West. I saw some of my books in the general store, but don't pick them up. If you were disappointed in Ned's, you are not likely to find anything redeeming in mine. But I console myself that we entertain folks, bring pleasure to some."

"I can see that. I know lots of folks read dime novels."

"The big market is east of the Mississippi."

"But wouldn't you rather write a story that was accurate in its history and geography and such? Buntline placed saguaro cactuses and Comanche Indians in Montana as I recall. Would it be that hard to put the Comanche in Texas and the saguaro cactus in Arizona?"

"I agree it would make the story more credible." Grant suspected he had probably written more outlandish things.

"From here on, why don't you call me 'Jim?'"

"I'd be pleased to if you will call me 'Grant.'"

"Grant. I've got an idea. Why don't you follow through with me on this case with the Sioux girl? I'm shorthanded, and maybe you can offer some ideas during the investigation, see something I am missing. Regardless, you'd have a chance to see how things really work—or don't work—in the real lawman's world."

"Yes, as long as I don't get in the way, I would like that."

"I tell you what. I'll swear you in as a deputy. You'll have a badge and the authority, but the county won't pay you a nickel. Eliminates any question about your being around."

Grant had to admit that the idea was seducing. "I still must meet my writing deadlines, so I couldn't be involved fulltime."

"No. No, I wouldn't expect that. Stop by when you are able. I'll get in touch if there is something you should really be involved in."

"Okay. This won't upset your other deputies?"

Tolliver called across the room. "Hey, Ozzie. Are you okay with Grant here signing on as a deputy?"

"That would be fine by me, Sheriff. Whatever you want."

It was obvious Ozzie had not missed much of the conversation. Tolliver said, "Ozzie's my chief deputy and only deputy. Being chief is good for an extra ten dollars a month. Town kicks in an extra ten if he acts as town marshal, too." He winked, "Leaves more in the budget for sheriff's salary that way." He paused a moment. "I was going to ride out to look over the crime scene again in an hour or so after I talk with the prosecutor. If you want to come by again, maybe you'd like to join me."

Grant said, "I would. I've got to go down to the furniture store and buy a desk if I can. I have another stop or two I can make if I've got time. I'll be back."

"It's hard to get the best of George Caldwell on a deal. Good luck."

"Is he tougher than Enos Fletcher?"

The sheriff laughed. "Nope. Did Enos sell you the grulla you hitched out front?"

"Yeah. It belonged to Hannah Locke. You said she is your prosecutor. She seems to leave quite a footprint in this town."

"Ah, Hannah. Now there's a challenge for you. Anyway, Enos likely got the best of you on the dollars, but you didn't buy some old plug either. That's a mighty fine-looking critter. When I saw you hitch that gelding out front, I figured that a man that would pick a horse like that wasn't the tenderfoot some might think."

From the sheriff's remark, he gathered that word of a tenderfoot's arrival might be spreading about Lockwood.

Chapter 16

SHERIFF TOLLIVER POINTED to the hazy outline of buildings backdropped by snowcapped mountains in the distance as Grant and Tolliver trotted their mounts toward Fox Creek where the Sioux girl's body was found. "That's the Pennock School. Three small classroom buildings. One they call a high school, probably thirty students. Majority don't go to school beyond eighth grade. I think one building takes fifth through eighth, and then the younger ones go to the other building."

As they drew nearer, Grant said, "I see some other buildings scattered about."

"They have small dormitories that house students that don't live in town. They are used mostly in the worst of winter, but some students stay the school term. They've got stables, of course. Not a bad arrangement for schooling. Bad thing is it's over a mile out from town. I've only lived here about three years, but I'm told that's because Quakers originally set up the school for Indians and didn't want them to mix with the whites, maybe for good reason since two Indian boys were lynched some years back. I don't know the whole story. Enos could tell you. He was here then. Another inspiration for your books."

"Was there a reservation nearby?"

"Nope. An old chief named Lame Buffalo headed a large band of Brule Sioux that had a village in the mountains. He believed that the white man's path was inevitable and that the children should be prepared for it. He encouraged education of the Sioux children, and the Quakers showed up to make it happen. The Quakers don't operate the school these days, but the name they gave the school stuck. You'll be hearing about the Lame Buffalo Association that finances much of the school and bought up land for sort of homesteading a lot of land in the valley by Sioux. The association got start-up money from some mysterious source, they say. Ethan Ramsey's wife, Skye, is a half-blood Sioux and seems to hold the secret to that."

"You are teasing me with a mystery, aren't you?"

"Could be."

They angled their mounts away from the school, riding across lush, spring grass. "Wait," Grant said, reining in his gelding as his eyes focused on the seemingly endless rangeland to the south.

"What do you see?" Tolliver asked.

"Cattle. Red and white cows and their calves. There must be hundreds spread out over the valley. I've never seen so many, and it's so calming to watch them grazing there with some of the calves nursing and others just lying down. I've seen cattle, of course, but not in a setting quite like this and so many in one place."

"Herefords. Some folks call them 'white-faces' because they are red with the white faces. Up close, you will see some black calves with the white faces. They are the result of crossbreeding a Black Angus bull with Hereford cows and heifers. You are viewing Skye and Ethan Ramsey's herd. Many of the big ranchers hereabouts are starting to cross the breeds and generally end up with black, white-faced cattle. That's what they call them—black, white-faces. Of course, some religiously stick with their purebreds which causes some problems on open range.

"You're starting to confuse me, but I'll add this to my list of things to learn about."

Ron Schwab

Tolliver said, "We'd better tend to business. We're going to move from this peaceful scene to a place that was the opposite of peaceful a few days ago. We'll have to cross the Fox Creek. It's running fuller from snow melt in the mountains but still not more than a few feet deep. Stay in the saddle, and you won't get those new boots wet."

Grant was surprised at the force of the of the crystal-clear water that rushed over the rocky creek bed between the banks, but as Tolliver had assured him, the mounts kept them well above the water and seemed unfazed by the crossing. Pine and aspen trees lined the opposite bank providing a closed curtain to any viewers from the school's side. They broke through the trees and dismounted, hitching Blue and the sheriff's sorrel to branches before the sheriff led Grant down a deer trail that snaked through trees and brush and opened into a grassy clearing.

"This is where they found poor Abigail. She was laying in the middle of the clearing where the grass is matted down. You will still see signs of dried blood in the grass. You can see there is a wide opening onto the rangeland over there." He gestured toward the south side, where Grant saw that trees thinned out enough to allow several horses to enter side by side.

"Looked like they led three horses in from hoofprints. That's why we figured three men or boys were involved," Tolliver said

They walked over to where the body had lain. "Not that much sign of blood. I was expecting more. I know it would have soaked in and dried, but there would usually be more residue. Was there a lot here when you saw the body?"

"Not a lot, now that I think of it."

"There should have been a bucketful with the throat cut."

"How do you know about blood?"

"War. Union infantry. Gettysburg."

"Confederate Cavalry. Gettysburg."

"Glad we didn't meet," Grant said.

"Yeah."

Apparently, Tolliver was willing to escape the subject, too. "Who found the girl?" Grant asked.

"Fellow named Jasper Tilgner. He comes out here to fish when he's not working. Let's just say Jasper spends a lot of time fishing."

"What time of day was this?"

"Early morning. Not long after sunrise. Jasper generally walks out from town, so he had to walk back to report what he found. Took him a spell."

"How long do think she had been dead?"

"Hard to say, but she was in school the day before and went home for supper and left her grandma's cabin about seven o'clock. Didn't say where she was going, or if she did, Grandma didn't hear. She's near deaf."

"Did she have a horse?"

"An old paint mare she rode back and forth to school. She was mounted when she left the cabin. The horse hasn't turned up."

"Why would she have ended up back here near the school?"

"The answer to that might solve the case," Tolliver said.

"I suppose you have considered she might have been killed someplace else and dropped off here?"

"Yep. But why would they leave her here?"

"What about her clothes?"

"She was naked, but her dress and underthings were strung about the clearing here. No shoes. Grandma said she was wearing her shoes when she left."

"I suppose you've talked to her schoolmates."

"Got a few coming to the office after school. The principal asked me not to come to the school. I understand that, and she gave me a list of five high school students who were friendly with Abigail. Perhaps you would like to interview one."

The sheriff was pulling Grant into the case faster than he wanted. "I don't know if I am ready to get that involved yet."

"You live in the same house. It's Jasmine Dupree. You could talk to her with her mother present."

Grant sighed. "I guess I could do that much."

Chapter 17

C ONTINUING WHAT SEEMED to be the start of an evening ritual, Grant and Moon sat at the kitchen table again nursing a concoction that Moon called birch tea. Grant found the sweet taste to his liking and quickly acceded when she prodded him to take a second cup.

"You will be my experiment. I have at least thirty teas I make from local plants. I keep the dried ingredients in jars. I suppose I have a year's worth. Jeb wants to package and sell the teas at his general store. I'm thinking on it, but then I am afraid it will become work and not fun. Birch tea relaxes you. It will help you sleep tonight. You apparently had a problem last night. I heard you yelling. My room is just below yours. I rushed upstairs to see if you were all right, but you were quiet by the time I reached your door. I decided you must have had a nightmare."

"I apologize for waking you. I hope I didn't disturb others. I do occasionally put up with nightmares. The war."

Moon said, "I don't think anyone else was bothered; Milton across the hall certainly would not have hesitated to complain if he had been upset. Is your nightmare always the same?"

"Yes, the one that causes me to yell."

"My mother interpreted dreams and visions. Some say I have that gift. Some Sioux visit me about such experiences. If you ever wish to talk about it, please do not hesitate to say so."

"I will think on that. But tonight, I want to ask your permission to speak to Jasmine. In your presence, of course." He had shoved his deputy badge in his trouser pocket before entering the house, preferring not to deal with questions it would have immediately raised. He placed the badge on the table. "I am now a volunteer deputy sheriff for Big River County."

"You did not waste much time taking on responsibility in the county. If you are not teasing me, I must admit I am surprised."

He told her of his visit with Sheriff Tolliver and their trip to Fox Creek. "My motives are a bit selfish, since I see the experience as an opportunity to learn more concerning the things I write about. Tolliver is interviewing Abigail's friends to see if they might know anything that would help track down the killer. He asked me to talk to Jasmine. Would you have an objection to that?"

"Of course not. If she knew anything, I think she would have told me. Her chores are done, so she is in her room studying. I will ask her to come in."

"I will try to be brief so she can get back to her schoolwork."

Moon got up. "Move to the dining table. I will be back with Jasmine shortly."

He moved into the dining room and sat down, more unsure now whether the deputy business was such a good idea. Soon Moon returned with Jasmine. The girl's dark eyes were wide and her face somber. She was obviously nervous or afraid.

He wished he could just call this off, but then she would be faced with an interview by the sheriff or someone else. Best for her to get it over. He pushed his chair back and stood, "Hello, Jasmine. Did your mother tell you what I want to talk to you about?"

Ron Schwab

She nodded her head. "Yes," she said, "but I don't know anything."

"Why don't you sit down, and I will try to make this brief?"

Jasmine sat across the table from Grant with Moon beside her.

"Jasmine," Grant said. "The reason we are talking to some of Abigail's friends is that someone may know nothing about the killing, but unknowingly might be aware of something about her that would provide a clue to who did this terrible thing. You would like to help, wouldn't you?"

"Yes. I just don't know anything."

"How well did you know Abigail?"

She shrugged. "I used to be her best friend up until last summer. Then she started pulling away and spent less and less time with me. Of course, I'm busy here at The Tipi and didn't have time to be with her as much as she wanted outside of school. I figured that was why she quit talking to me so much and started avoiding me. She started missing school this year, too. I doubt if she was there more than half the time. She used to be a very serious student. I don't think she would have come back next term. I'm just guessing. She didn't say as much, but that's how it usually comes about."

"Did she have any boyfriends?"

Jasmine chewed on her lower lip and seemed reluctant to answer.

"Jasmine," Moon said, "answer the question."

"Not real boyfriends. I don't know this for a fact, but some said she was seeing boys over where they found her body. I overheard boys joking that for a quarter they could meet Abigail over there and . . . she would let them have a poke." She lowered her head, avoiding Grant's eyes. "This is so embarrassing."

"Don't be embarrassed. This is important information. You do want her killer brought to justice, don't you?"

"Of course. She didn't deserve the terrible thing that happened to her. She was a sweet, tender-hearted girl once. I should have tried harder to be friends again. And I know some of the things she did were to help care for her poor old grandmother. They didn't have anything but that little old shack they lived in. Tribe members dropped food by sometimes to keep them from starving, and Abigail worked temporary jobs when she could find one."

Moon said, "We hired her here sometimes when we were extra busy or had a special clean up. She was a good worker and fun to be around."

Jasmine said, "Bird Dancing, her grandmother, insisted Abigail stay in school, but her mind started to fail with her body, and I know she had no idea Abigail wasn't going to school but half the time."

"Can you think of anything else?" Grant said. "I may want to talk with you again, but this could help more than you know."

"I can't think of anything. May I leave?"

"Certainly. And thank you for talking to me."

She started to rise and then sat back down. "I thought of something else. Last summer, one of the last days we spent some time together, Abigail told me something that I thought was very strange."

Grant said, "What was that?"

"She said as soon as they would take her on, she wanted to go to work at The Doll House."

"That's a fancy saloon that maintains a busy whorehouse," Moon said. "The previous owners got into big trouble with the law and were uprooted by the Pinkertons. I doubt if this bunch is much better. I will tell you about it another time."

"Thank you again, Jasmine," Grant said. "You have helped a lot, at least provided the beginnings of a trail perhaps."

Chapter 18

"HAVE YOU FOUND a place to live yet, Brady? My mother could show up any day now," Samantha said. They shared a bench on the covered veranda of the log house. It had been nearly a month since Sammy's return to Lockwood.

Trouble bristled. Sammy had come across the footbridge. The Yates house was separated from the Morris residence by no more than a quarter mile; the Yates residence sat on the north side of the North Laramie River and the Morris property on the south. Before Caleb and Millie Morris left Wyoming, the two had traipsed back and forth over the footbridge for as long as Trouble could remember.

"You trying to push me out? You said your ma would send a telegram before she and your brothers left Iowa. That would give me a couple days head start. What little

I got can be out of here in a few hours if need be. You're darn lucky the railroad traded the place back to you."

The railroad had originally purchased the house and quarter section for its line to Lockwood, and Samantha's parents had retained the adjoining quarter to the south. A year later, the railroad decided the south tract suited the track better and paid boot to trade the home parcel back in exchange for the other land.

"I was glad that happened," Samantha said. "Iowa was never home to me, and I always dreamed of coming back here. Of course, I didn't want daddy to die for that to happen." She teared up. "I miss him every day. Anyway, I'm not pushing. I'm worried about you finding a place to live. I wish you would move back in with your mother after I move over here. She wants you there in the worst way."

"I love Ma, but it ain't going to happen." He waited for her to correct his grammar, but she said nothing. "I'm going to move in with Bushwa Sparks if you've got to know."

"Bushwa? I remember him. You could smell him coming before you saw him."

"He's got an extra room in his cabin. It's got a cot and room enough for me to put my personals. Like this place, it's several miles out of Lockwood up in the foothills, as the crow flies not more than three miles from here. You booting me off the land, too, or do I get to farm the place this crop season?"

"We want you to farm it just like you have been. You've given Mama a good return."

"Well then, I can leave my farming equipment in the barn, the mules, too, if I can hire one of your brothers to look after them at a fair price."

"I'm sure that won't be a problem. Levi is twelve years old now, always hungry for a dollar—like somebody else I know. Jake's ten and almost as big as his brother, which upsets Levi to no end."

"Tell him I was late stretching out, too, but I jumped past six feet almost overnight, Ma says."

"I doubt that. But I'm still not used to having to look up at you. Seems strange somehow."

She might have not grown taller, Trouble thought, but she wasn't some stick figure anymore. Sammy had grown more than a little bit in the right places. He didn't suppose they could take up skinny dipping together again like they did in the old days before their folks said, 'no more.' "I just can't quite believe you're back and going to be living in this house again."

"Get used to it. I can't imagine ever leaving these mountains and this valley for more than a few weeks again." She was quiet for a few moments before she spoke again. "Your mother asked me to talk to you about something. For some reason, she thinks you've got good business sense."

"You don't agree?"

"I'm withholding judgment. Just hear me out. Sarah's thinking about closing her dress shop again. You haven't been around enough to notice, and she wouldn't complain, but her affliction is numbing her fingers. She's got the shakes worse than they've been for a spell. Not terrible. It comes and goes, but she needs nimble hands and fingers for her work."

"Damn. Why doesn't she tell me these things?"

"Why don't you ask? She's about three minutes across the footbridge."

Sammy always did speak her mind. That much about her had not changed. "I'll run over and see her after I do chores. What's this business thing you wanted to talk about?"

"First, you should understand that your mother's business is not making any money. She and Jim live off his wages and the dab of rent she receives from the farm ground on her quarter section. You're renting that. You know over a fourth of it is forest. You can't be farming more than thirty acres. And the rest is grass that isn't likely carrying more than fifteen cows with calves at side."

"You've sure got Yates business figured out, don't you?"

She shrugged, "Maybe you aren't the only one who knows a thing or two about business. Anyway, Sarah's got two problems. First, is her ailment that comes and goes. Second, the competition has changed. Oaks General Store now sells dresses and all kinds of ladies' garments that are shipped in from back east. Sarah, especially since she has slowed some, can't turn out fitted dresses and jackets fast enough to meet demand, so the business goes to Oaks."

"The demand's there but not the supply. Adam Smith says somebody is going to come up with the supply to make a profit."

"Exactly. And right now, some factory in Boston or New York City is doing it. Why not do it right here at home? Your mother owns the building in town, and she knows everything about needlework and dressmaking. She even designs dresses herself without the need of store-bought patterns. Sewing machines are expensive, but we can buy three commercial Singer sewing machines for three hundred dollars each."

"Whoa. I thought Ma wanted you to ask me questions."

"Hear me out first. I have already spoken with Mister Gaines at the bank. I have half the sewing machine money saved up from raising and selling pigs on the Iowa farm. Pa let me have a share for doing all the work when I wasn't in school. He called them 'mortgage lifters' because you can get in the business quickly and turn the money over fast."

"Wonder why I never thought of that?" Trouble said.

"You don't have all the ideas in this world, Brady Yates. Now let me finish. I will furnish the machines, and Sarah will provide the building. We will go into a fifty-fifty partnership that will be called 'Sarah's Fashions.' We will hire two or three more women. Your mom will teach the workers how to use the machines properly and will design and supervise, select the materials to order. I will do the bookkeeping, sew some and handle sales. I will have the summer to get things started and then I will have to work around school another year. I've talked to She-Bear—I guess she's Carissa now—and they will stock their store with our garments. I am going to contact stores in Denver, Cheyenne and other towns. I might have to travel some to get things started. Anyhow, I think we can make good profits at this. Now, what's your opinion?"

"I don't know anything about making dresses. First thing that comes to mind is your cost. You will have to have your cloth and materials shipped in, and you will have wages to pay. Can you match the quality of the general store's providers and sell to Jeb Oaks at the same cost?"

"Easily. Wages might be about the same back east, but if we don't get too big for our britches, we can hire better quality workers. Most women here have had to sew for themselves and families, and they are used to hard work. Some of the big factories in the east have hired on children. Cheap labor, maybe, but they will be unskilled for a long time before they pay their ways. Better to pay a little more and hire folks that have skills and are willing to offer a good day's work. And the companies back east have big shipping costs for the items sent back here. We wouldn't have any of those costs for items sold in Lockwood and not near as much for those sold nearby."

"Well, it sounds like you got it thought out. I don't see any reason not to give it a try. I can't make a good case not to do it given all the projects I've taken on."

She smiled and leaned over and gave him a peck on the cheek. "You just saved us a big fuss, Brady."

Chapter 19

LETTERS FROM ERASTUS Beadle and Percival Garth
arrived the same day. The Beadle letter included
two typewritten copies of a ten-page contract,
the carbon copy so faint that a magnifying glass would
be needed to read it. Garth's letter outlined a proposition
that was enticing but he feared was a bit too speculative
for this time in his life. He worried that his trip west, although he found a certain peace in this place, had burned
out his sense of adventure for now. He reread the Garth
letter and placed it on the scarred and stained top of the
sturdy, rolltop desk he had purchased from Lockwood
Furniture and Funerals.

His writing hours had been extremely
productive during his month at The Tipi, and he
was finishing two manuscripts he had started prior
to heading west. Another was half completed, so he

would be able to convert his work to cash quickly once he signed a new contract with Beadle.

He would be joining Moon downstairs soon for evening tea, which had evolved into a ritual that required no invitation. He enjoyed her company, and she had made it clear that she looked forward to this time each day. He thought she was an exceptionally attractive woman, who seemed unaware of her allure, but he was determined not to pursue romance and risk losing the first woman he could recall having thought of as a close friend. Two failed marriages reminded him also that he could not rely on either his judgment or behavior when it came to the opposite sex.

When he went downstairs, Moon already had placed the teapot and cups on the kitchen table. When he walked into the kitchen, he found her drying dishes. He still helped with dishes when he ate late, but the previous night she chased him off, insisting that her tenants were not expected to do household chores outside their rooms. Besides, she admonished, he was supposed to be working on a book. True enough, but he was struggling. Incentive tended to sleep when he did not have a contract and dollars coaxing him on.

When Moon joined him at the table, she asked, "Progress on the book today?"

"Not much, but some reasons to write arrived in the mail."

"Reasons by mail? That's interesting."

"Contracts from Beadle and Company for a dozen dime novels, one every other month for two years. Half by P. J. Bowie and half by Jake West."

"You can write that fast?"

"That's not a problem once I set my mind to it. I've done a book in a month more than once. Dime novels are short. As you have seen, not much time is spent on research. I'm not sure about the contract, though. It provides for a flat fee per book and complete release of the copyright to the company, which I have done in the past."

"Is that a good thing? I know nothing about the financial side of books but giving up a copyright seems worrisome. Of course, I have no idea exactly how they work."

"I don't know what I should do, and the laws have changed over the years, but essentially the author has rights to publishing of his works for twenty-eight years and is entitled to an extension for another fourteen years. Some filing with the government must be made to receive the extension. None of this concerns me if I sign a contract selling my rights, of course."

"So you must make a decision."

"It gets more complicated because of another proposal. I met another smaller publisher from Omaha on the way out. He said I should be retaining copyrights and insisting upon royalty payments from Beadle. I also got a letter from him. He would like for me to write a full-length novel under my own name, something that would appeal to a broader readership. Such a book would require authenticity and be at least five or six times the length of a dime novel."

"Could you make as much money?"

"I would receive an advance that would be more than I earn from two or three of the dime novels, but it could be a long wait for royalties." Beadle's proposal would yield four hundred dollars per book, and he figured he could get by nicely on twenty-four hundred dollars per year. He doubted there were many folks in Lockwood who enjoyed an income as high as that figure. Many likely did not reach one thousand dollars in a year's time.

Moon smiled. "I can't keep up with you. Have you considered consulting with a lawyer?"

"Yes. I wondered about Ethan Ramsey at Ramsey and Locke."

"Ethan has a statewide reputation, but he is in Cheyenne the next month. He is a member of the territorial legislature, and they are trying to put together a plan that will convince Congress to grant Wyoming statehood. I don't say this because she is my friend, but Hannah Locke is a very respected lawyer. She could help you. We have two other lawyers in Lockwood, but one handles mostly coal company business matters, and the other doesn't have more than a year's experience."

"Miss Locke and I did not have a very pleasant encounter when we completed the horse purchase. Frankly, I didn't care for her much. She was very unpleasant, just short of rude."

"Hannah tends not to be very trusting when she first meets someone, but she's very kind and easy to talk with when you get to know her. She told me that she felt she had handled your meeting clumsily. Anyway, I don't have any other local recommendation I can make."

"I guess I have nothing to lose. I'll stop by her office tomorrow and see if I can make an appointment. I'll take the original of the Beadle contract and the Garth letter and leave them for her to look over before I meet with her."

A loud, frantic hammering at the front door interrupted their conversation. Moon sprang to her feet, "I will be right back."

When she returned, Deputy Ozzie White trailed her, a grim look on his boyish face. "Ozzie needs to talk to you," Moon said.

"What is it, Ozzie?"

"Big trouble at The Doll House. One of the ladies killed. Two gunmen held up the barkeeper and are holed up in the place. They're holding another gal hostage. Sheriff says he needs both his deputies. That's me and you."

Grant considered his deputy job mostly an honorary one that allowed the sheriff to share information. He had not planned on the possibility of gunplay or killing. He got up, "My Winchester is upstairs. I'll run up and grab it."

"If you got a sidearm, you better bring it, too. I'll go over to the stable and start saddling that grulla of yours. Tack next to the stall?"

"Yeah. But if he makes a fuss, just wait for me."

"Okay, but I generally do better with horses than people."

Grant hurried upstairs two steps at a time. When he entered his room, he retrieved his holstered derringer from the chest drawer and strapped it over his shoulder and across his chest. He owned no other pistol. This would have to do, and it was slightly better than nothing in a situation of this sort. He slipped into his buffalo hide jacket, picked up his Winchester and headed back downstairs.

Moon met him at the foot of the stairway. "Grant, you don't have to do this. You didn't bargain for this type of situation. My God, have you ever shot a man?"

He looked at her with sad eyes. "Thirty to forty, I suppose. I never really kept count."

Her eyes widened, and she responded with stunned silence as he moved toward the front door.

Chapter 20

GRANT AND OZZIE White dismounted and hitched their horses at a rail a few buildings west of The Doll House just off Main Street. Grant was not about to risk Blue being struck by a stray bullet.

"So where do we find Sheriff Tolliver?" Grant asked.

"Last I knew, he was hunkered down behind a turned-over table just inside the doorway. Most of the customers was pouring out of the place then. The gunmen was holed up behind the bar with Ginger, one of the whores. She's not much more than a kid. Sheriff had them pinned down, but they want free passage out or they claim they will kill her. They likely ain't bluffing. They already killed one, but the Sheriff said he could try to talk them down for a spell till I got help."

"And I'm the only man you thought of?"

"Only one nearby. Jeb Oaks would have jumped in, but he lives a few miles out of town."

"There's got to be a back way out of the building. I don't see any horses here. They must have their mounts out back."

"There's a big customer stable there for putting up horses. Public can't gawk at who comes and goes. Some folks who visit the whores like to keep it private-like."

Grant looked skyward. Almost a full moon, clear sky. He had carried out sniper tasks under worse conditions. "I'm going around behind. Tell the sheriff to agree to let them vacate the building if they will leave the young lady behind. I'll try to take them down when they come for their mounts. I am betting they head out the back door, but I will be there either way. Can you get to the sheriff without taking a bullet?"

"Yeah. He ain't far from the door. I'll dive and roll."

The young man was constructed like a scarecrow and average height, so he would not make much of a target, and he looked like he might be able to move with good speed. "Okay. I'm going to head around to the back. I'll wait a spell but if nothing happens, I'll see if I can slip in the back door. Our priority should be to protect Ginger."

The building sat on a northeast corner but opened off a side street to the east, so Grant stepped out onto the street and walked south toward the street intersection, passing a crowd gathered outside. He looked behind the building and saw a huge barn-like structure set some twenty to thirty feet behind The Doll House. That would be the private stable. It appeared that the place lured a good number of men who preferred to keep their visits private. He assumed most entered from the back entrance as well.

He walked down the pathway that led toward the stable, his Winchester in his hand, ready to swing to his shoulder quickly if circumstances called for it. He was nearly to the building's rear when gunfire exploded from inside, guns cracking repeatedly, signaling that shots were being exchanged. He raced toward the back of the building and caught sight of the big door, deciding to burst through and join the fight. He started to open the door when the gunfire ceased and was replaced by a deathlike silence. He backed away, concluding it would be prudent to wait a bit before entering.

He moved to the stable, seeking cover in its shadow. The Doll House door opened, and two men emerged. A big man carrying a bag in his left hand was in the lead, stepping cautiously and his head swiveling as his eyes tried to pick up a trap. He was followed by a smaller man whose fingers clutched the wrist of a whimpering, sobbing woman.

Grant slowly positioned his rifle, aiming it at the big man's head. "Stop where you are, gentlemen," he said. "I don't miss at this range. You must choose to live or die."

The men froze, their faces turned toward his voice, obviously picking up his shadowy form now. The big man said, "Put your gun to the whore's head, Rocky." Then he spoke to Grant, while reaching for his holstered pistol. "Who the hell do you think you are, mister?"

"Take that six-gun out easy like and drop it on the ground. And you, Rocky, you toss yours down, too."

The big man went for his gun and squeezed off one wild shot before Grant's slug drove through his right eye and toppled him to the dust, the bag slipping from his hand and spilling some of its contents on the ground. As Grant guessed he would, Rocky reflexively shifted his pistol away from the young woman's head to fire at the assailant, but Grant's rifle cracked and sent a slug tearing into the hapless man's neck. His knees buckled, and he pitched forward, landing across his partner's legs.

The woman was frozen in place when Grant stepped out of the shadows and approached her. He said, "Don't be afraid, ma'am. Everything's all right now. I'm Deputy Coolidge."

When he reached her, she fell into his arms, clutching him so tightly he almost dropped the Winchester. "Thank God," she said, her body shaking uncontrollably. "Thank you. Thank you. I thought I was dead. I ain't prayed like this since I was a little girl. God sent you. I know He did."

She left Grant speechless for a moment. "Ma'am, I've got to know. What happened inside?"

She stepped away. "I'm sorry. I'm just thinking of myself. The sheriff's down and so is Ozzie. I think the sheriff's badly hurt, Ozzie not so much."

"I've got to get in there. Can you get that bag and whatever fell out? I'm guessing it's gold coin and paper money."

"Yes. I can do that. Go ahead. I'll be right in."

Grant entered the building and rushed down the hallway which apparently led to the front bar and gambling area. He passed a lamp-lighted stairway which he suspected led to the upstairs bordello, allowing a visitor to enter without being seen by the front room customers. When he reached the barroom, he saw the sheriff sprawled out on the floor, back-down, in a pool of blood. Ozzie sat with his legs stretched out and his back propped against the wall some ten feet from the sheriff, conscious. Three or four men peered through the open entryway, curious but not moving to assist.

Ozzie pointed at the down sheriff, signaling that Grant should tend to Tolliver first. Grant knelt beside the sheriff and confirmed that he was still breathing. He instantly saw the blood-soaked britches and the blood flow from a tear in the inner thigh. Artery, and Tolliver had to be near to bleeding out. He yanked the bandana from his own neck, twisting it tight about the sheriff's thigh until the bleeding eased to a trickle.

He knotted the bandana, and before examining the sheriff further, yelled at the men in the doorway. "Somebody high-tail it across the street and tell Enos what's happened and that we need a buckboard over here quick. I'd like another to notify the doctor we're on the way. For God's sake, get me some volunteers to help with this."

That seemed to awaken the onlookers. A gray-haired man said, "I'll get Enos. My boy's out here. I'll send him to tell Doc Weintraub."

Ozzie said, "Stick with Jim. I'm okay if I don't try to get up. It's my head. Somebody took me down from behind with a pistol butt, I think. Then he must have shot the sheriff."

This was not making any sense. Grant leaned over the sheriff. "Jim, can you hear me?"

Tolliver groaned and opened his eyes. "Backshot." His eyelids fluttered, and his eyes shut again.

Grant, trying not to disturb the thigh wound more than necessary, gently turned Tolliver on his side. He found the entry wound in the sheriff's back below the shoulder blade. There was scant blood on the shirt fabric enclosing the wound, and he decided not to disturb it. This was a physician's job. He got up and peeled table-cloths from two tables, tossing one over the sheriff and rolling up the other to cushion his head. He had seen more than his share of wounds and mutilations during the war, and he judged that Tolliver had a fair chance if he had not bled out too much. His face was pale as a white sheet.

He moved toward Ozzie when two men parted the crowd outside and burst through the doorway. The obvious spokesman was a tall man with a thin, black moustache. He was attired in a blue suit and string tie and wore a gray Stetson hat. He was accompanied by a man that a dime novelist would label a gunslinger, a wiry man with a neatly trimmed reddish beard, reptilian, green eyes and a holstered gun resting on each hip.

"What the hell is going on here?"

"Who's asking?" Grant replied, bristling at the new-comer's hostile demeanor.

"Winston Colbert. I own The Doll House. I've been in Cheyenne on business and return to find the place shot up, blood all over the place and, worse, no customers."

"Well, Mister Colbert, you'll find worse. I'm told there is a dead woman upstairs, and I promise you will find two dead men out back. I am the acting deputy sheriff of this county, and I have wounded men to tend to. I will speak with you later. I suggest you and your friend find yourself a bottle behind the bar and go sit down at a table someplace. I don't want you messing with the crime scene just yet."

"Why, you insolent bastard."

Grant turned away and walked over to Ozzie and knelt beside him. "Let me look at it," he said.

Ozzie turned his head so Grant could see the back of the young deputy's scalp. "All I remember is somebody pushing my hat off and suddenly everything going black. I don't recollect feeling anything. I just woke up dizzier than a loon and my head pounding like a smithy had my head on an anvil. Seems not to be hurting so much now, but my head still spins when I move it."

"You've got a hell of a knot and a small gash up there. Docs have told me that it's not all that bad to have the swelling, but we'll let Doctor Weintraub decide that."

"I'm ready to load. Do I dun the county for this?"

It was Enos Fletcher with several big men trailing him. "Yeah," Grant said, "send your bill to the county."

Grant assisted with moving the sheriff and Ozzie onto the mule-drawn wagon. "I'll drop by the Weintraub Hospital later," he told Enos. "I guess my work here isn't finished." Unfortunately, he had no notion about what that work entailed. What would U.S. Marshal Buck Tyree do?

Chapter 21

H E WALKED BACK into The Doll House and saw that Winston Colbert and his companion had vacated their chairs and were moving in his direction. Instinctively, he did not like this man.

When Colbert approached again, he asked, "Are you done here, Deputy? I need to get this place cleaned up and back in business."

"I'm not. First, I've got to see the body upstairs. Also, money was stolen from behind your bar. I recovered it from the men out back. A lady named Ginger took custody of the money."

"Ginger? Why does she have the money?"

"She was taken as a hostage by the robbers. I was pressed to get back in here, and she was to follow with the money. Some of it had spilled onto the ground."

Colbert turned to the gunslinger. "Ryker, go round up Ginger and the money. I don't trust that little bitch."

Grant said, "She was just outside the back door when I last saw her. She was going to follow me in, but when she saw the wounded men, she probably retreated down the hall. She might even be upstairs."

"I'll take a look-see out back first," Ryker said. "Maybe I'll recognize the dead men."

"I'd appreciate it if you would take me upstairs and show me around, maybe help me find the body and reassure the ladies it's safe now," Grant said.

"Whatever it takes to get you the hell out of my business place."

Winston Colbert did not seem to be warming up to him, but Grant consoled himself that the feeling was mutual. They climbed the winding staircase to the second floor, pausing at the midway landing so he could obtain a bird's eye view of the enormous room below. Taking in the chandeliers, the massive bar and the gambling and drinking-dining areas separated by invisible curtains it seemed, he was struck by the elegance of the place. He had unfortunately visited many taverns and saloons and had seen nothing finer. The drab exterior of the building certainly camouflaged the interior. The man who attacked the lawmen would have entered from the front door. He made a mental note to identify some of the out-side onlookers to see if they remembered someone entering during the gunfight.

At the top of the staircase, they were met by a portly, mustachioed man wearing a striped shirt and bow tie. Grant guessed him to be a bartender.

"Orv, what are you doing up here?" Colbert asked. "Get your ass downstairs and get set up for business."

"Those outlaws drug Ginger down to the bar, and I took off down the hall and came up the back way. I wasn't in the mood for dying."

"Why didn't you take the money with you? I'm betting there was two hundred dollars in the till under the counter."

Orv's face flushed. "More like five hundred, Boss. Didn't make it to the bank this morning."

"We'd damn well better get that money back or you're going to be slave labor until I'm paid. Have you seen Ginger?"

"Nope. Not since them outlaws drug her behind the bar."

Grant intervened. "A woman was killed up here. Where do we find the body?"

There were two hallways that led from this juncture, one south and one west. The bartender with a fling of his thumb signaled west. "Third door on the left side. Ruby. I could hear her screaming from downstairs. She and Ginger agreed to take on both men in the same room, and I guess it didn't work out. When the men left with Ginger, Sugar checked, and when she saw what happened, she headed for the sheriff's office."

"They shot Ruby?" Colbert asked.

"Knife. Ain't pretty. I saw all I could take from the hallway," the bartender said.

Grant shuddered. The blade again. He could almost feel it plunging into his chest. "I would like to speak with Sugar after I look at the body."

As they walked toward the room, he noticed that doors were ajar now along the hallways. The women, who had doubtless been in hiding, were now surrendering to their curiosity. A dusky woman dressed in a low-cut gown stepped out into the hallway. Grant guessed her to be mulatto, but she could pass for Mexican or Mediterranean lineage if she chose. It mattered not; stunning described her sufficiently.

"I am Sugar. I won't look at Ruby again, but I will wait out here and speak with you when you are finished."

"Thank you. I won't be long." He went to the closed door, but Colbert did not follow. He suspected the owner wanted to coach the witness some. He did not care. He was already treading in deep water.

Grant opened the door, entered the room, and was greeted by the naked body that lay face up on the bed. He stepped over to the bedside and saw that the bloody head dropped away from the shoulders at an angle that would have been impossible if she had not been nearly decapitated during the knife sawing away at her throat. Unlike Ginger, Ruby would have been in her mid-thirties, perhaps older. It helped that he had witnessed mutilations of every kind during less than a year of infantry service, but somehow seeing the ghastly wound inflicted upon a woman far from the battlefield made it more difficult to bear. He bent over her and took her hand. "I'm sorry, Ruby. Rest in peace."

When he left the room, he found that Ryker had joined Sugar and Colbert. The anger flaring in Colbert's eyes did not bode well.

"Ginger hasn't turned up. Neither has the money. This is on you, deputy. I'll be suing you and the county if I don't get my money back. You put the money in Ginger's care."

Grant decided to ignore the man. Words would only bury him faster in this quicksand he had walked into. He turned to Sugar. "Ma'am, I would like to speak with you alone."

"I want to be with her. I'm her employer," Colbert said. "But not her lawyer."

"We can use my room," Sugar said, nodding for him to follow.

"We've got bodies to get rid of. What are you going to do about it?" Colbert said.

Grant said, "You've got two choices: get George Caldwell down here or let them be."

"I'm not paying to bury anybody. Ruby already owed me money, and the other two stole from me. Not my responsibility."

Grant said, "Tell Caldwell that I'll take care of Ruby's burial and a marker, too. Maybe the county will do the others. He will know about such things, I'm sure."

Sugar led him into her room. It was clean and had a slight cinnamon scent. The decorating theme was decidedly yellow in varying shades, walls, bedspread and the frilly lace that fringed two stuffed chairs that faced a small tea table. The ceiling was half covered by a mirror.

"Sit down," she said. "I'd offer coffee or a drink, but I doubt if my boss would approve."

It felt good to sit down and regroup a bit. "That's fine. I would just like to chat with you a few minutes, and then I'll be on my way. I need to see how the sheriff is doing."

Sugar said, "I don't know much about any of this. I just found Ruby after the two men left with Ginger."

"Had you seen the two men here before."

"Uh, I don't remember. They could have been here, I suppose."

"Did you see a third man? Someone else shot Sheriff Tolliver downstairs. It doesn't seem likely he left by the front entrance, and I should have met him when I came down the hallway if he tried to escape by that route. I am guessing he came up the staircase, went down the back stairway and made for the door after I got to the public room in front."

"No. No. I didn't see anybody else, but I was in this room most of the time."

"He must have encountered Ginger. She was either taken hostage again, or she was somehow involved in all of this."

"I wouldn't know anything about that," Sugar said almost too hastily.

It struck him that Sugar was a poised, well-spoken woman, something that could not be said for the prostitutes he encountered in bordellos during his drinking years. It was sheer luck that he had not contracted something from the menu of venereal diseases in those days. He sensed that this woman knew more than she was telling him, but he would call that to the sheriff's attention for a possible follow up interview.

Grant said, "I would appreciate it if you would talk to the other women and see if anyone has information that might be helpful. Contact the sheriff's office with anything that might shed some light on this. They should be concerned since one of their friends was murdered."

"Of course, but this was so unexpected, I would be surprised if anyone knows anything."

He attempted to elicit more details from her for another five minutes before he surrendered. Colbert's talk with her had obviously been effective. It almost seemed that the man did not want the crimes solved.

Chapter 22

GRANT ENTERED A large, two-story house which a sign said was the Weintraub Hospital. A girl with olive-tinted skin that he guessed to be about Trouble's age sat in a waiting room chair next to a woman he surmised was Sarah Tolliver. Trouble sat on the other side of his mother. Trouble stood when he saw Grant walk in.

"We're waiting for Doc," Trouble said. "Ruth—she's his wife and nurse—said he would be out with a report in a few minutes." He gestured toward his mother. "This is my ma, Sarah."

Sarah Tolliver nodded and gave him a nervous smile. She was an attractive woman but on the frail side, although she was likely no older than himself.

Grant doffed his hat. "A pleasure to meet you, ma'am. I'm sorry for the circumstances."

"Ma, this is the fella I told you about. Grant Coolidge. He's one of Jim's deputies, and he writes some of the dime novels I read." He paused. "Oh, and this here is my friend Sammy, uh, Samantha Morris."

The girl rolled her eyes. "Hi, Mister Coolidge. Just call me Sammy. Brady's told me all about you." She smiled. "Some of it might even be true."

He instantly liked Samantha Morris. A man could not fault Trouble's taste in ladies if he was keeping company with both her and Jasmine Dupree, but the boy might be on a course to earning his nickname.

A door opened, and a tall, white-coated man with angular features and wire- rimmed spectacles stepped into the room. He looked at Grant questioningly. "I am Henry Weintraub," he said.

Taking the cue, Grant said, "Grant Coolidge, temporary deputy sheriff."

"Jim wants to talk to you but not tonight. Check back first thing tomorrow afternoon, and we'll see. But if it is okay with Sarah, you can hear what I've got to report."

"Certainly, that's fine," Sarah said. "If Jim's talking, I take it that's positive."

"Two wounds. A slug imbedded in the muscle below his shoulder. I think it's a thirty-eight, same as the thigh wound. Nothing vital hit with the back slug, and removal was quite simple. He will be sore for a good spell, and we will have to be alert to infection. That's his biggest risk. The thigh wound is a greater complication."

"What do you mean?" Sarah asked.

"The slug tore into the femoral artery—that carries the blood supply to the lower body. It hit some bone as well. Jim would not be alive if the deputy here had not got a tourniquet above the artery. He would have bled out right there on the floor. Came close enough to doing that, I would guess. I will need to keep him here at least a week to see that he drinks more fluids than he wants to replenish the blood supply and to continue dressing and treatment of the wounds. The thigh wound needs special care. His leg is at risk if infection sets in. I want to monitor it. He may need a cane or crutch for a good spell when he is up and moving. He can forget about returning to work for at least a month."

Grant asked, "What about Ozzie?"

Weintraub said, "I should be able to turn him loose in a few days, but he will have to take it easy for a week. Keep him in the sheriff's office for a spell maybe. He took a bad blow to the back of his head, but the skull is intact, and I expect his dizziness to start subsiding by this time tomorrow." He turned to Sarah. "Now, Sarah, if you would like to visit Jim for just a bit, I will take you to his room. He was under anesthesia and is very weak, so don't expect much response."

"I'm just grateful he's alive." Her eyes locked with Grant's. "Thank you, Grant. We won't forget your part in this."

Chapter 23

GRANT RETURNED TO The Tipi just after midnight and was surprised to find Moon waiting in the parlor, sitting in the rocking chair next to the lamp table with a book in her hands. He sat down on the cowhide-covered settee, claiming a spot nearest the table.

"Would you like some tea?" she asked.

"Thanks, but I think not. What are you reading?"

She held up the dime novel. "The book you left this morning. *The Brightest Star.* It's different than the others. P.J. Bowie gave Marshal Tyree a romance with a Comanche woman whose band must have got lost and ended up in Montana."

She was teasing him about his geographic mishaps. He had told her to point out errors, and she was taking him at his word. "I promise that I am going to have a new awareness about such issues."

"It was a very good book, seriously. You don't give yourself enough credit as a writer. I cried when Lark was killed. Tyree loved her so much, but, of course, he must ride away into the sunset to his next adventure. However, he will never forget this woman and will carry her in his heart forever. Now, tell me about your night. You were gone a long time."

Grant gave her a quick summary of The Doll House drama. "It appears Jim Tolliver will be taking a leave from his job. Ozzie should be back to work in a few days. I am sort of in no man's land. I don't consider myself an official deputy, and I want nothing more to do with the job. Tomorrow, I will find out how to dump this badge."

"Killing those two men bothers you, doesn't it.?"

"Yeah. I had enough of that in the war. I was used often as a sniper because I had certain prowess with the long gun, a Sharps rifle in those days. There was distance, and it didn't seem real then, but in the field when battle was up close, you could see the faces of the men you shot. Gettysburg was like working in a livestock slaughterhouse. I was almost grateful I was wounded and sent home."

"You were wounded?"

He rubbed the left side of his chest and shoulder. "Bayonet. Your friend Hannah Locke's brother saved my life. It left me hating knives and anything with a blade."

"Your nightmares?"

"Yeah. The bayonet blade is always getting ready to plunge. I have no right to whine. I came home in one piece. Many left an arm or leg behind or were buried in an unmarked grave in a cow pasture or cottonfield."

"Don't be so hard on yourself. You are not whining. Sometimes it is better to share our pasts."

"And yours?"

"Another time perhaps."

"Well, I guess we'd both better get some sleep. I still need to get the writing proposals and contracts to your lawyer friend tomorrow. First, I will go to the sheriff's office, though, and see about feeding the prisoner. I guess I will stay on duty there until I talk to the sheriff later in the afternoon. I'm very confused about all this and the limbo I am dealing with. I don't handle uncertainty well. I just want to get back to my work where I can play God and make the decisions for my characters."

He stood up to leave, and Moon joined him at the foot of the stairs after turning off the kerosene lamp. She took his hand briefly and said, "You are a good man, Grant."

She gave him a chaste peck on the cheek before heading down the hallway to her bedroom.

Grant climbed the stairs and went to his room. It was unseasonably warm, and the room was stuffy, so he opened the window to let in some of the cool breeze drifting down from the mountains. He stripped bare, tossing his clothes on the chair and slipping under the sheet and blankets. He dropped off to sleep in minutes.

Then the soldier with fixed bayonet visited again, coming at him slowly like a puppet dancing on strings, and Grant was frozen by fear, unable to run, incapable of defending himself. He screamed, but his pleas died in his throat. All he could do was embrace the blade and receive it into his chest.

The image faded and he was aware of a hand on his shoulder, shaking him gently, and a voice whispering, "Grant, Grant. It's okay."

He opened his eyes and saw Moon's face above his before he felt her lips touch his and her body move upon him and her nakedness press against his own flesh. "Say nothing," she said softly before her lips covered his again and his own body awakened and responded.

The first time was over quickly. The next was leisurely as they took the time to touch and explore. There were no words between them and finally when sated they slept.

When he awakened at sunrise, she was gone. The sheets beside him were cool. Had this been a dream? Then he saw several strands of black hair on the pillow next to his.

Chapter 24

AT BREAKFAST MOON behaved as if nothing had happened between them, so he took her cue and kept the conversation casual. Regardless, he found himself nervous and anxious. He did not know what last night had meant to this mysterious woman who had quickly become his best friend in Lockwood. He more than liked her, and he could not deny that he was physically attracted to this exotic beauty. But mere lust had not worked out well for him in the past.

At the sheriff's office, he passed the food box through the bars to the man who was now identified as Hubert Grainger. The Chowdown held a contract to provide meals for the prisoners, and a schoolboy had delivered a box of cold flapjacks, eggs and sausage a short time earlier. The coffee making was the deputy's chore, and Grant expected to hear complaints. Serving breakfast was nothing compared to emptying Grainger's chamber pot in the privy out back earlier and then washing out the thing. Thankfully, a deputy sheriff out of Denver was scheduled to pick up the prisoner in two days. Good riddance. They had been boarding this man a good month.

He heard the door out front open and close, so he hurried down the short hallway. When he stepped into the office area, he was greeted by the banker, Matthew Gaines and a darkly tanned, white-haired man whose attire announced 'rancher.' The latter had probing eyes that were blue as the mountain sky. Grant doubted an ounce of fat could be located on the man who seemed far from surrendering to his years.

"Good morning, gentlemen," Grant said. "What can I do for you?"

Gaines smiled and said, "Plenty. Grant, this is Con Callaway. He's a rancher five miles west and chairman of the County Board."

Callaway stepped forward and extended his hand, giving Grant an iron grip that he tried to match. He feared that he had failed miserably.

Callaway said, "Pleasure to meet you, Grant. I've heard good things about you."

Grant claimed the sheriff's desk and invited the men to sit down. Callaway said, "You are probably wondering what the hell we're doing here."

Grant shrugged, "The thought had crossed my mind."

Callaway continued, "Doc Weintraub sent a rider out to the Double C last night and asked me to get into the hospital first thing this morning. The rider told me some about what happened, and Matt and me have been trying to piece it all together. Anyhow, Jim insisted on talking to us. The Doc gave us ten minutes."

"I was to talk to him this afternoon if he's able."

"Don't bother." He reached into his vest pocket and plucked out the gold sheriff's badge. "Jim gave us this. He's taking a leave of absence. He'll take the badge back when he feels he can do the job again. That might be a spell—a month or more."

Gaines spoke. "I'm just here to back Con. You know I'm town mayor, but the board chairman has the authority to fill vacancies in county offices. Jim said we should convince you to serve as acting sheriff."

Grant was incredulous. "You can't be serious."

Callaway said, "Hundred dollars a month. That's more than Jim gets paid from county funds." Grant wondered what other funds the sheriff tapped. Contingency perhaps?

"Why me?"

Callaway said, "Nobody in town with lawman experience. Ozzie ain't ready and said he would resign as deputy if we insisted he take the acting sheriff's job. You showed last night that you can handle a gun, if need be, but more important, you can take charge. Besides, you were already looking into things, asking questions and such. You know more about The Doll House case than anybody. Tell me who could come in cold and take over better than you. Grant, this town and county needs you right now. You step up now, and we won't forget it."

What in the hell was he thinking? Was he trying to be Marshal Tyree? "No more than two months, and if I decide I'm not up to it, I will resign before."

Callaway slid the gold badge across the desk. "Consider yourself sworn, Sheriff Coolidge."

Chapter 25

GRANT SUDDENLY HAD acquired responsibilities he had not bargained for, but he was not about to abandon his plans for grubbing out a living as a writer. He considered signing the Beadle contracts and sending them back, but he decided to see what the lawyer had to say. He did not relish dealing with Blue's former owner again, but he opened the door and entered the front room of the Ramsey and Locke office, glad that he would only be leaving papers for review this visit.

He was greeted by the fuzzy-cheeked clerk he encountered almost a month earlier. His name was Hamilton Fish according to the cedarwood placard on the counter. Fish brushed some errant strands of blond hair off his forehead and got up from his desk when Grant stepped in.

He tendered a welcoming smile and said, "Sheriff Coolidge. So good to see you again. How may I help you?"

Grant reached into his worn canvas bag. "I would like to leave some papers here for Miss Locke to review and then make an appointment to meet with her about them."

"Well, why don't you just wait here a minute, and I will see if she is free to speak with you now. It might save time if you spoke with her first before she looked at your papers."

"That's really not necessary as far as I am concerned." The young man disappeared down the hallway before he finished his sentence. He shook his head in disbelief. He had been sheriff less than an hour, and the news was traveling like a shooting star. A contraption called the telephone was starting to take hold in some larger cities. He could not see how it would serve any purpose in Lockwood, Wyoming.

He did not have time to sit down before Hannah Locke appeared wearing a rust-colored skirt and jacket that went nicely with the copper-colored hair that was tied back with a green ribbon and cascaded over her shoulders. It seemed that the west had more than its share of pretty women, or perhaps he had been living like a hermit too long.

She smiled when she stepped out and offered her hand. It was an engaging smile, one that she had not shared during his first visit.

"Good to see you again, Sheriff Coolidge. Ham says you would like me to review some contracts for you. Why don't you come in my office and tell me about them?"

"Please, call me Grant."

"Okay, Grant. I'm Hannah."

He followed her into her private office and took one of the chairs in front of her desk. To his surprise, she sat down in the other, angling it so they were facing each other almost knee to knee now that the barrier of the desk had been eliminated.

"Before we get down to business," she said, "I want to apologize for my behavior the last time you were here. I fear I was not very pleasant and possibly uncivil. It was no excuse, but I was not happy about selling Blue to a stranger. I hated to let him go. I should not have gelded him and kept him for a stallion. The sale put me in a mood. I hope you will find that he is a very special animal."

"I am learning that. We have bonded, and he will not be sold while I live."

"I can't tell you how much that pleases me. Also, one of my failings is that I tend to be a suspicious sort. Ethan chides me for what he calls the ice on my shoulder on occasion. Anyway, I'm sorry."

"No need to apologize. I must admit that many folks find me a bit standoffish at first meeting. I am not comfortable meeting people or mingling with crowds."

"Perhaps we have a few things in common then. I must confess, too, that you come recommended by my best friend, Moon Dupree. She speaks very highly of you. She told me about your intervention with the robber who might have otherwise killed her. She also swears you are a kind and honest man. My first thought was to warn her to be wary of premature judgment, but she has dealt with enough of the other kind that she requires no warning. Enough. What did you want my assistance with?"

He pulled a copy of the proposed Beadle contract and the original of the Percival Garth proposal from his bag and handed her the papers. He gave her a brief summary of his conversation with Garth and the man's suggestion that he was not being paid enough by Beadle. "I haven't paid much attention to the business side of my writing. I've just been grateful I could make enough to subsist, but I would like to be paid whatever I'm worth, and I gather Beadle has made a decent amount of money from my books."

"You don't intend to spend your life playing Buck Tyree as a real-life lawman then?" Her greenish-blue eyes twinkled and a mischievous close-mouth smile appeared.

"Hardly. But what do you know about Buck Tyree?"

"I am in love with him, that's all."

His brow furrowed. "I don't understand."

"I think I have read all of P.J. Bowie's novels and most of Jake West's. Of course, I have read most of Ned Buntline's novels, at least more than fifty of them. I have all the books on shelves in my home library. I've read the Tyree books three or four times."

He could not believe this. "You read dime novels?"

"I love them. I read statutes and court decisions all day long. I'm not looking to read Shakespeare when I relax before bed. Dime novels can be finished quickly, and they entertain, some decidedly better than others. It's the story I care about. I don't fret about some of the factual inaccuracies." Her eyes fastened on his. "I don't say this because you are a prospective client, Grant. Your novels are the best of the better. And I suspect you have a healthy female audience because you don't treat women like helpless idiots in your stories."

He did not care about the motivation for her words. It was difficult for a writer not to savor praise for the product of hours of lonely work. "I appreciate the kind words.

I am just a bit taken aback that a lawyer would be reading my work."

"You might be surprised how many lawyers and other people read your novels. They disappear from the shelves of the general store almost as fast as they come in. I have a standing order with Jeb to set aside one of each title as they come in. I think he has a few other such orders."

"Well, I would like to have you read the Garth proposal and the Beadle contracts and give me your thoughts. It's time for me to turn the business side over to someone else."

"I can do that. Set up an appointment with Ham for three days from now. It won't take me long to study the documents, but we need to do a bit of research on copyright laws. We have one of the best law libraries in the territory, and Ham is a top-notch researcher. We are fortunate. After another year of clerking, he will take the bar examination and is committed to staying on with our firm."

"Can you give me some idea of what fees to expect?"

"I intended to discuss that with you. My time is billed at five dollars hourly. Ham's time for research is billed at a two-dollar rate. Before your total bill would reach one hundred dollars, we will contact you at the sheriff's office before we proceed further. I am confident that the initial work won't reach that threshold."

He flinched inwardly, wondering what kind of a trap he might be stepping into, but today's Hannah Locke was far different than the one he met several weeks earlier. Moon trusted her. He decided he would. "That is agreeable. I'll set up an appointment on the way out."

He started to rise when Hannah spoke again. "And, Grant, if there is anything we can do to assist in your investigation of either of the recent killings, please contact us. We can't share client information obviously, but we know a lot about the poisonous snakes that lurk hereabouts, and I am the current county prosecutor.

"I do have a question."

"Yes?"

"What do you know about Winston Colbert and Bart Ryker?"

"They are among the poisonous snakes. Watch out for them. Ryker is just a hired gun, sort of a personal guard for Colbert. A man who requires a constant guard? Makes you wonder, doesn't it? Colbert bought The Doll House a few years back after the previous owner took the owl hoot trail, as they say. He has lawyers in Cheyenne, and he tosses a lot of money around, in my opinion more than his operation would have after expenses. I am guessing he is involved in something else, but I have no idea what. Watch your back with that man and his hired gun."

"I'll do that."

Chapter 26

LATE AFTERNOON, GRANT visited Jim Tolliver at the hospital. The patient was sleeping with the help of laudanum at the time, so he stepped over to speak with Ozzie who was in the adjacent bed separated by a curtain. He was in good spirits and advised his acting boss that he would be on duty at the jail the next day. Grant told him that would be Doctor Weintraub's decision.

He retrieved Blue from Fletcher's Livery and was headed back to The Tipi for supper but would return to the jail and spend the night on the cot along one wall in the sheriff's office. When a prisoner was in custody, it was policy to have an officer spend the night, usually Ozzie. The previous night, the prisoner had been left unguarded. Fortunately, there had been no incident beyond the incarcerated man's complaints that he would have been trapped in the event of fire.

He arrived in time to eat with the early shift, which he preferred because only he and the teacher, Milton Lockhart, generally ate early. Often, Moon joined them as she did tonight. Fried chicken was the main dish for supper and it, and all the vegetables, were delicious as usual. He knew that a pie or cobbler would show up soon. Again, he fretted about his waistline. This had never been a problem before, but he had never eaten the quantities he was consuming in Lockwood these days.

Lockhart sat at the head of the table, Moon and Grant positioned next to him, so they faced each other.

Lockhart looked at Grant, "Rumor at school is that you are the new sheriff."

"Acting sheriff till Jim Tolliver can get back to work."

"Don't see a badge."

"In my pocket. I wanted to tell Missus Dupree before I pinned it back on."

Moon said, "I heard. Trouble brought a load of firewood by. He told me. Jasmine knew as well. I wondered if you were going to say something or keep it a dark secret."

"Not any chance of that in this town."

Lockhart said, "You going to do something about our schoolgirl?"

"It's on my list. I'm sure you know there was another killing."

"A whore. She doesn't count. I was told you killed a few yourself."

"I'm sorry, Milton, I cannot discuss this. There is an investigation going on. We're still sorting this out."

They ate in silence after that. After Lockhart wolfed down a slice of cherry pie, he got up and went to his room without another word.

"I think he is miffed at me," Grant said.

"Residing in the same house as the sheriff can bring him attention he probably rarely gets. Firsthand information about the investigations. Top source for gossip, that sort of thing."

"I am sorry to disappoint him, but I can't have him reporting details to the teachers at the school—if I ever collect any details. I don't have any sense of where I'm going with this job right now. I am stumbling around in a maze."

"Just be careful. There is something strange going on here."

"That much I've figured out. By the way, I will be returning to the office for the night. We've still got a prisoner we are holding, as you know. He will be out of here in a few days, and Ozzie plans to be on duty tomorrow.

Before he left the office this morning, the county board chairman said I could hire another deputy temporarily if I can find one. Let me know if you think of anyone."

"Bushwa Sparks."

"Sparks?"

"Just a thought. He served in the Mexican War as a young man. He was a Confederate soldier. He's lived in this county a long time. He knows everybody and every inch of this valley and surrounding mountains. He's a shrewd devil. You've met him. You said you liked him."

"Do you think he would take it on?"

"If you approach him as a friend who needs help, yes."

"I'll ponder this."

"Now," she said, "we should talk about last night." She got up and walked over to the stairway, looking up the steps that led to the second-floor landing.

Grant did not wish to talk about last night, but he watched Moon as she moved, imagining the form beneath the simple, cotton dress. He saw little of her in the soft glow of moonlight that filtered into his room last night, but he would gladly settle for what his touch had told him if he could share another night with this creature. He feared that his living in the same house as Moon Dupree could become an untenable distraction.

Moon returned to her chair. "I wanted to be certain that our friend Milton was not spying from the top of the stairs. I did not see him, but we should speak softly."

"I understand."

"About last night. We should speak of it."

"I suppose but let me say it was very special between us. I will always remember."

"It is not the end for us unless you wish it to be." Her dark eyes found his.

"No, I don't want it to be the end."

"I have not been with a man since my late husband over five years ago. I carry no disease, and I am past the time for conceiving a child."

"Uh, okay. It has been several years since I have been with a woman, and I do not have a disease. As to a child, I guess I could still do my part." He grinned sheepishly and could feel a flash of blush on his cheeks. This was the strangest conversation he could recall having with a female. It was like a business meeting about intimacy.

"We will be two friends fulfilling needs," she said, "for whatever time we have."

"However you wish it to be."

"It is not always what we wish. Destiny will decide. Who knows? Maybe there will be more than I now sense. I hope we can continue our evening ritual of tea. We will know at those times whether we can snatch some time to share later. We must be together in your room. Jasmine's is next to mine, and I cannot bring myself to reveal our trysts to her, not now anyway."

"That is fine. What about Milton across the hall from me?"

"I will be forced to visit late. If he learns, we must be prepared for gossip. Can you endure that?"

"A small price," he said.

"It is settled then. Now you must return to work. Will you be here for breakfast in the morning?"

"I will wait until somebody from The Chowdown brings the prisoner's breakfast and then I will come here to eat and to change clothes."

"You will not get your bath tonight. We can have water ready for you in the morning, if you like."

"That's not within your bath time rules."

"I have the right to make exceptions. If you come for breakfast a bit late, Jasmine will have left for school, and the other renters will be at their jobs."

That thought coupled with the tortuous office cot would assure a sleepless night, he thought.

Chapter 27

"OZZIE WAS OVER here looking for Bushwa. The so-called sheriff wants to talk to him," Enos told Trouble when the new owner-to-be rode up to the stable. "He's out at his place today getting his ground tilled up for a big garden along the bottom land near the creek. That's what I was helping him fence last week."

"Cropping rocks ain't easy."

"Soil has built up some there from flooding over the years."

"Them same floods can wash the dirt and crops away."

"Bushwa is an optimist. He figures to grow corn and melons and sell them to Jeb at the general store."

"You and Bushwa always got money on your brains."

"Oh, I think of other things now and then. Just don't talk about them."

"Yeah, that little filly, Jasmine Dupree. What's Sammy think about her?"

"Nothing to think about. Me and Jasmine aren't anything special to each other. Just talk sometimes, meet up at a public dance."

"That's enough to stir up a good hair pulling. I ain't seen one in a coon's age. Might be worth going to one of them dances."

"You'd be wasting your time unless you've got your eye on one of those widow women. You'd need to see the barber to trim your hair and whiskers, take a bath."

"Ain't looking for a woman. Last thing I need. Are you still set on taking up residence in the hayloft?"

"Yep. You've still got your room in back. I'll fix breakfast for us. Do some other meals when I'm around, but we'll just be on our own more often than not."

"Won't matter none to me. I been on my own for a long time."

"Anyway, I've got to run out to Bushwa's place and let him know I won't be moving in. He won't care. He was just doing me a favor anyhow. He likes life alone up there, and with all my businesses, I need to be in town. Just as well that the Morris family is booting me out of their place. When I'm out to Bushwa's, I'll tell him the sheriff wants to see him."

"What about the paperwork on the livery?"

"I see the lawyer this afternoon to go over anything. Did you get a lawyer yet? Miss Locke says you ought to have one." Trouble knew that the old codger could not read more than a few words. He had seen Enos sign papers by printing the letters of his name almost legibly.

"Don't need no snake of a law wrangler. Your lawyer can just go over things when we sign. I'd trust her or Ethan more than most of them crooks, which ain't saying much."

"Well, I'm going to head out to Bushwa's. I'll stop at the sheriff's office and let Grant know that I'll tell Bushwa he wants to talk to him."

"Ain't my concern."

When he hitched Tag, his sorrel gelding, to the rail in front of the sheriff's office, he noticed that Grant Coolidge's gelding was tied there, so he figured that duty must have taken the acting sheriff out of the office today. Often, he left the horse at the livery most of the day. It had been three or four days since the shoot-out at The Doll House, and Trouble had heard nothing about any developments in the case. Maybe he could wangle something out of Grant.

He entered the office and found Grant standing and gazing out the window as his step-pa was inclined to do. Ozzie was at his desk and looked fit enough.

"Morning, Trouble. What brings you here this morning?"

"Heard you are looking for Bushwa Sparks. Found him yet?"

"Nope, but I haven't looked too hard."

"I think he's out at his place today trying to be a farmer."

"Can you tell me how to get there?"

"Better than that. I'm headed out that way to talk to him. I'd be pleased to have you ride along if you want."

"I'll take you up on that invitation. How far out is his place?"

"Don't know in miles, but a good half hour in time. Slow going when you hit the foothills. He's at the high end where you start the climb into some steep mountain country."

"I haven't been up in the high country yet. I hope I can do that as soon as my sheriff's job is over."

"Be glad to show you some things that a man ought to see."

"I just may take you up on that offer." Grant turned to Ozzie's desk. "Ozzie, I'll be gone for a few hours. Solve all the problems while I'm gone, would you?"

"I'll do my best, boss, but don't count on it."

A fast gallop across grassland to the southwest edge of the North Laramie River valley took the riders to the foothills. Trouble pointed to a clear creek that sent water splashing and tumbling over its rocky bed as it emerged from the rugged hills that were essentially stairsteps to the lofty peaks that rose in the background, "That's Fox Creek. I've never seen a fox up here, but that's what the old mountain men called it, and it carried on to becoming official on the county records. It runs right past Bushwa's cabin. Problem is that the banks are too steep to follow it. We'll take a wagon road just past the creek that twists like a snake up into the hills."

"Is it his private road?"

"Well, I wouldn't say that, but the county doesn't keep it up either. Most of it up to Bushwa's place is on government land, but folks just cross it to get to where they're going. It probably reaches a half dozen cabins up this way before it straightens out some and heads to lower country. When you hit the flat, there's an old trail that forks off to Cheyenne and Laramie, but even by horse or wagon it takes a few days longer than the old stagecoach road. And of course, with the railroad now, I don't know what fool would use it."

"Seems like an out of the way place for Bushwa to live."

"He likes it that way. Bushwa wants to get hold of the land between here and his place if the government puts it up for bids. Most of Wyoming Territory is still owned by government. A lot of it nobody wants, but there is all kinds of competition and a fair amount of skullduggery that goes on to get some of the properties that can be turned to profit. Had plenty of that a few years back when coal was discovered in the mountains."

"On government land?"

"Some of it. Government bureaucrats were taking bribes to help get land into the hands of those who paid the highest price to the men with power. Adam Smith said that's the nature of government management. We start competing for the favor of the government instead of the market."

"You are a student of Adam Smith?"

"Banker Gaines introduced me to his books when I was just a kid. Smartest man I've met yet, Mister Gaines." It occurred to Trouble that he might have offended Grant Coolidge. "Of course, I don't really know you that well yet."

Grant laughed. "I'll concede to your banker friend—on economics anyway. I haven't read much of Adam Smith."

They reined their horses onto the wagon road and began their climb into the foothills.

"You really should read *The Wealth of Nations*. You come to understand what is making this country grow, how businesses come to be and such. Why you should watch your back as soon as politicians say they're going help you out."

"Maybe I will, but I wanted to ask you about Jim. I didn't get over to the hospital to see him today. Have you spoken with him?"

"Saw him before I checked in with Enos. Doc says he's going to live. He's past the dangerous time for infection to set in. I'll help Ma take him back to the house day after tomorrow. I guess that bullet tore out a chunk of bone, too, and he might end up with a limp and a cane for good. But he'll be able to sit in the saddle and handle his guns. Being a lawman is what he knows, and he's not ready to leave it behind if that concerns you."

"Yes, selfishly it does. I don't want to do the sheriff's job a day longer than I'm needed."

"Can't say that I blame you. Can't make any money at it."

They rode their geldings at a walk up the wagon trail, twisting and turning between stone escarpments at places. Pine trees began to dot the landscape and grew thicker as they went. "The clearing's up ahead," Trouble said, "and we're in luck. Bushwa is on the porch."

Grant said, "He's sitting in a rocker. Doesn't look like he's tilling."

As they approached the sturdy-looking log cabin, Trouble waved and yelled, "Hey, Bushwa. You won't get a garden planted sitting on your ass."

As they rode up, dismounted and hitched their horses, Bushwa said, "I'm done with the garden business. I worked hard last night to get the ground ready, planted some seeds for corn and melons and the like. Looked out this morning, and crows covered the plot helping themselves to breakfast on my seeds. I let them go ahead and have their fill and walked out after they flew off and saw that deer had been stomping all over the plot, too."

Trouble said, "So you got to start all over?"

"Hell no, I ain't. I figured to fence the deer out before stuff started to grow, but that won't keep the crows out, and I'll bet the coons and possums and rabbits, and every creature known to man will get the word by day's end. I can't make any money doing this, and I can't afford to spend summer carrying on this kind of war. I surrender."

"Sorry it didn't work out, Bushwa."

"I shoulda knowed better. Been in these parts long enough to see what was coming. Hell, folks in town even got this trouble, but the gathering of people helps keep some of the animals at their distance. Now, if you two rode out for cake or cookies, I can't help you none. I'm guessing this ain't a social call."

"Well," Trouble said, "I came to tell you I won't be renting the room in your cabin here. I decided to set up a nest in the loft at the livery."

"Live with that crazy old fart, Enos? Sleep with the smell of horseshit drifting up your nose?"

"There's worse things." He did not retort that Bushwa's odor was not likely to be an improvement. Besides, he had never found horse manure offensive. Maybe it was a matter of what you were accustomed to.

"Well, it's your choice, boy."

"I just figured I should be nearer to my businesses. I didn't want to lose an hour or more on the trail every day, and I work till after dark lots of times. And rent's free at the livery."

"Aha. Now you're finally truthing me. It's the rent. You don't want to let loose of a damn nickel, do you?"

"Uh, I think Sheriff Coolidge wants to talk to you." He turned to Grant. "Would you like some privacy, Grant? I can take a stroll down the hill and see how Bushwa's garden is doing."

"No, that's not necessary." Grant spoke to Bushwa. "I need your help, Bushwa. You can do a great service to me and to our county. I would like you to take on the job as my temporary deputy."

"Me? I ain't never been a lawman."

"But you've seen more than your share of war. You know this county and the people here, and you come highly recommended. I've got some killings to solve, and there are things going on that just don't make sense. I'd be indebted to you if you could help me out."

"I'd be paid?"

"I'm authorized to pay twenty dollars a week, and you can take time to look after your real estate investments when you need to."

Trouble could not resist commenting, "Dang sight more than you're going to make off that garden."

Bushwa's mouth twisted in a snarl. "Don't need no comments from a reneger."

He did not think Bushwa was truly angry at him, but he figured it would be years before the ornery cuss let him forget about it.

Bushwa said, "When do I start?"

"How about tomorrow morning whenever you can get in."

"I get to wear a badge?"

"I've got one waiting for you."

"Okay. I'll come claim it tomorrow."

Chapter 28

HANNAH LOCKE SAT at her desk, staring hypnotically at the azure sky outside her office window. She had two appointments this afternoon, neither of which she considered routine. Brady Yates was first. He had recently turned sixteen and was engaged in more enterprises than most men or women would take on during a lifetime. He was smart as a whip, and she could not think of anyone who worked harder. His ambition was boundless.

Yet, he was five years from attaining legal age to contract and deal with property. Thus, with Brady's consent, she would sign a declaration of trust naming him as sole beneficiary. As trustee, she would take title to real estate, enter contracts and be the legal owner of his enterprises until he was of age. Arrangements had been made with the banker, Matthew Gaines, and she was confident she had all the details worked out.

Her preference would have been for Gaines to act as trustee, but he had declined. She supposed that he found it awkward given that he was Brady's biological father, a fact that Brady had only recently learned. Few were aware of this, but as a lawyer she was acquainted with many of the ghosts and demons that haunted her clients' pasts. This information never passed her lips, and most was omitted from her files, so others would not discover a toxic bit of history.

Her other appointment was with Grant Coolidge. She worried about her lack of experience with copyright law, but she considered herself second to none when it came to contract drafting and analysis. She doubted if there was a copyright expert west of the Mississippi River, and she would give her best effort to this new client. Hamilton Fish had done his usual thorough job of research and tracked some information that might be significant.

Grant was an enigma. She knew little about this man. A writer. A few weeks in town, and he becomes sheriff. Her best friend, Moon Dupree, seemed to be talking less about the man, and she found herself wondering if something was happening between the two. What really troubled her was that she felt a twinge of jealousy at the thought. Coolidge was a handsome devil, who seemed unaware of the effect his looks might have on a woman—which made him even more alluring. Worse, she felt an undeniable attraction to this man she barely knew. She shook off the thought for the moment. Her experience with men had been wretched.

"Brady Yates is here, Hannah. Are you ready to speak with him?" Hamilton Fish asked from just outside her open door.

She swung her swivel chair back to the desk, facing the doorway. "Yes, just send him in. He knows the way. We shouldn't be long."

Shortly, Trouble entered the room and went directly to one of the chairs in front of the desk. "Hello, ma'am. I was fearful I would be late. I've been out to Bushwa's place with the sheriff."

"I hope Bushwa's not in trouble with the law."

Trouble chuckled, "Hardly. Not the kind you're thinking of anyhow. Grant's hired him on as a deputy sheriff."

"Really?" She had difficulty seeing that rogue wearing a deputy's badge. On the other hand, he was a tough old bird and wily as a fox. Perhaps that was the kind of deputy called for with the current turmoil in the community.

"Yeah. Old Bushwa seems fired up about the notion."

"Now about the livery business. Is Enos still in the saddle for the deal?"

"Yep."

"Has he hired a lawyer that I can deliver the papers to?"

"Says he doesn't have any use for lawyers."

Enos had a lot of company, she thought. She had learned early on that there was little public affection for her profession. That was saved for the physicians. "Can Enos read?"

"Not much. But he trusts you enough to go over the papers with him when he signs."

"I don't like handling it that way. I will be signing the documents, too, as trustee. We've been through all this. You do understand that I technically own the businesses until you are twenty-one?"

"Yes, ma'am."

"You have free rein to run the livery, but I do have responsibility to know what is taking place. Do you keep track of the income and expenses, have a list of your inventories for your enterprises, that sort of thing?"

"In my head."

"I will need written reports monthly. If you don't want to do that, we should find someone who will. I know it's an extra expense, but you must do this for all your businesses."

"That's what Mister Gaines says. He will loan me the money for the down payment, but he wants to see business records until the loan is paid. He says I should have ledgers for all the projects. I don't have time for that stuff. I know when I'm making money. But I guess I'll have to do something. I know somebody who might do this."

"A bookkeeper?"

"Sammy Morris. Her family's moving back here. She's good with numbers. I'll ask her."

"I remember Samantha. They lived across the river from your mother's farm. She is about your age, isn't she?"

"Yeah. We both have another year of school unless I get the boot earlier. I don't go much."

Hannah was not going to press the boy on that issue. School or not, Brady Yates was not going to starve in his lifetime. "Well, if Samantha agrees to take the job, tell her to speak with me, so I can explain what she needs to do. I will pick up an accounting journal and ledger I would like her to use at the Oaks General Store. I have a book with accounting instructions I can loan her also."

"This is getting too complicated. How do I finish the deal with Enos?"

"You have passed your sixteenth birthday, and I have the paperwork ready, if Enos wants to get this done. Can you be at the livery tomorrow morning?"

"I guess so. I was planning to ride out to talk to Taylor Brown about buying his sawmill. He's losing business because he can't get the work out. Competition is going to drive him out of business if he doesn't get things turned around, and he's too feeble to do it himself."

Another project? She did not want to hear about it. "Bring a draft from the bank for the down payment. I will meet you and Enos at the livery at ten o'clock."

"Yes, ma'am. I'll head out to the sawmill after that."

Chapter 29

"I SHOULD BE at the sheriff's office right now, but I will still need to make a living when that work's done. I gather you have looked at Beadle's contracts and the Garth proposal. What do you think?" Grant asked.

Hannah said, "As to Beadle, I think you can do much better. Ham has done a lot of research and investigation and exchanged wires with a friend in Cheyenne who worked in the publishing business at one time. Is the Beadle contract the same as you have always signed?"

"Yes. I am sure it is."

"Then Beadle owns the rights to the Bowie and West pen names as well as the copyrights to all the books you have written."

"Yeah, I always understood that."

"That means Beadle can hire any writer to do the dime novels under those names. That reduces your leverage tremendously. Ham has projected that each book sells over a hundred thousand copies. He bases this on the number of copies Jeb says he sells and the country's population without considering that sales are probably greater east of the Mississippi."

"I can't believe there would be that many readers."

"Your dime novels have been selling for a quarter. A ten percent royalty would earn twenty-five hundred dollars."

She could see that he was nearly speechless at what she was saying, so she decided to continue. "I doubt if they will negotiate on a royalty basis now, but you should be able to earn much more than they are paying you. They run the risk that another writer would not hold your readers with his stories, eventually making their copyrights worth less."

Grant said, "I like knowing what I will be paid anyway."

"You should also reserve the privilege of writing for other publishers under pen names or your own, if you wish. That would allow you to strike a deal with Garth. For the moment, I suggest focusing on negotiating a contract with Beadle and advising Garth of your interest in working on projects with him. Keep that door open.

Finalize something with him only after you have nailed down the Beadle contracts."

"How much do you think I could get from Beadle?"

"I think you should seek a thousand dollars per book on a new contract."

"That would give me the option to take on whatever other projects suited me. If you are correct, I have been a lousy businessman. I don't want to deal with this. I just want to get this sheriff's job done and spend the rest of my life writing my books. I came west hoping to simplify my life. In a few weeks it has become so complicated I feel like I'm running in a maze."

"I'm sorry."

"Not your fault, but you can help me."

"I will try to."

"I want you to contact Beadle and make the best deal you can get. When the contracts are ready, show me where to sign."

"Are you serious? My time and your bill will start to add up."

"Do it. I would also like to have you contact Garth and explore what might be worked out with him." He stood up. "I don't want to deal with publishers. This is in your hands now. You know where to find me."

Hannah said nothing. Grant walked out the door.

Chapter 30

WHEN BUSHWA AMBLED in for his first day as deputy, Grant plucked a badge from the desk drawer and pinned it on the man's filthy buckskin shirt. "You are declared a deputy sheriff," Grant said.

"No ceremony or nothing?"

"That's the best I can do."

"Well, what do I do now? Don't see no desk. You and Ozzie have claimed the only two for your sleeping places."

"You're going to help me shake some trees."

"What do you mean?"

"We're going to visit The Doll House."

"Well, before we do that I ought to run across the street to the barber's and get my hair and beard trimmed some and maybe even try a bath."

"You won't need a bath for this visit."

"If you say so."

As they walked along the boardwalk toward The Doll House, which was a good four blocks distant from the sheriff's office, Bushwa asked, "What's my part in what you're up to here?"

"I am paying a call on Winston Colbert, the proprietor of the establishment. He's got a man who seems to always be close by like a bodyguard of sorts."

"You're talking about that weasel, Bart Ryker."

"Then you know the man?"

"Seen him around. Heard about him. He's been with Colbert from the beginning, him and some other gun slicks that hole up in cabins on the slope above my place a mile or so. They ride past from time to time. Never speak, even when I say howdy."

"You never mentioned those men before. How many?"

"You never asked. I seen a dozen different ones. Don't know if they're all up there at the same time. Like I say, we don't chat none."

"You said 'cabins.' There is more than one?"

"Used to be sort of a community up there when I first come years ago. Three men, as I recollect and a dozen women betwixt them. Called the females 'wives.' I don't know the niceties of it. Built the cabins and lived up there three or four years. Vacant for a lot of years, occupied by coons and possums and rats and such. Looked like solid buildings, but they must have been half filled with animal shit by the time those men moved in a few years back. Strange thing, though. Past year, lots of covered wagons pass by going up that way. Couldn't say how many. Not home that much. Must go over the mountaintop and down the other side, which is a bunch of damned foolishness. If they wasn't taking the train, the old stage road out of town through the valley would be quicker."

"Interesting. I need to find out how that property is titled. Could you make a sketch of where it's at?"

"Better than that. I'll go over to the county recorder's and get official word."

"Do you think those men are on Colbert's payroll?"

"Don't know. I just know Ryker goes up that way once or twice a week, and I seen one of them go in The Doll House three or four times. Of course, that could be for a drink or upstairs business. But you never told me my part."

"Just look mean and like you're ready to go for your gun. I want Colbert to know I've got somebody covering my back."

"That's easy enough."

They pushed the batwing doors aside and entered the saloon. Grant noticed there was no trace of the shootout that had taken place three days earlier. There was a scattering of morning drinkers at the tables, some playing cards. He could remember many mornings alone and nursing a whiskey bottle in his room, but he had been a rare social drinker. One thing he liked about separation from his roots was that nobody in Lockwood knew of the pathetic drunk who had staggered along the streets of the little Ohio river town ten years earlier, the would-be writer who abandoned the whiskey bottle on his thirtieth birthday.

He walked up to the bar where the man he had encountered upstairs the night of the killing presided. "Good morning, gentlemen. What suits your tastes today?"

"I would like to speak with Mister Colbert. Official business," Grant said.

Before he replied, the bartender reached under the bar, pulled out a pencil and paper scrap, wrote something on the paper, folded it and pressed it into Grant's hand. "I'll check with the boss," he said, slipping out from behind the bar and heading down the hallway Grant had come down after his altercation with the gunmen.

Grant furtively unfolded the piece of paper that he had been given and read the message: 'Help.' He stuffed the note in his shirt pocket.

The bartender returned. "Mister Colbert will talk to you. His office is first door on the right down the hall."

"Thank you." He gave the bartender two nods of his head, hoping he understood that the message had been read. He had no idea how he was going to help the man or why he needed it.

He stepped into the hallway, Bushwa a few paces behind. Ryker stood outside an open doorway, which he took to be Colbert's office, arms folded over his chest.

Ryker said, "Go on in. Alone."

"Wait here," Grant told Bushwa.

He entered the office, where Colbert sat at a massive desk that Grant instantly envied. He could fill that bare desktop with stacks of manuscript pages and other clutter in no time. The door closed behind him.

"Sit down and state your business, Coolidge. I'm a busy man."

"I'll stand, thanks." He noticed that Colbert's chair was raised from the floor somehow, so it appeared more like a throne than comfortable working furniture, assuring that the occupant would tower over persons seated on the other side of the desk. "I'm still investigating the murder and robbery here the other night, and I have a few questions and requests."

"You can ask. I'll decide whether to answer."

"I'd like to know more about Ginger—where she came from, how long she had been at The Doll House."

"I don't know anything about her past. She showed up about six months back. Ruby interviewed all the girls, decided who to take on. I suppose she would be what some places call a madam. We referred to her as the upstairs manager."

"Do you think Ginger knew the killers before they showed up here, that maybe a robbery was planned, or they had a reason to kill Ruby?"

"Seems unlikely, but I wouldn't know."

"The man who shot the sheriff obviously did not kill Ginger, not here anyhow. She did not leave Lockwood on a train. We have confirmed that. Cheyenne is a long ride by horseback from here. I'm guessing she is somewhere in the county."

"Sheriff, I hear you are a damned yarn spinner. Well, I don't want you making up stories about The Doll House or the people here. I don't give a damn what became of Ginger. She's gone, the money's gone. End of that story. I just want to get on with my business. Now, if you're done . . ."

"I would like to speak with Sugar again before I leave and later some of the other ladies."

"Sugar's gone."

"Gone where?"

"Wouldn't know. Disappeared the day after all the commotion."

"Why didn't you report it to our office?"

"Hell, people come and go all the time. They got a right to do that the last I heard."

"Mister Colbert. I'm not very comfortable about your cooperation with the investigation. I would think you would want to dig out the cause of the murder and shootings, so that you can head off any future problems. Frankly, I get the sense you are hiding something. If you aren't going to be helpful, I intend to do my own digging till I find out what this is all about."

"Just remember this isn't a storybook. You don't get to decide the end of this story and what happens with the folks you are pestering here. Don't make a nuisance of yourself."

Grant turned and walked out the door into the hallway where it appeared Bushwa and Ryker were engaged in a stare down.

Chapter 31

BACK AT THE sheriff's office, Grant spoke with his deputies and showed them the message he received from the bartender. "I'm not sure what to make of this," he said. "My first thought is, of course, that he fears for his life over something, but I must consider that he might be bait in a trap. Regardless, I need to try to speak with him alone. I want to find out where he lives and what his work hours are. I'm thinking I might pay a visit tonight."

Bushwa said, "I'll check on that. I'll start with Enos Fletcher. The Doll House front is within sight of the livery. Enos will know something or think of somebody that does."

"I heard the man called 'Orv' the night of the killing. What's his last name?"

"Jones. Orville Jones. He' s been here since Colbert took over The Doll House, but he's sort of invisible outside the saloon. Ain't seen him about town more than two or three times. Guess that would have been in the general store."

"I'll let you figure out how I can talk to the man privately." He turned to Ozzie. "And you, Ozzie, I want you to go to the railroad station and talk to the ticket agent and find out if Sugar has bought a ticket out of Lockwood since that night."

"Sugar?"

"I don't know her name. She's one of the ladies at The Doll House."

"Oh, that Sugar."

Grant furrowed his brow and squinted one eye. "So you know her?"

Ozzie's face turned crimson. "Well, I seen her around. I don't frequent the place or nothing."

Bushwa said, "I seen you coming out of there one night, and with drinks costing double anyplace else, I don't see you going there to socialize with a bottle."

Poor Ozzie. Time to give him a break. "Just find out if Sugar left on the train."

Bushwa said, "I'll go check on that property title before I visit Enos."

"While you are doing that, ask the county recorder to verify ownership of The Doll House property."

"I'll do that." He led the way out the door.

With his deputies gone, Grant welcomed some alone time. He needed to sort things out. The world he was now engaged in was not one created by his imagination. Real people were dying, and bona fide criminals were causing it. He wrote his stories without an outline, often not knowing what the next chapter would bring until it appeared on the paper in his handwriting.

On more than one occasion he had written himself into a corner and had to struggle to set out the remaining narrative to make sense of the plot he had contrived to that point. He felt like he was in such a corner now. Why in blazes had he agreed to take on this task? He was no lawman, and his novels made the lawman's work too simple. He always knew who the bad guys were, and Marshal Buck Tyree always disposed of the villains with a gunfight. Tyree had incurred a dozen or more flesh wounds, but his adversaries consistently ended up on Boot Hill.

Grant decided to stroll down to the Gaines Bank and see if Matt Gaines was available. The man seemed to know the town that he governed. Perhaps the banker carried information stored in his head that he was unaware could be significant to the case. Besides, he had come to enjoy Katy's welcoming smile when he walked into the bank.

Grant had come to realize that Katy was not being flirtatious. Cheer was just a part of her nature. He had learned from Moon that Katy was keeping company with a serious beau, and he hoped the young woman retained her good nature when she married the young cowboy who had won her heart.

Before he got out of his chair, Bushwa burst through the door. "Ain't been to the stable yet, Grant. Picked up some information at the recorder's office."

"Sit down. I'm listening."

Bushwa sat down in front of the desk. "Just thought I would let you know what I learned at the recorder's office, so you can chew on it some. Figured you ought to have something to do while your deputies take care of the real work."

"So why don't you tell me about it?"

"Colbert ain't holding title to The Doll House. Not the place up above mine neither. Same guy now owns both."

Grant was getting tired of Bushwa building the suspense. This was not a novel for entertainment. "What in the hell is the man's name?"

"Don't get crabby with me, boss. The name is Rayburn Cox. And guess what?"

Grant's silence replied.

Bushwa got the message. "His address is Santa Fe. That's in New Mexico Territory, you know."

"I heard rumors to that effect. Did you learn anything else about the owner?"

"Nope. That's all that was on the public record."

"I don't know what this does to help us, but I would sure like to know how this Rayburn Cox fits into the puzzle. I would think he was just a landlord if all he owned was The Doll House real estate, but his ownership of the other property suggests that he has a greater role in whatever is going on."

Bushwa got up. "Well, I'll be heading over to talk with Enos."

"Thanks, Bushwa. I'm glad to have this information. I've just got to figure out what to do with it."

Grant sat at his desk nervously tapping his pencil on the desktop. How could he find out who Rayburn Cox was? He could think of no person he knew who resided in Santa Fe, certainly no one he could contact to make an inquiry. It occurred to him that lawyers had something of an unofficial network of colleagues throughout the country who could be contacted to assist clients with business in other states or territories. He wondered if Hannah

Locke might be able to assist. It could not do any harm to ask.

He left his office and walked down the street to the Ramsey and Locke office building. When he entered, Hamilton Fish looked up from his desk and nodded.

"Can I help you, sheriff?"

"I would like to speak briefly with Hannah sometime, hopefully yet today if she can find time for me."

"Just a moment." He got up and hurried down the hallway. When he returned, he said, "She's available now. It will be just a few minutes."

Momentarily, Hannah appeared. "Grant, come on back."

He followed her to the office, and when they were seated, he said, "Sorry to barge in like this. Sheriff's business."

"So I bill the county?"

"Well, I don't know. I would need to talk to the board chairman. Just add it to my bill. I'll deal with the county later."

"I'm not serious. On the house for now."

He told her about Rayburn Cox and his concerns about the man. "I need to find out about this gentleman without him knowing he is the subject of my inquiry."

"Understandably. I do know a lawyer who could possibly help us. Her name is Jael Rivers. She practices in the Rivers and Sinclair firm. Her husband, Josh Rivers, is the senior partner. Sinclair is Danna Sinclair. They may be the only firm in the country that includes more than one woman in the office. I met Jael at a conference in Denver, and we became quite good friends, partly because we were the only two women in attendance. She has handled some client business for me in Santa Fe, and we correspond from time to time."

"So you could send her a telegram?"

"I could. I wonder if we should. How urgent is this?"

"Not terribly, I guess. The case is moving as slow as molasses anyway, and I have other problems ahead of this on my list."

"I'm concerned about confidentiality. If this man is somebody important, he might have connections with the telegraph office there. In that case he might get a warning about an inquiry, and Jael might never see the message."

"That makes sense, but I can't wait weeks for a mail response."

"Can you wait a week?"

"I suppose."

"Let me check with Dayton Roberts at the post office. We have excellent rail connections south to Santa Fe. I will see what kind of priorities we can obtain on delivery. I can send a letter and explain the circumstances in a way that would be impossible by telegraph, and Jael can give a more detailed response."

"Okay. Once again, I will just leave this in your hands. Thanks. I do appreciate this."

"I hope it helps. I have a bad feeling about these killings. I fear we haven't seen the end of it all."

Chapter 32

"SUGAR DID NOT leave on the train. Ticket agent said he would have knowed her," Ozzie said. "Office ain't open nights since all we get is day passenger trains."

"At least that eliminates one possibility unless somebody else bought her ticket and she slipped into the passenger car without being seen. Seems unlikely, though. We must assume she's still around Lockwood someplace. I just hope she's alive."

"You worried somebody kilt her?"

"It is possible. Colbert did not like the idea of my speaking to Sugar outside his presence."

Grant strolled over to The Chowdown and picked up three lunches while Ozzie brewed a fresh pot of his mud coffee. Grant vowed he would drink the coffee before, not after, he ate his apple pie. When he returned to the office,

Bushwa was sitting in one of the captain's chairs in front of the sheriff's desk.

Grant placed the lunch box on the desktop and removed three roasted beef sandwiches and the pieces of pie. "Contingency fund pays for lunch today, boys." Ozzie had explained that the contingency fund was kept in cash in a lockbox absent a lock under the sheriff's desk and usually paid for lunch for any of the lawmen on duty. Grant had no hesitance, considering the paltry salary he was paid, in maintaining the tradition.

Bushwa said, "Just keep that gun-powder coffee away. I don't want a hole blowed in my gut."

Grant saw that Ozzie was hurt by the jab and said, "I'll take a cup, Ozzie. I can't imagine what Bushwa's brew would taste like. You do fine with the coffee," he lied.

Bushwa grunted and plucked a sandwich from the desktop.

Grant took a bite from his own sandwich, savoring the taste a few moments. He had certainly been a good distance from starvation since he crossed the Mississippi. Marshal Tyree was often on the brink of starvation during his pursuits, eating half the population of rabbits along the way. This lawman preferred beef and apple pie.

"Well, what did you learn from Enos?" Grant asked Bushwa.

"How about we eat first?"

"How about you tell me now, while we eat."

"Jones almost always leaves The Doll House at midnight weekdays. Saturdays Enos ain't seen him leave. Enos calls it quits about that time, so he figures Jones works late that night. I'll tell you this. Don't go in The Doll House's front door late at night. It's within sight of the livery, and Enos will often be perched on his bench like a big old crow seeing who's going in and out. I reckon the man could mine a fortune in blackmail if he chose. Likely a lot better pickings at that back entrance, though. Enos don't like the competition from the saloon's stable. Besides, he'd really know who was going and coming if they had to put up the mounts there."

"Where does Jones live?"

"Got hisself a room at Sally's Bed and Board. Decent place. Serves three meals, and he don't go into work till about three most days. We was lucky to catch him there on a morning shift. Likely somebody didn't show for work."

"I take it he walks to and from work. Otherwise, he would go out the back to the saloon's stable to get his horse."

"Well, ain't you a smart devil? Yep. It's only about three town blocks to Sally's off on a side street. He walks right past Enos's bench, says 'howdy,' trades pleasantries about the weather and such but don't do more than slow down a mite. Enos would love to wangle more from him, but the man don't let loose with words easy."

"Pass the word to Enos that I'm going to be at the livery tonight about nine o'clock. I'll explain what I want him to do when I get there."

Bushwa said, "I'll be there to back you."

"I don't think that will be necessary."

"Likely not. But I'll be there. I'll claim one of the cell beds for the night. Ain't none occupied the last I saw."

"No, take your pick."

"I'll do that, and if you ain't got other chores, as soon as I finish this pie, I'm going to go back and take me a nap."

"An excellent idea." Grant was ready for a respite from conversation with the contrary cuss. Bushwa made it clear that he did not defer to rank, and since the man was doing him a favor with his presence, Grant figured he had no right to expect blind obedience, nor did he want it while he muddled through the job that had dropped upon him.

They finished eating in silence, and Bushwa disappeared through the doorway that took him to the cells leaving Grant and Ozzie in the office. Grant said, "I'm going to go talk to Matt Gaines a spell if he's available. I'll check back here before I go to The Tipi. I'll have supper there tonight before I head over to the livery."

Ozzie said, "Well, Grant, today is clean-up day here, so I thought I'd clean the privy out back. It's going to take some extra scrubbing with Bushwa being around. I notice his aim ain't too good with his pizzle. Hope he's better with a gun."

"That doesn't sound like fun."

"Ain't that bad. I fill the bucket from the pump next to the horse tank out front, take some lye and sprinkle it on the two-hole seat, scrub a bit and rinse it off. Be good till his next trip. I ain't about to talk to the old rascal about it. Maybe you would."

"We'll see," Grant said noncommittally, but he considered such a conversation unlikely. Odd, the kinds of things that become a part of a sheriff's duties. This issue would have never faced Buck Tyree. He was too busy shooting bad guys.

Chapter 33

MATT GAINES INVITED Grant into the bank president's office as soon as Katy informed him of the sheriff's arrival. They were no sooner seated than Katy appeared with her seemingly perpetual smile and two mugs of coffee. "Now you let me know," she said, "if it's too strong or not strong enough."

Grant took a sip that scorched his lips, but he welcomed it. "Perfect," he said before she went out the door. He hoped it would help wash away the acrid office coffee that lingered even after the pie.

"What can I help you with, Sheriff?" Gaines asked.

"Maybe nothing. I'm still working mostly on hunches, but I'm speculating that the role of The Doll House in the killing of Ruby Name Unknown is more than just the location of the crime. I am considering that Abigail Doe

Eyes's murder could be related and that this is a small piece of something much larger."

"Now, you have piqued my curiosity."

"I hope to know more tomorrow, and I will try to keep you informed. I trust you will keep Mister Callaway, the board chairman, up to date. Technically, he's my boss, I guess."

"Con's honest as a looking glass. But don't tell me anything that shouldn't be passed on. He is a good friend and better customer."

"I understand. Did you ever hear of a man named Rayburn Cox?"

Gaines' brow furrowed. "Yes, according to the territory's banking records, Rayburn Cox and his brother, Elmer, are the shareholders of the Lockwood State Bank, my competitor. And, yes, it is called the 'state bank' even though Wyoming is still a territory, a designation born of optimism, I guess. Banks must be registered with the territory governor's office, and all owners must be listed. When the bank changed ownership a few years back, I made it my business to find out who the owners were. I was certain that the president, John Unger, a local young man, would not have had the money to make the purchase. Is this relevant to your investigation?"

"Could be. Are you aware that Rayburn Cox owns The Doll House real estate and some mountain property?"

"I had no idea. I suppose that's why we've never done any business with The Doll House. Many businesses maintain accounts in both banks in a small town like this. It's an opportunity for competitive lending, and merchants hope to obtain some reciprocal patronage. Of course, there are some who are loyal to specific banks, and we appreciate those who choose to work exclusively with us. We go out of our way to reward that loyalty. I'm sure the Lockwood State does the same for customers who select that institution. So, I gather the bank ownership adds another piece to your puzzle?"

"That's a good way of putting it. It's still a puzzle, but what you have told me could be very important. And I just stumbled onto this information. I wonder if that's how a lot of cases get solved. Lucky stumbles."

Gaines laughed. "It would not surprise me in the least. Skill and hard work will carry a man a good distance, but I welcome a lucky stumble whenever it happens—and it has happened to me more than once during this lifetime."

Grant stood, reached across the desk and shook the banker's hand. "Thank you, Matt. If you think of anything else about the Lockwood State Bank and The Doll

House connection, I would appreciate it if you would let me know."

"I certainly will, Grant, and for what it's worth, I think we drafted the right man for sheriff."

Chapter 34

MOON WORRIED ABOUT Grant. He had returned for supper at The Tipi, and now they enjoyed their ritualistic tea at the kitchen table before he returned to work. He had become consumed with his sheriff's job, almost forgetting, it seemed, that he was a writer, not a lawman. She saw him as a kind and gentle man, racing from a past that was not nearly so sordid as he imagined. Two failed marriages. Post-war years of drunkenness, all long behind him.

He had killed men and nearly been killed during the war. That past was the demon that haunted him as it likely did many combatants. It was also the one he rarely mentioned. She did not press. That was a core component of the strange relationship she had with this man. Neither probed the other for personal information. Disclosures were made voluntarily and spontaneously.

Tonight, Grant had not been talkative, but they were comfortable with long silences. She knew his mind was on his sheriff's duties and whatever task faced him later this evening. She decided to draw his obsession away to another topic. "I have never told you how I came to be in Lockwood. Are you curious?"

Grant looked up from the teacup he had been staring at. "Of course."

"Frenchmen have shaped my life three times. The first was my father. The French traders and trappers played important roles in settlement of the west and especially the mountain country. Many took up Indian wives, leaving the woman and the couple's children behind when the man moved on. My mother was Brule Sioux, one of Lame Buffalo's band. My father, Pierre Couture, was such a trader, only when he returned to St. Louis he took my mother, me and my little brother with him. I was six years old at the time."

"That explains why you speak English so perfectly."

She smiled. "I was educated in St. Louis for ten years. There were other half-bloods there, but we attended white schools. My mother and brother died during a smallpox epidemic when I was eight, and my father raised me. I speak French well enough and get by with the local Sioux dialect now, but English is my language."

"I'm surprised you didn't remain in St. Louis."

"My father died the year I finished my schooling. He was a good man and was attentive to my upbringing. He was a better father than businessman, however, and creditors took most of the property when he died. I was fortunate, though, that I salvaged five hundred dollars from his estate. After that was settled, I felt the mountains of my early childhood calling. We only had stagecoach connections then, but I found my way to Lockwood. It consisted of no more than a trading post, a stagecoach relay and half dozen houses when I arrived. There was also a tiny schoolhouse and ten-bed dormitory some distance away at the school's present location. A Quaker woman was operating the school alone at the time, the other teacher having died, and she agreed to take me on as a teacher for room and board—'room' consisting of sharing a single room with her in the dormitory building where a kitchen and dining area was also located. Enough of my story for tonight."

Grant said, "I hope to hear more of it someday."

"It gets more complicated as time rolls on."

He nodded. "Life has a way of doing that. Certainly, mine has."

She hoped she was not one of his complications, but why would she think otherwise? He had become one of hers.

Grant pulled his timepiece form his trouser pocket and glanced at it. "I need to leave in fifteen minutes. I'm meeting Bushwa at the livery at nine o'clock." His face was grim and taut, and that did nothing to pacify her concerns.

"We hope to meet up with an important witness tonight, somebody who might help me make sense of the killings of Ruby and Abigail."

"Do you think the same killer is involved?"

"If not the same individual, a part of the same scheme, whatever it might be."

"I hope that you find some answers."

"We'll see. Don't wait up. It will be well after midnight when I get back."

She supposed he was saying it would be too late for lovemaking. It would never be too late on her part, but she understood that he was trying to be considerate. To hell with lovemaking. There was no way she would sleep until she heard him come through the door.

Chapter 35

GRANT LED BLUE inside the Fletcher's Livery stable where he found Bushwa and Enos standing in the alleyway quarreling about something. "Sorry to interrupt, gentlemen, but I would like to put up my horse for a few hours."

"Pick an empty stall," Enos said. "That will be a half dollar."

Bushwa said, "That's what we're fussing about. I told this old thief we shouldn't have to pay him a damned penny. We ain't customers. We're here on law business. A half dollar for a few hours. This old coot has a habit of stealing and just can't break it. He don't own this place no more. Him and Trouble and the lady lawyer was just finishing signing the papers when I come over this morning."

Enos said, "Trouble ain't said nothing about policy changes. I work for him now, and I ain't changing the rules till the boss says so."

"He's going to have a hell of a lot of fun trying to boss an old fox like you. He's going to wish he'd never got hold of this place," Bushwa said.

Grant placed a silver dollar in Enos's hand. That will take care of two horses." He looked at Bushwa. "Contingency fund." He could see the disappointment in the man's face. He was learning that Bushwa loved to quarrel. Arguing was a game he was unable to pass up. He and Enos were near twins in that regard.

Grant and Bushwa unsaddled their mounts and led them into stalls. When the horses were watered and offered a handful of grain that Enos grudgingly surrendered, the men met in the alleyway. Grant said, "We're going to have a long wait, but I don't want to risk Jones leaving The Doll House early."

Bushwa said, "And how are we going to know when this jaybird heads out?"

"You're going to be up in the hayloft. Open the doors just enough to give you a view down that side street where the main entry to the saloon is located. Let me know when you see him coming this way on the boardwalk. Take your Winchester up there with you and stay posted and keep a lookout till I'm finished with the man."

"I'll have it ready. Are you expecting trouble?"

"It's always best to expect it. If he follows his usual route, he will cross the street, turn west and walk past the livery. Enos, I would like you to take your usual place on the bench as soon Bushwa says Jones is on his way. I will be hidden behind the wall adjacent to the entryway."

"Am I getting paid for this?" Enos asked.

"No."

Enos did not protest, evidently sensing that the acting sheriff was in no mood to dicker. "So I'm sitting there on my skinny ass. What do I do then?"

"When he greets you, tell him I want to see him inside and to step through the door opening."

"And if he don't want no part of that?"

"Nothing. He continues down the street."

They waited quietly. Cloud cover drifted down from the mountains, hiding the moon and starlight and dropping a shroud of blackness over the town. Grant thought the darkness could be a blessing, making it easier for Jones to slip into the stable unseen. On the other hand, it would be more difficult for Bushwa's eyes to pick out and identify the man so that he could alert Grant to the bartender's approach.

Grant heard Bushwa's booted foot stomping on the loft floor above him. "Get seated on the bench, Enos. I'll be just inside."

Without a word the liveryman hobbled to the bench and sat down. The old-timer seemed unfazed by the intrigue, and his calm demeanor might keep Jones from being spooked, Grant thought.

Grant caught a glimpse of the shadowy figure crossing the street on his way to the livery corner before he pressed his back against the stable's inner wall and listened. The bartender spoke first. "Good evening, Mister Fletcher."

"Howdy. Sheriff's inside. Step in quick-like. I'll keep watch out here."

The man responded instantly and stepped through the wide entryway. Grant moved out to join him. "Let's keep walking down the alleyway."

When they reached the middle of the building, Grant said, "Over to the side in the vacant stall. We can't be seen by a passerby there."

Jones said, "I don't think I'm in my right mind to be doing this."

"Your note said 'help.' I gathered you were a man with a problem."

Jones sighed. "I want to leave The Doll House and this town, and the sooner the better."

"Why don't you just pack and go?"

"I wouldn't have given you that note if it was that easy. I know too much. I came with Winston Colbert when he set up shop here. I met him in Kansas City when I was tending bar there. He offered me twice what I was getting paid to come out to Wyoming. Said all I had to do was tend bar and keep my mouth shut. After Ruby was killed and the shooting the other night, I realized it ain't that simple. Ruby knew more than was good for her health, too."

"Are you saying Colbert killed her?"

"Not personally, but he ordered it done. I can't prove it, but those men you killed were a part of the gunslinger army he keeps hid away up in the mountains. Tom Avery, the outlaw that shot Sheriff Tolliver, is another. The robbery was a clumsy cover. Be assured Colbert got his money back."

"You are saying that Colbert ordered the attack on his own place? Why?"

"I'm guessing it started with Ruby making a threat, holding him up for money. Her candle did not burn bright. Her death was also a message to any of us who know what's going on to think again before taking it to the law. I am a dead man if Colbert finds out I'm talking with you, but I figure I'm near the top of the list anyhow. I want out of here."

"You really don't think you could just buy a train ticket and leave?"

"He would send his wolves after me. They would go to the station agent, find my destination and be right behind. I thought of buying a horse and taking off, but I'm a town boy. I'd be lost a few hours out and end up dead anyhow."

Grant said, "I will try to help you, but tell me what's going on at The Doll House."

"Well, I don't understand it all, but Colbert is freighting Indian girls for whore houses, some as young as twelve. There are rich customers who will pay a lot of money for the young ones, and they like them on the dark side. The Doll House has special nights when word is sent to the interested men that the young ones are available. Colbert uses some of his girls here before shipping them on."

"I haven't heard anything about missing Sioux girls in this county."

"One dead, though."

"Abigail Doe Eyes?"

"Don't know her name. Doubt if she gave her real one when she came here wanting work. She was thinking of cleaning and the like, I'm sure. I'm sorry to say I sent her to Ruby. I don't think the girl bargained for the work Ruby put her into, but she must have liked the money because she left days and came back nights, maybe three times a week for a month. When Colbert found out she was a local, he threw a fit, slapped Ruby around, screamed at everybody. I guess he was worried about word getting out about town that he was using young girls here. That would cause the law to look closer at his business, I suppose."

"So, Colbert ordered the girl murdered."

"Just my guess. Can't say for sure who did it, but you probably killed two of them already—Gus and Rocky. Don't even know their last names. If there was a third, I'd bet on Tom Avery. They were the men for the dirtiest jobs. Rocky likely did the killing. He always carried a nasty-looking skinning knife."

"Can you tell me more about the night Ruby was killed?"

"I was damned confused that night when men I knew were tearing up the place, killing Ruby and robbing the lock box."

Grant said, "Conveniently, Colbert had been out of town, so everybody would have figured he didn't have anything to do with it. What about Sugar?"

"Highest of the high-class whores. Colbert's exclusive, too. Don't know what happened to her, or Ginger, neither. Dead maybe. Just don't know."

Grant asked, "The freighting of young Indian girls. How does that work?"

"Don't know. I just know some were drug in here for maybe a week at a time, and the special customers would show up, most by rail from Cheyenne. I suppose telegrams went out when the girls were to be available. As near as I could tell Lockwood was sort of a relay stop. Indian girls—maybe some orphans, possibly others captured like animals, brought a few at a time from reservations up north. Then Colbert's men loaded them on wagons and hauled them south to Laramie or Cheyenne. Ruby told me once they went to Denver and then Santa Fe. That's where they were sorted out like cattle and some sent on to Mexico or Texas, wherever the market was. Ruby somehow was on the inside of things."

Grant spoke to Jones for a bit longer before deciding the man could not help with much more in the way of specifics, but he had laid out the basis of the case, which reached well beyond several murders. Analysis of the crimes involved were beyond his expertise. He was aware, however, that his jurisdiction did not extend beyond the county line. He needed legal advice soon. Tolliver had been a U.S. Marshal. If the man was up to it, time for consultation had arrived. Perhaps Hannah could help.

"What do I do now?" Jones asked.

"I can take you into protective custody, lodge you in a jail cell under guard until we figure out how to protect you and move you away from here to a safe place. You would have to agree to be available as a witness."

"They'll know I've talked if I'm in a jail cell. One way or another, Colbert will get to me unless you've got an army to surround your office and jailhouse."

The man was entitled to the truth. "I have two deputies and myself. I might be able to round up some more help."

Jones said, "I don't think my life is in immediate danger. I would like to go to work tomorrow as usual. You come up with a plan for my protection. I will meet you here tomorrow night when I get off work."

Grant did not like the idea of letting the key witness out of his sight, but his grounds for holding the man based on information that was in large part speculative was flimsy. Also, he could not guarantee Orville Jones's safety in the jail without making other arrangements. "If that's what you want. I'll see what I can come up with in the way of more support. I still think the jail is the best place for your protection until we can move you to Cheyenne or elsewhere. You have your things packed and be ready to move out of your room tomorrow night."

Chapter 36

WHEN GRANT RETURNED to The Tipi after his meeting with Jones, he walked in to find Moon reading in the parlor. She put her book aside and got up and greeted him with a warm kiss. "If you would like company or need to talk, I'll join you in bed in a few minutes."

"Both," he said, noting that she was barefoot and already in her cotton robe, probably naked beneath it. The thought distracted him from his worries. He gave her a quick hug and headed up to the bedroom while she turned off the downstairs lamps.

When Moon arrived and slipped between the sheets, they delayed their talking until more urgent priorities were addressed. Afterward, Moon curled up like a purring cat and he spooned up against her propped up on his elbow, head resting on his hand and the other arm flung over her waist.

"Time to talk?" she asked, her voice soft, still seductive.

"Yes. I'm hoping you might see something that I'm overlooking in this tangled plot."

"I'm listening."

He told her about his meeting with the bartender. When he finished, he said, "My first concern is to protect the witness. I'm uneasy with him returning to The Doll House for even ten minutes. I've got to have a solution by tonight. Every time we meet increases the chances the wrong person catches on to what he's up to. That makes him a dead man."

"Why don't you talk to Hannah first thing when you head for your office? She's county prosecutor and she's going to become involved in whatever happens. Besides, I have the greatest respect for our sheriff, but it seems to me that some of this goes way beyond his job responsibilities. She won't take it kindly if she gets pulled into a legal mess to sort out and wasn't given a warning."

"You're right, of course. If I represent the law in this county, I'd better have some back up. I was surprised, though, when I learned she is the prosecutor."

"They cannot keep a prosecutor here. It's a parttime job, and the two firms, Ramsey and Locke and Houseman and Rich, alternate every two years assigning one of their lawyers to act as prosecutor. If there is conflict with a client, the other office furnishes a special prosecutor. Hannah says it's just the lot of small-town lawyers. They sometimes are forced to wear hats they would not otherwise choose."

"My first meeting with Hannah did not go so well, but the second time, I think we made peace."

"You and Hannah are a good fit. You will become very special to each other in time."

What a strange thing for a woman lying naked with him in his bed to say, Grant thought. She often talked of the future in ways that made it seem that a spirit guided her path through life, giving her a clairvoyance not granted to others of humankind. "I don't know about that, but I trust her to give me good legal counsel. That's enough."

She rolled over, pulled him to her and pressed her lips to his. "Let's not waste our time together."

Chapter 37

WHEN MOON AWAKENED, the sun was just starting to filter through the curtains. Grant was sleeping soundly, a soft purr rising from his breathing. She had only a moment to savor the peaceful look on his handsome face, before she smelled the succulent aroma of biscuits and bacon drifting up the stairway. Oh, my God. Jasmine was preparing breakfast for the renters.

She swung her legs out of bed and snatched up her robe. Grant stirred and raised himself up on one elbow. "Moon?"

"I've got to run. Jasmine has started breakfast. She's going to know about us." She bent over and kissed him softly. "See you at breakfast."

"Uh. Yeah. Okay."

She opened the door and darted into the hallway, slamming into Milton Lockhart and nearly knocking him off his feet when she shoved him against the opposite wall. She stepped back. "Mister Lockhart, I am so sorry. I was waking Mister Grant."

Lockhart stared at her with wide eyes. "It appears so," he said.

She looked down and saw that her robe had pulled apart, leaving nothing to the man's imagination. She could think of nothing to say, so she tugged it about her, turned and raced down the hallway. When she reached the bottom of the stairway, she saw that Jasmine was setting places for the several renters who ate first shift. There was no way to put off facing her.

"Good morning, Mother. I hope you slept well," Jasmine said, her voice cool.

Mother, not mom. What to say? She would not lie. "I hope you slept well, too."

"I will finish with the early eaters, but Mister Riley will be bringing the school carriage by in less than an hour. You might wish to change before you serve the others."

"Uh, yes, I will do that immediately." She rushed for her room.

After donning some undergarments and changing into a respectable olive-drab dress, Moon slipped on a pair of low-heeled shoes and joined her daughter in the kitchen. "I can take over now," she said.

"Good, I need to gather up my school things and go out and wait for Mister Riley."

"Jasmine, we will talk about it tonight."

"I do not wish to talk about it, and I refuse to talk about it. Whatever you have been doing with Mister Coolidge the past several weeks is none of my concern." She walked out of the kitchen.

So Jasmine had already guessed. She was not entirely surprised. Most fifteen-year-old girls would not be naïve about such things. And what her forty-seven-year-old mother did with an adult male was indeed none of the daughter's concern. Moon decided she was relieved not to be faced with engaging in a conversation about 'it.' She would not surrender a minute of any time Grant was willing to share with her. Life was too short and precious. She thought of the single vulture that had been circling the house for two days now. A sign, but for whom? She feared its message might be for Grant.

Chapter 38

"THIS IS A very serious situation," Hannah said. "And complicated. We must get a U.S. Marshal here.

Hopefully, there is one available in the Cheyenne office, but it might take a week at best, maybe a month, for someone to show up. Jim Tolliver's a former marshal. If you like, I can ride out to the Yates farm and get Jim's permission to send a telegram under his name requesting assistance from Cheyenne. I can follow it up with a letter giving a brief summary of the federal issues involved here."

"And what are those federal issues?"

"Wyoming is a territory, so the federal courts have jurisdiction over many of the serious crimes, but if there is a scheme to abduct and transport Indian girls across state and territorial lines, that is clearly a federal crime. Also, I have been reading articles in the Cheyenne newspaper about girls disappearing from the reservations. The Bureau of Indian Affairs is looking into this supposedly, but I can imagine how quickly that investigation would be moving, and it is likely a road to nowhere."

"I don't know much about the reservations."

"Well, Lockwood, isolated as it is, would make a perfect conduit for moving Indian children south. There are natural trails from most of the reservations to the North Laramie Valley. There is the huge Fort Washakie Reservation to the north that includes Shoshone and Arapahoe. In Montana there is the Crow Indian Reservation and in the southeast corner of that territory is the Northern Cheyenne Reservation. Farther east into South Dakota, you find the Sioux reservations. There are a good number of orphans among the tribes, and the populations are spread out over vast areas. Dollars would likely find ample locals who would capture prey. If we can be part of ending this disgusting and totally immoral activity, I will gladly put my other work on hold to help."

Grant assumed that 'other work' included his own. His writing career seemed to be floating in mud these days.

"I will gladly leave it to you to pursue the U.S. Marshal Service. My priority is to preserve the witness. I feel I must get him to safety tonight. We need his help if we are going to piece the puzzle together. I sense he knows more than he has told us. He may not even be aware of some of the things he knows until we have a chance to question him, which I would like to have you involved with."

"Gladly. Here's another thought. Talk to Trouble Yates about scouting out the place where Colbert has men hiding out. If he is not at the livery, Enos should know where he is at. Trouble knows this country better than anybody, even Bushwa. You don't have to give him a lot of details, but anything you say is safe with him. I am going to speak with some folks and see if I can round you up a few volunteer deputies. If this blows up too soon, you may need more men on standby with guns."

"That would be good. I won't count on it, though." He started to get out of his chair, but she lifted her hand signaling he should stay.

"I'm not finished. I received a telegram yesterday afternoon."

"From your friend in Santa Fe, I assume."

"No, she will respond by mail. That will be another two or three days, if we are lucky. The message was from your friend, Percival Garth. He wants to come to Lockwood to discuss publishing possibilities with us. I am to name a date."

"I don't see how I can set a date with this case pend-ing. Things change by the hour it seems. Perhaps we should put him off a month or two."

"I don't recommend it. Harvest the fruit when it's ripe. Garth is the fruit, and he seems anxious to make a deal with you. I would like to set something up in another week and ask him to allow two days. Meeting place will be at my office, and if you are not available, I will meet with him. We can discuss possibilities you would be open to before he arrives. You haven't known me long, and I un-derstand if you are not comfortable giving me that much rope."

Strange, Grant thought, he had come to Lockwood short on trust when it came to relationships with wom-en, and after a few weeks' time, he was practically turn-ing his life over to a pair of females. "I trust you, and it would suit me fine to never set eyes on Percy Garth or the Beadles. I just want to write my books and deposit the drafts at the Gaines Bank."

"Well, I would prefer we both meet with Mister Garth for a short time, but if he has proposals that interest you, I can hammer out the details with the man. I am inter-ested in the rights you might have to use your pen names with other publishers besides Beadle or to contract with others. I know that you said that the contract Beadle sent recently was the same as the others, but it would be nice to compare to be certain. Do you have copies of your book contracts?"

"Uh, no. I might have once, but if I did, I lost them when I was getting rid of things before I left Ohio." He saw the disapproval in the lawyer's eyes, but she spared him a scolding.

"Well, before we sign any new contracts with Beadle, I will insist we see the old contracts just to verify that you have surrendered copyrights and privileges to use the pen names. If you did not, that would make a huge difference in our negotiations."

"I never gave a thought to any of these things."

"That's what you are paying me to do. By the way, Ham will have your first bill ready for you on the way out. No hurry about paying it." She paused and smiled. "As long as we have your draft within the next five days."

"Well, I can pay when I leave if it does not require more than I've got in the bank."

"Just teasing you. You might be surprised at the figure."

That could mean anything, he thought.

Chapter 39

GRANT DID PAY the lawyer's fees, and gladly since the ninety-dollar figure was at least a fourth of what he had feared. To his naïve mind it appeared the services were being performed with some efficiency.

Before going to the stable to locate Trouble Yates, he stopped at the office to confirm there were no new problems on the sheriff's desk. He found Bushwa dozing in Ozzie's chair with his feet propped upon the desk.

When Grant came in, Bushwa pushed his hat back and swung his legs off the desk. "Good morning, boss man. Figured you must have slept in this morning."

"I had a meeting with the prosecutor."

"Who's that?"

"Miss Locke."

"You don't say? Lucky devil. That woman's prettier than a little red heifer in a flower bed. Hard seeing her as the old maid that she is. I'd say starting the day with Hannah Locke beats a cup of coffee all to hell. Course that ain't saying much when it's Ozzie's coffee."

"Where is Ozzie?"

"He rode out to his ma's place. She's got a little farmstead a few miles northeast. Sets out in the south edge of Ethan and Skye Ramsey's Lazy R spread."

"I assumed he was a local boy, but I never asked about his family. I should have."

"You never asked about mine neither."

"Figured you didn't have any that would claim you. Besides, in the short time since we've met up, you haven't been exactly shy telling me anything you wanted me to know about."

"Don't get testy, sheriff. Anyhow, Ozzie's ma is a widow woman, buried three husbands so far and ain't fifty yet. Ozzie's pa was the first. Sioux killed and scalped Abner when Ozzie was a tyke. Second husband left her with a small ranch that Ramsey bought a dozen or so years back, carving out the farmstead so she could live there. Third husband was a fence jumper. She caught him in bed with another woman and splattered his brains against the bedroom wall with a shotgun. His female friend would've met the same end, but Maggie had to re-load, and the young woman got away. Left town on the first stage out."

"And they didn't send her off to prison?"

"Nah. Old Will Bridges was sheriff then and was more or less judge and jury, too. He declared the shooting self-defense. Nobody seemed to mind. Folks thought a lot of Will."

"Sounds like Ozzie isn't forced to look after her too much."

"No." He chuckled. "Hell, no. She ain't hard on the eyes neither and has always got a few bachelors or widowers courting, although I think a few is after her whiskey."

"What do you mean?"

"She's got her a still, too. Does a helluva trade. Cow-boys up and down the valley drop by Maggie's place for cheap spirits. I stop by now and then myself. I've given thought to courting her, but I hear she's kinda persnick-ety about her man friends bathing and such. Don't like beards. I know one feller that had the barber clear his whiskers off just to get the favor of that female. Didn't do no good. I think she expects to rule the roost. That just wouldn't work out for me, so I'll settle for her corn liquor and a look now and then."

Grant decided he would like to meet Ozzie's mother someday, but that was low priority on his list right now. He told Bushwa about his plans to survey the outlaw hideout. "I would have you lead me there, but I don't want you gone from here that long."

"Trouble's the man for that anyhow. I don't know the country that good off the trail. You want to get up on Coyote Ridge where the coyotes make their music at night. I could get you there from the main trail, but you'd better talk to Trouble about a back way."

"I guess I'd better see to tracking down Trouble. Be thinking about how we might convince Jones we can protect him if he comes with us tonight."

"Better get some more of your contingency money out. Trouble ain't gonna give up his time for nothing." Sheriff Tolliver was not going to be happy with the fate of his contingency fund when he returned.

Chapter 40

TROUBLE FOUND SAMMY at his mother's dress shop, where she was busy packing boxes with ladies' garments. She looked up when he entered the building. "What are you doing here?"

"That's a nice greeting. 'Good morning' would have been friendlier."

"I didn't mean it that way."

"I wanted to talk to you about some business."

"Do you ever talk about anything else?"

"You likely don't want to talk about Adam Smith and the economists."

"You are right about that. What's the business you want to talk about? I'm packing your mother's inventory. Jeb and Carissa Oaks have bought it all for half its worth, but we've got to clear it out, so we can set up sewing machines for the dress operation. Oaks has agreed to buy from us exclusively for a start. I'm going to Cheyenne next week to line up some shops there. With school out the end of this week, I've got a lot to get done."

"Well, I wanted to see if you could do some bookkeeping for me. Miss Locke says I need to find somebody to keep books on all my projects and especially the livery. I'm too busy to keep books, and I hate putting numbers down on paper anyhow. I do just fine working the numbers in my head."

"And you thought I could do it for you?"

"Well, I'd pay you, of course, if you wanted me to."

"Wanted you to? I wouldn't take that on for free, not when I've got my own business to run."

"Well, I've been thinking."

She rolled her eyes. "That's dangerous."

He blushed. "I ain't told you this before. During the years you've been gone, you've sure turned into a pretty thing."

Her eyes widened, "You have never, ever told me anything like that. Thank you, I guess."

"And we were best friends as kids all those years. I still think of you that way."

Sammy said, "I wasn't sure where we stood these days. To be honest, I had hoped it would be that way again. What's your sweetheart Jasmine going to say about this?"

"Ain't going to say anything. She ain't my sweetheart, never was. She just caught my eye now and then. And she's making eyes at another boy down at the school now." Her eyes narrowed and her lips pursed, and he knew instantly he had said the wrong thing.

"So I am your second choice? I am so honored."

"Now don't get riled, Sammy. I ain't good at this sort of thing."

"I'm not clear on what this 'sort of thing' is."

"I would like for us to get married."

She yelled, "What? Are you crazy? Is this a proposal?"

"Well sort of. If you want it to be."

"Well, I don't. And the answer is 'no', not now anyway. You are just a boy."

"I'm sixteen, same age as you. A lot of girls get married at your age."

"At sixteen, a female is a young woman. A male is still a boy. You won't be a man till you are at least eighteen, maybe older."

"Now if that doesn't beat all. I do a man's work, make more than most men's wages."

"There are other things that make a man."

"Well, if you're thinking babies, I can darn well do that, too."

"Stop. I didn't know you had such a filthy mind."

"I guess I'd better be going."

Sammy said, "Wait, Brady. I'm sorry, I've been sort of huffy with you. This just struck me so sudden. You are special to me, and I always hoped we could be more special to each other. Do you want to court me?"

"Court you? You mean like we might get married sometime?"

"Yes. But you can't ask me till we are both at least eighteen. And I would expect you to be a little romantic, like take me to a dance sometimes, maybe go for rides or walks together like we used to—get acquainted again."

"Well, I'd like that."

"It would be nice if you would kiss me sometimes, give me some flowers, that sort of thing."

"I would really like that—the kissing." He grinned.

"But understand right off. No boy or man is going to poke me until I've got a wedding band on my finger."

Two years was forever, he thought. "Uh, yeah, I understand, I guess."

"No guessing about it. So do you want to court me?"

"Yeah, I do."

She stepped over to him, reached up and pulled his head to her. She pressed her lips to his, and they lingered until he feared he would collapse. He was embarrassed with his arousal and was almost glad when she stepped back.

"Then you may court me," Sammy said. "And during that time, I will break you of saying 'ain't.'"

Two years. Two years. Ma always told him not to wish time to pass. Each minute is one less we have on this earth. He would willingly forfeit two years of minutes if he could get to that eighteenth birthday sooner.

Chapter 41

"THERE HE COMES," Enos said, nodding toward the west on Main Street. "He didn't take his critter, so I knowed he wouldn't be long."

Grant saw Trouble ambling down the boardwalk absent his usual hurried pace. He appeared to be studying the boards beneath his feet and he walked as if preoccupied about something.

When he reached the livery entrance, he looked up. "Howdy, Grant," he said, looking at him questioningly.

"Hi, Trouble. I need your help—today if possible."

"I'll help if I can. I've got stall cleaning to do this morning. I got two men working on fencing out at Callaway's spread and thought I'd go out and lend a hand, but nothing says I got to."

"I need you to give me a county tour. I'll explain later." He figured Enos did not need to know his agenda. "I'll drop by The Chowdown and get two lunches packed. Get your horse saddled and come by the office in an hour. I've got Blue hitched in front of the office, and he's getting impatient. Do you have a telescope?"

"Yep. Always keep my spyglass in the saddlebags."

When Trouble appeared at the Sheriff's office an hour later, the two mounted and rode toward Fox Creek, where Trouble said he had a favorite lunch spot. When they broke through the birch and aspen that lined the creek and came upon the stream, Grant instantly approved of the young man's selection. It was an idyllic spot with a grass carpet that lined the edge of the bank. The white-capped water rushing over the rocks dropped over a three-foot fall and hummed a constant background melody that Grant found soothing.

They staked out Blue and Tag along the bank where they could access grass and water and then found shade and settled in by the creek to eat. Both were silent for a spell as they enjoyed The Chowdown's standard lunch of roasted beef sandwiches, supplemented with Saratoga chips and ginger cookies. "I hope this is enough for you," Grant said.

"Anything is enough. I forget to eat a noon meal half the time. Sammy's always scolding me about it just like she used to before they went back to Iowa for almost three years."

"Sammy. She's the young woman who was at the hospital with your mother when Jim was being cared for. Seemed like a nice girl. Pretty, too."

"Yeah, that's true enough, but she's a bossy sort. A fellow's got to just plug his ears sometimes. I just don't understand the female sex, I guess. Do you got the ladies figured out?"

Grant laughed. "You are talking to a man who has been married twice and divorced both times. No. I'm still learning."

"How old were you when you got married the first time?"

"Twenty-five. Divorced at twenty-nine. Married again at thirty. That lasted six months. My fault with both. The first was eighteen when she married me. She was a good woman and deserved better than she got."

"And the second?"

"I think neither one of us deserved as bad as we got."

"Well, I'll let you be the first to know. I'm courting Sammy, but I can't ask her to marry me till I'm eighteen."

"That sounds very wise. You had both best be sure."

"Yeah, I guess. What you got in mind for me to do today?"

"I want to look over the site of three buildings some distance up the trail from Bushwa's cabin, but I've got to do it without being seen. Do you know the place?"

"Sure do. Been by there more times than I can count. Occupied by a bunch of unfriendly types lately. I bypass it when I go up that way, which ain't often."

"I want to get above that cluster of buildings and see if I can get an idea of what's going on there. Get some idea of the lay of the station in case we must move in on the place at some point. That's why I asked about your telescope."

"We can do that. It's a rough ride up a back trail. There's an overhang farther up that would give a decent look with the spyglass, but all you'd see otherwise are a bunch of scurrying ants."

Grant said, "Is this the place Bushwa called Coyote Ridge?"

"Yep. That's it." He hesitated. "County paying for my time? I'd say three dollars for an afternoon."

"Contingency fund." Grant scrambled to his feet. "You take the lead. I'll follow."

Trouble, astride his sorrel gelding, led Grant along a narrow trail that edged the foothills taking him farther west than he had ventured yet. As they moved at a slow trot, his eyes scanned the green valley and the distant mountains that framed it, wondering if there would ever be a time when he was not in awe of the majestic beauty that surrounded him in this place. He edged Blue up beside Trouble and remarked, "This country is like my idea of heaven. I can't imagine someone like yourself ever wanting to leave this valley."

"Well, not for long anyhow. But sometimes in the winter you think you're visiting hell when you got snow up to your ass and there's work to be done."

"I hadn't thought about winter."

"Oh, there ain't much prettier than these snow-covered mountains, but you'd better get through a long winter before rendering your judgment."

The slopes became increasingly cloaked with pine and aspen trees as they commenced a climb into the foothills. Trouble said, "This is why I want to get into the lumbering business. Almost half of my ma's little farm is trees, good lumbering stuff, too. Besides the pine, there's a fair number of cedars and more walnut than anyplace in the territory, I'll bet. Lots of oak, too. Next government auction, I got my eyes on some land that ain't nothing but trees. No chance of coal there, so it should go cheap, maybe for a little of nothing. If you got some money to invest, we should talk."

"I'll keep that in mind." He had a hunch that this young man's enterprises might be a good place to put some money if he got ahead of the other expenses that were growing faster than his income.

"When we put these foothills behind us in a bit, we've got a steep climb ahead. Most of it is through trees, but we'll have about two hundred feet out on the mountain's edge with what seems a bottomless drop. How are you on heights?"

"Not good." That was an understatement. He was terrified of high places and got shaky climbing a ten-foot ladder to get onto a rooftop. He found it difficult to write about high places and generally kept his novel heroes well-grounded.

"You got lots of company. I don't mind high up. I'll tell you when we get there, and you just close your eyes and give Blue his reins. He'll follow me and do just fine."

From that moment, Grant obsessed about the trail on the mountain's edge they would be traversing. Close his eyes and leave it to the horse? That notion gave him no comfort. For a time, he almost forgot his mission.

As the horses plodded up the narrow, snaking trail through the timber, it seemed to Grant that time moved like watching an hourglass. Then he noticed that the forest began to thin and be replaced by rock and that a huge precipice jutted out from the sheer stone walls that blocked their course.

"That's the north side of Coyote Ridge," Trouble said. "We ride along the wall a spell, and then come to the ledge-trail I was telling you about."

Grant looked off to the northeast, where the thinning of the trees now offered an ample view. He could see the mountain peaks on the other side of the valley and the winding North Laramie River, a tiny blue ribbon running between the ranch ranges and patches of farm ground, but just below was what appeared an abyss. And then he caught sight of the beginning of the trail above it, no more than four feet wide at this point. He felt as if he was embarking on a journey that would replace the nightmare that had retired since Moon entered his life.

Trouble must have sensed his apprehension. "The trail here will take us to the top of Coyote Ridge. I know another that won't bother you a bit we can leave on. Might be near dark when we get back."

Grant nodded. "I'm closing my eyes. It's up to you and Blue to get me over this thing. And I will not complain about getting back late."

"Don't worry about a thing. We'll do fine."

He closed his eyes and relaxed his hold on the reins, resisting the urge to yank tight. Blue moved ahead, and

Grant could feel every step, hear the horseshoes striking on hard stone when he figured they must have moved onto the ledge. Marshal Tyree would think his cowardice a disgrace. Maybe he would put the damned lawman in a similar place someday, expose a flaw for a change. That thought and the plotting of another novel distracted him for a few minutes but not long enough.

"We're about there," Trouble said, after what was likely five or ten minutes on the ledge but seemed like a day. "Let Blue stay the boss till I say otherwise."

Soon, he felt the gelding step up and lunge forward. He swore that his heart stopped for an instant, but then the horse's quieter pace told him that they had reached softer ground.

"Okay, sheriff, you can open your eyes now and let Blue know you are back in charge."

He opened his eyes and saw that they appeared to be on a grassy, flat-top ridge that ran for some distance along the base of another tier of mountains. He tossed a look over his shoulder to get a glimpse of the end of the cliffside trail they had just traveled. That was enough. "I've got to admit I'm more than embarrassed about my reaction to the trail."

"No need to be. With me it's snakes. I don't care how big or little, poisonous or not, if I catch sight of one, I'm on the run. Makes it worse that Sammy loves the dang things, knows all about every snake in the world. Picks up and plays with those that ain't got the poison in their fangs. She can handle a rattlesnake, too, given time. She had a conniption once when I shot one of the devils. Says they got their place in nature. Well, they can stay away from my part of nature."

Grant appreciated Trouble's understanding and restraint from ridicule, but he was not about to confess that he feared snakes as well. So would Marshal Tyree by the time Grant got done with him. "So, where do we find the overlook?"

Trouble dismounted. "Follow me."

Grant swung out of the saddle and fell in beside his young friend, leading his mount. In less than ten minutes, they reached a jumbled stack of boulders, which had apparently dropped during a landslide upslope. "We can stake out our horses in the meadow. There will be water for the critters before we're halfway down. You get up on top of those rocks with the spyglass and that will clear you from the overhang so you can see the building site without crowding the edge."

They staked the horses, and Trouble retrieved the telescope from his saddlebags and handed it to Grant. They clambered to the highest point on the rockpile, and then Trouble pointed eastward where a plume of smoke drifted into the sky before fanning out and disappearing. "Aim for the smoke, follow it down and you'll find what you're looking for."

Grant found a flat-topped boulder to perch on and let himself down. Trouble made a place for himself lower on the stack. He was comfortable with a telescope from his sniping days and pressed the instrument to his eye and focused until he captured a full view of the layout. A strange set-up. Three identical rectangular log buildings shaped like train boxcars, only three times the size, were placed to form a 'U'. It appeared that all had four small front windows and a small, uncovered porch. There were no rear windows in the one backed in his direction, and he assumed the others matched.

The buildings reminded him of Army housing he had seen at established forts. It would be interesting to know, he thought, what the original builders and occupants had in mind for the place, how they earned a living. He envisioned a commune of sorts, something like the original New Harmony in Indiana. Perhaps he could do a novel in such a setting.

His telescope picked up two men sitting on a bench in front of the building at the bottom of the 'U,' apparently just chatting. He shifted the focus away from the structures and found an expansive barn or stable with a corral on the far side that connected to a fence that led into a meadow that dropped over a slope. A half dozen steers, and several horses and three mules grazed in the visible part of the pasture. He assumed that there were more beyond his sight line and likely some horses stalled in the barn for prompt availability.

Along the near side of the barn were two big Conestoga wagons of the type that had carried settlers west. This verified stories of possible transport of captive Indian children via this route. It occurred to him that the existence of wagons here suggested that some such abductees might be housed in one of the buildings. As he understood Jones, this was a collecting place, and he supposed one or both wagons were put into service when a full load of human cargo was accumulated.

The wide barn door was pushed open, and six mounted men rode out, taking the trail that he surmised would pass Bushwa's cabin. He thought it possible that his deputy might encounter the riders if he had made the trip out to check on his home and pastured critters. Another man shut the barn door, so that tallied nine men he had seen counting the two on the bench.

He started to put the telescope down, when the door to the building with the bench opened and a man stepped out. He gave a quick hand wave to the men on the bench and headed for the stable. Soon, the door opened again, and a woman stepped out onto the porch. She appeared to be speaking to the two. The man nearest the door got up and followed the woman back into the house. Grant had met the woman before. Her name was Ginger. He wondered if Sugar was here, too.

Grant spoke to Trouble. "I've seen enough. Do you want to grab a view?"

"As long as I'm here, I might do that." Trouble scrambled up the boulder stack and took the telescope while Grant made his way down. When Grant stepped onto level earth again, he walked out to the grass to retrieve the horses.

He started to pull Blue's stake from the ground when Trouble called, "I suppose you saw those Indian girls when you were looking down there?"

Grant wheeled and hurried back to the rockpile. "What Indian girls?"

"Three girls. They came out the door of the near cabin and went around back to one of the privies. Looks like the girls are taking turns. There's a man with them toting a rifle. Appears to be a little guy."

Grant worked his way back up the jumbled boulders and took the telescope and pressed it to his eye. After a moment's focusing, he said, "Yeah, they're girls alright. I see two, but I suppose the third is in the privy. I'd guess these two would be twelve or thirteen, but I'm no good at guessing ages. What do you think?"

"That's about right. The other would be a few years older, I think."

"And there could be more," Grant said, thinking out loud.

"Seems likely. I don't know what this is all about, but you look like it's weighing heavy on you."

"That's a real understatement. Maybe I haven't been pushing things fast enough. Now that I know about this, I can't just scrape it off my plate. I've got to deal with it, and soon."

Chapter 42

WHEN HE AND Trouble returned to town a good hour before sundown, Grant stopped at the sheriff's office to confirm that both his deputies were still available for night duty. Bushwa had not returned from the visit to his cabin yet, but Ozzie was at his desk with a checkerboard and checkers laid out on the desktop.

"Who's winning?" Grant asked.

"Me. I'm red. Of course, I'm black, too. Tried to draw Bushwa into a game, and he wanted nothing to do with it. Sometimes he can be a grumpy old cuss."

"So, are both of you planning to be here with the prisoner tonight?"

"Yep. Bushwa was going to bring his bedroll from home. Thinks our jail beds are too hard, wants some more padding."

"I'll be staying over, too. I thought I'd put Bushwa in back, and you and I would do shifts at the front. That back door at the end of the hall must be five or six inches thick, and with two steel bars locking it nobody's coming through without a lot of noise. We'll put our prisoner in the windowless, back cell, and Bushwa can lodge in the next."

Ozzie said, "Miss Locke stopped by. She said to tell you that she's got three men and two females that will spell us at the jail over this next week. She didn't have to tell anybody why. They just stepped up."

"Females. You're not serious?"

"Miss Locke herself and Jeb Oaks's wife, She-Bear— some call her 'Carissa.' Old She-Bear is a warrior legend around these parts and ain't nobody better with a Winchester than Hannah Locke. She helped defend the jail from a lynch mob once. Of course, Jeb's an old buffalo soldier, and you can count on him. Banker Gaines is ready to step up, and Con Callaway's son, Bobby, and a few volunteer hands from the Double C will help. Miss Locke is going to talk to Skye Ramsey at the Lazy R, and she's sure to offer a few men. Miss Locke's making a list of every man we can call on and where to find them. We just need to get our man over here and hold him through the night."

Grant shook his head in disbelief. "With all this help, I don't know how I ended up as sheriff."

"Because you seem to have a knack for taking charge and deciding what needs to be done. Most folks look for somebody to follow. Oh, I forgot to mention. Miss Locke left something for you. It's hanging on the coat hook next to your desk."

He stepped over and slipped the pistol from the holster hanging from the gun belt there. "An old Army Colt revolver. It's been around a spell but appears to be well cared for."

"It's a gift and Miss Locke told me she would be offended if you didn't wear it. She said you would know how to use it. She picked it up at Oaks General Store with that box of cartridges on the desk. Said a sheriff shouldn't be seen carrying a puny Derringer around."

He had not fired one since the war, but he strapped on the belt and holster and tested the feel of the gun in his hand and found he was surprisingly comfortable with the weapon on his hip. How well he could handle it was another question. Like swimming maybe: you never forgot how. Regardless, Grant hoped he would not be forced to fire it. He much preferred a rifle.

Grant had been planning to return to The Tipi for a quick supper when the door opened and Bushwa appeared. "Howdy, boys," he said. "Ain't talking about me, I hope."

"Not this time," Grant said. "Ozzie's just telling me about the folks that have volunteered to help with guarding the jail while Jones is under our protection, but I'm afraid it's getting more complicated."

"What do you mean?" Bushwa asked.

Grant told him about the girls he and Trouble had seen at Rayburn Cox's property above Bushwa's place. "We also caught a glimpse of Ginger. My best guess is that she's engaged in her usual business. Whether she is there of her own accord or not, I can't say. I would sure like to know if Sugar's there."

Bushwa said, "What about the Injun girls you seen?"

"We've got to get them out soon, I am thinking. At least while they are in Big River County, we've got some claim to jurisdiction. We can't wait for the federal people to get involved. It might be weeks, if ever."

Bushwa said, "Well, the three of us ain't enough guns to do it."

"We would have to see if some of the folks on the volunteer list are willing to help out."

"You mentioned the six gunslingers that rode out while you were watching."

"I didn't say they were gunslingers."

"They are. They rode by my place while I was out there. I seen the devils go by from the stable door. Don't think they seen me. One was Ryker, so it's a good bet Winston Colbert sent him to fetch the others. Don't like this a damn bit where we're hoping to make off with a witness tonight."

Grant said, "We can't be certain Jones will show, and I cannot imagine his mentioning his plans to anyone else. I suppose there is a chance someone saw him enter the stable and talk with us. I'm tempted to march into The Doll House, arrest him and take him into custody, but if he has changed his mind that won't help us get his cooperation."

"Them hired guns could be up to anything. Most likely, Colbert has another job for them. Maybe they're talking about moving them Injun kids out," Bushwa said.

"That's a possibility. We'll stick with our plan for now. I'm going back to The Tipi for a quick supper. The two of you can eat in shifts if you like. Tell The Chowdown to put it on the sheriff's bill. The contingency fund can pay since I've got you working late tonight."

Bushwa said, "Late? Hell, you got us set to work all night, and we don't get a nickel's more pay."

"Maybe I can get you bonus pay from the county board when this case is closed down."

"I ain't counting on it. That Con Callaway treats the county coffers like it's his own blood he's giving up."

That might not always be bad, Grant thought, but he was not in the mood for an argument.

Chapter 43

THE GRAY BLANKET of dusk was settling on the river valley as Grant rode Blue at a walk to The Tipi. He would arrive at the tail end of the last supper shift. Perhaps there would be a few minutes for some private moments with Moon if the others had eaten. He had not spoken with her since the embarrassing encounters after oversleeping this morning. He carried his share of guilt for any discomfort she might have suffered over the episode.

As he rode down Main Street toward the road that would take him beyond the town proper to The Tipi, he heard footsteps on the boardwalk off to his right and tossed a look over his shoulder. A man backed up next to a building, leaned against it, dug some fixings from his pocket and commenced rolling a cigarette. With the fading light, Grant could not make out his face, but he was a tall man wearing a white hat with a flat crown and unusually wide brim. The only other hat like that he had seen was on one of the riders who left the Cox place. He looked back again just before he reached the road and saw that the man's face was aimed in his direction as he drew on his cigarette. Grant was almost certain he was being followed, and he found the idea unnerving, another new experience that he was not prepared for.

He considered going back and confronting the man, but to what purpose? The stalker would deny he was following him. It might be best to let the man think he had been undetected. What bothered him most was that the follower was likely going to identify his place of residence. On the other hand, he assumed that would not be a difficult task if anyone asked a few casual questions about Lockwood. There would be no such thing as an anonymous abode in this town.

He put up Blue in the stable, deciding he would walk back to the livery and enter from the rear in order to escape notice by any of The Doll House people. Also, if the man who appeared to be following him waited outside The Tipi, it would be easier to elude him afoot.

When he entered the boarding house and walked into the dining room, he saw that Moon sat alone at the kitchen table nursing a cup of coffee. He walked into the kitchen, "Too late for some supper?" he asked.

Moon looked up, and he recognized instantly that something was wrong. Her eyes were glazed with tears and the flesh about them were swollen. She had obviously been crying. She got up from table. "I've been saving some supper for you. I know you have sheriff's business tonight, but I was hoping you would stop by. Everyone else has eaten and gone up to their rooms. A few are probably sleeping already, and Milton Lockhart is no doubt reading. He didn't say a word when I served his food; just sat there with a smirk on his face."

"I'm sorry, but that's not what you're distressed about."

She retrieved a bowl and plate from the cupboard, went to the woodstove and began dishing stew from a big kettle there. "Stew and biscuits and cherry pie. Sit down at the kitchen table. It's cozier here."

He sat down. "Are you going to tell me what the problem is?"

She placed the plates of food on the table and poured him a mug of coffee before taking the chair across from his. "Jasmine didn't come home after school."

"You must be worried sick."

"Yes. I don't know what to do."

"Has she done this before?"

"Yes, rarely. It's always after we've had a fuss. She's mature in so many ways, taking on all the responsibility she does here. Yet the child in her erupts sometimes." She nodded at his plate, "Eat before it gets cold."

His appetite had disappeared, but he started picking at his food to pacify her. "When this happens, is she usually gone overnight?"

"Sometimes she has ended up at her friend Ann Pickett's house. I would check but it's located on a small ranch about five miles out. She would have to ride double on Ann's horse to go there, so I don't think it is likely she is at the Pickett place. And it would not be unusual for her to show up after midnight. I just have a bad feeling about this. And, of course, Abby Doe Eyes's murder sends my imagination on a rampage."

"Understandably. But you know that there is no reason to expect anything like that. Was she angry with you this morning—about us?"

"I don't know. It was apparent that it was no surprise. She had at least suspected. My late appearance for breakfast obviously was confirmation. She was cool, but there was no tantrum or outburst. I told her we would talk about it. She said she did not wish to discuss it. The school coach—it is an old stagecoach—came by and she left."

"Does the coach usually bring her home?"

"Sometimes. But the coach does not wait. She will walk sometimes. She doesn't mind walking a few miles, especially in the spring."

"We should check with the driver."

"Yes, if she doesn't turn up tonight. But the after-school driver could have been anyone from the school. I would need to speak with the headmaster at the Pennock School to find out who drove the coach tonight—likely a teacher from the school."

He reached across the table and took her hand. "I feel responsible for this."

Her dark eyes met his, and he saw fire in hers. "That is ridiculous. I chose to come to your bed. If I had not done so, we would probably still be sitting here chatting about the weather. I am not sorry about what we shared, not a minute of it. I would never have missed it."

It startled him that she was speaking past tense. This was not the time to raise that question. "I have a job to do tonight, and it may require me to stay overnight at the sheriff's office. Regardless, as soon as I can get away, I will come by and find out if Jasmine has come home. If not, I will organize a search first thing in the morning starting with a visit to the Pickett ranch. But there is something else I must warn you about."

Her eyes narrowed. "What?"

"I think I was followed here tonight. I'm quite certain the man is keeping track of my whereabouts, and when I leave, he will try to stick with me. But please, do not go outside. Do you have a gun?"

"A Derringer and a double-barrel shotgun."

"And you can use them?"

"Damn right."

"Keep them loaded and handy. If somebody seems to be trying to break in, run upstairs and wake that young man, the one who works for the butcher."

"Paul."

"I noticed he carries a hog-leg at his side."

"I think he uses it at the slaughterhouse for cattle, but he at least knows how to shoot it. And I have a hunch that 'hog leg' is another westernism you are collecting for a novel."

Grant rolled his eyes. "Bushwa's term for a sidearm. He is a dictionary of the unique western language. Anyway, just promise me you will wake him if you sense trouble."

She sighed. "I will, but it sounds like you are the one who should be careful."

He stood up to leave. "I will be, and I will get back here as soon as possible. We will find Jasmine, and she will be fine. I promise."

"Don't make a promise like that. You cannot control outcomes, contribute maybe, but this is not like writing a novel where you get to play God." She rose from her chair and went to him, and he took her into his arms, and he held her close while they shared a lingering kiss.

Moon said, "I swore I would never let this happen with another man, but I loved you, Grant Coolidge, P.J. Bowie, Jake West or whatever your name is at the moment."

"And I love you, Moon Dupree." Again, she had spoken in the past tense.

Chapter 44

GRANT STEPPED OUT of The Tipi's front door and onto the porch, making no effort to conceal himself. He decided he wanted to be seen by the man who had been following him if he was still out there, thinking that he might draw the stalker away from the boarding house before he attempted to lose him.

He walked slowly, following the road that would take him to the intersection with the street that dead ended near the rear of the large livery tract. He was learning that western boots did not adapt well to long walking distances or that his needed a lot more breaking in. He looked over his shoulder intermittently as he moved as he maintained a leisurely pace but saw no sign of a follower. When he reached the intersection, he cast his eyes about carefully before he turned toward the livery.

Ron Schwab

He had little confidence in his own detection skills but saw nothing suspicious behind him, so he headed the five or six blocks toward his destination. When he arrived at the livery, he saw Enos and Trouble talking at the front entrance when he slipped into the stable's rear doorway. He did not expect Bushwa's appearance until later. He checked his timepiece. Ten minutes past nine o'clock. He anticipated his deputy's arrival in another hour or so.

As he approached Enos and the new livery owner, he said, "Good evening, gentlemen." Both started and turned to face him, evidently not hearing his footsteps behind them. Enos said, "Good way to get shot, Sheriff, sneaking up on an old man like that."

"Sorry, Enos. I figured you heard me coming down the alleyway."

"Hearing ain't so good these days."

"Yeah, unless a man said something he did not want heard," Trouble said.

"I didn't expect to run into you again," Grant said.

"Guess I didn't tell you I'm living here now. In the hayloft."

"I see."

"I got kicked out of the place where I was living. Sammy's mother owns the house, and she and her two boys are coming in on the train tomorrow. They will be taking over the house along with Sammy. The gal I'm courting wanted me out, so she could do some cleaning before her ma settled in. Said I keep house like a pig. Won't deny it, but I wasn't there that much. Washed the sheets once a month if I thought of it and swept it out a time or two. Not like I brought any livestock into the house—except for an orphaned newborn calf for a week or so."

"Well, it doesn't appear your new lodging will require much housekeeping. Did Enos tell you we got some business going on here along about midnight?"

"Yep. He explained that Bushwa would cover the loft opening toward the street. I've got my Winchester up there. Thought I'd bring it down and watch the rear just in case somebody is on to Jones coming here."

The idea made sense to Grant. "That's a good idea. I'd appreciate it if you would do that. I had somebody following me earlier this evening. I'm sure he was one of the men I saw leave the compound up in the mountains this afternoon."

"That can't be good," Trouble said.

"Not likely."

While they waited for Bushwa, Enos settled on his outside bench, and Trouble took up his post at the far end of the long stable. Grant went back to join him for a spell.

"Trouble, I wanted to speak with you privately for a few minutes."

"Nobody near but us and the horses. I'm guessing you wanted to be out of Enos's hearing range."

"Yeah. What I've got to talk about may amount to nothing, and I'd rather not start a lot of talk if it comes to nothing."

"I understand that."

"Jasmine Dupree had not come home from school by the time I left the boarding house. If she's not there when I get back, I'm going to take up a search. You show up at school occasionally you told me, and your young lady friend, Samantha, I gather is more consistent with her attendance. Is there anything about Jasmine I should know?"

"Well, I was sweet on Jazzie for a spell, and I like her lots, but she flirts with a lot of boys, and they flock after her like male dogs chasing a bitch in heat, if you know what I mean."

"I do."

"Anyhow, when Sammy came back to Lockwood, it took about three days for me to see that her and me were meant to be. But Sammy's been keeping kind of a watch on Jazzie. I think part of it's because she knew I had eyes for her for a spell. Of course, I still like to look at Jazzie, but I know better than to mention it to Sammy. If I did, there would be hell to pay."

Trouble's story was taking too much time, and Grant sensed it was leading to something significant. "You hinted that Sammy might have seen something involving Jasmine."

"Oh, yeah. She said some feller on horseback has been waiting for Jazzie after school. He's half-hidden in the pines on the north side windbreak, but for the past week or so, she heads right for that rider, and he pulls her up behind him and off they go."

"She must get home in time to help fix supper, or at least Moon hasn't complained. Has Samantha mentioned anything about the rider's age?"

"She said he's too far away to tell. Not an old man, though. Sits tall and straight in the saddle."

"Did she mention the horse's color or anything like that?"

"Yeah. A buckskin. From its size, she thought the critter was a gelding or stallion."

That helped some. Grant could not recall seeing more than two or three buckskins since his arrival. One had belonged to the county board chairman, and he was many winters from young. He remembered seeing one in the livery stable a week back. "I saw a buckskin gelding in a stall here a week or so ago."

"That would have been Miss Locke's horse. She's partial to buckskins. That one is out of her buckskin mare and stallion. She's hoping the stallion will turn out some more for her. She generally runs ten to twelve mixed mares in her herd."

"Well, I hope Jasmine shows up at The Tipi, so the rider becomes irrelevant. She wouldn't be the first gal who was seeing somebody her mother was clueless about." And he would see that mother was informed.

Trouble said, "I just hope she's all right. She's one of the smartest kids at the school, works hard at the boarding house. I keep thinking of Abby Doe Eyes, and now I'm worried."

"I'm sure she's fine," Grant said, not believing a word of his statement.

When Bushwa made his appearance through the rear doorway, Grant said, "No sign of anybody out there?"

"No. You expecting somebody?"

Grant told him about the man following him earlier and the missing Jasmine. "There is something going on here. I'm concerned that Colbert is a step ahead of us. It's possible that he suspects Jones of trying to make a break. Maybe somebody saw him come in here last night, or he said something to the wrong person. People have a way of finding out things in this town that mystifies me."

Bushwa said, "You're making too much of it, Grant. What travels fast is news. This ain't news. Ain't the sort of thing folks learn about."

"I hope you're right, but we had better be ready for anything. I'm glad we've got Trouble here to cover the back of the stable."

"You might like to know we've got more help if we need it."

"What do you mean?"

"Hannah Locke and Jeb Oaks and She-Bear are just up the street at the general store, armed and ready for gunplay. They hear a shot and they're out the door and headed this way."

"Well, let's get in place and be ready just in case Jones shows up early."

Chapter 45

"Something strange going on out there, Sheriff," Bushwa called from the loft.

"Like what?"

"I didn't give it no mind before, but there's a high-sided buckboard sitting kitty-cornered across the street. I just saw a man's head pop up for a second. I don't think he's just taking a nap in the wagon, and there could be more."

"Well, Jones could be coming anytime. Just keep your eyes on the wagon."

"He's coming now, staggering more than walking, though."

Enos Fletcher stuck with the bench, but he had to be nervous, exposed as he was. From just inside the open entryway, Grant said, "Enos, get up and walk in here, easy-like."

Enos hobbled in and picked up the shotgun he had left leaning against the wall next to the door. "I thank you kindly for that, Sheriff. Wanted to do my job, but I got the prickles on the back of my neck something fierce."

Grant's first glimpse of Jones was when the bartender reached the corner across the street. The man was, indeed, wobbly on his feet as Bushwa had suggested. He was not going to make it to the livery without help. Grant set his rifle down and started racing across the street to assist the man. He heard a rifle crack from behind him, glanced at the buckboard and saw a man topple out. A second gunman fired at Jones, and the bartender straightened and kept on moving toward Grant. It seemed to be raining gunfire now, reminding him of the war.

He got to Jones just as the man took another slug, apparently low because he could barely stand now. Grant wrapped his arm about the man's back, and half lifting and part dragging, started moving him toward the livery. They made the middle of the street when he saw the horses and their riders charging down Main Street toward him, no more than half a block distant. At that instant, Jones collapsed, and Grant was unable to hold him up. He knelt beside the man and drew his gifted Colt to face the oncoming riders, who were firing at him now.

Again, he was at Gettysburg, the air resounding with the cracks and explosions of gunfire and acrid with smoke. He expected to die, but his mind was numb to it. There must be six to eight men, and they would ride him over soon. He fired the Colt, and to his amazement, two riders dropped and then another, and another. A man astride a buckskin broke through the melee and headed for the accidental sheriff and his fallen witness, his pistol spitting lead. Grant felt a slug tear through his hat, as he squeezed the trigger of his own weapon and saw the gunman vault from his saddle. His rider no longer in charge, the buckskin veered away.

Suddenly, an eerie silence settled over the street. He bent over Jones who lay crumpled at his knees. He saw the labored rise and fall of his chest, but the moonlight was not enough to give him a decent view. "Orville, Orville, can you hear me?"

A raspy voice croaked, "Yeah, I hear you."

"Where are you hit?"

"Right hip. Back. Hurts like hell."

Bushwa stood above him now. "You okay, Grant?"

"Yeah, but we need to get Jones here to Doc Weintraub. Would you see if Enos can get a critter or two hitched to the wagon?"

"That wagon's going to be making a lot of trips before the night's out, and Doc can forget about sleeping, and we're going to need an army of deputies for guard duty. Undertaker is going to have a good night, I would guess."

Bushwa had just disappeared into the livery, when Grant saw Hannah Locke step off the boardwalk and walk his way. Booted, wearing a wide-brimmed hat and attired in snug denim britches and a buckskin pullover shirt, she had a Winchester cradled in her right arm. When she reached him, he said, "So I wasn't taking two or three men down with a single shot. I thought that Colt you left me had special powers. Anyhow, it saved my life. Thank you."

"I did not want to lose a new client, and I can't say you did not take down an extra man or two, but Jeb and She-Bear and I were cranking out lead as fast as we could. It wasn't quite fair. The riders didn't know we were hidden in the walkways between a few of the buildings along the way. We saw them collecting at the intersection near the general store and headed out the backway and set up to greet them if they moved toward the livery. Jeb and She-Bear are checking now to see how many are still alive. They're lucky. Not all that many years back, the lady would have taken scalps."

"You took them all down?"

"Six went down during the gunfire. Two got away to tell the story to their boss."

"I can't prove it yet, but I'm guessing that would be Winston Colbert. Could you stay with Mister Jones for a bit? There's not much more we can do for him here but be with him. He fades in and out. I want to take a look at the guy over where that buckskin's hanging out. If he's alive, he may know something of Jasmine's whereabouts."

"Jasmine's missing?"

"She did not come home when school let out."

"Oh, my God. Moon must be frantic."

"Well, she was worried, that's for sure. But she was staying calm when I spoke with her. I told her three hours or so ago that I would get back as soon as I could to start a search if Jasmine had not come home by then."

"I will be going with you."

"We are going to need guards for the hospital."

"Jeb knows the names of the volunteers. He will help your deputies get a schedule worked out and contact the men."

Hannah knelt beside the wounded bartender and Grant got up to look at the man who had almost run him over with the horse. He lay in the dirt just in front of the boardwalk on the streetside opposite the livery. The body was motionless, and he quickly confirmed the man's death. He would not have been more than twenty years old, a blond handsome young man who would no doubt have attracted a teenage girl's attention.

It sickened Grant to think he had taken the life of one so young, even though the rider had obviously been set on killing him. He was likely just a boy, possibly orphaned and alone, who fell in with the wrong crowd. Of course, he could have been something else, too, such as a cold-blooded killer who murdered without remorse. Regardless, it seemed likely he was the one who had been meeting Jasmine after school, and that did not bode well for the girl. The horse nickered and caught his attention. He reached out and clutched the reins before stroking the critter's nose and muzzle.

He eyed the animal's underbelly, and confirmed he was a stallion, tall and thickly muscled, an exceptionally quality horse for a mere boy. Of course, there was the possibility the buckskin had been stolen. He led the horse back to Hannah and saw that Bushwa and Trouble were easing Jones into the wagon.

When Bushwa saw Grant walk up, he said, "Two others up the street we're going to pick up. Enos will drive the wagon, and me and Trouble will walk along and help load. You coming?"

"I'll be along a bit later. Get Ozzie to go over and help guard the hospital. I don't expect an attack now, but it's best to be ready."

He turned back to Hannah and saw that that she was entranced by the buckskin, running her fingers over the stallion's back and down his withers and shoulders.

She looked at Grant. "He's a powerful beast and gentle as a kitten. What is going to become of him?"

"I have no idea. I guess I will need to check with my bosses."

"I think such animals are generally sold by the sheriff and the proceeds added to the contingency fund. I want this one. My fillies up for breeding next are daughters of my current stallion, so I can't use him. This guy would be perfect."

"Hannah, I can't make promises. We have other business right now. I see at least three other horses roaming the streets that I hope Enos and Trouble will corral when they have a chance."

"Sorry. I do get caught up with my horses."

Suddenly, a bell started clanging from the west.

"Fire," Hannah said. "They are calling the volunteers. I smell smoke drifting in from the west. We take that seriously with the forests covering the mountains and much of the foothills. Fortunately, we've had a wet winter and spring. I think this is a town fire."

They looked at each other and mouthed the words together. "Moon."

Chapter 46

GRANT SWUNG INTO the saddle of the buckskin stallion and reached down and grasped Hannah's hand while she scrambled up behind him. "My horse is hitched in front of the office," she said.

He kneed the horse forward, and they raced down Main Street, leaving it to the deputies and the Oaks couple to clean up the remaining human carnage. When Grant reined in at the Ramsey and Locke office, Hannah slipped off the buckskin, retrieved her own mount and soon fell in beside him. The smoke burned his eyes now, and he saw the flames shooting skyward, illuminating the dark sky behind the downtown commercial buildings that blocked his view, confirming, however, that the fire was engulfing The Tipi.

"Moon would have been up waiting for Jasmine or me," Grant called to Hannah. "She would have escaped."

"I pray you are right."

When they turned onto the road that led to The Tipi, they encountered the inferno with a melee of men and a few women fighting a hopeless battle. A single pump wagon with two men on the pump and three manning the big hose was sending sheets of water onto the burning, exterior house walls. A bucket brigade had formed at the outdoor pump in a futile effort to extinguish the blaze at the base although the empty doorway seemed clear now.

They dismounted and hitched the horses to tree branches on the opposite side of the road. Grant saw Milton Lockhart, still in his nightshirt and his face pallid, sitting trance-like at the base of an oak tree. He rushed Lockhart. "Milton, where's Moon?"

"She saved my life. She risked her own, to wake me and the others. I would have died. Oh, dear God. This is hell."

"Milton, where is Moon?"

He stood, tears streaming down his cheeks. "She didn't come out. She went into your room; she said she was getting your manuscript satchel. She screamed at the rest of us to get out."

Grant wheeled and raced for the boarding house. Hannah yelled after him. "No, Grant. Don't be a fool. Grant. Don't."

He passed Matt Gaines on his way to the charred hole that had been the door. Matt appeared to be commanding the battle against the fire, and he ordered Grant to stop. Others screamed at him as he leaped onto the porch. One of the half-burned boards collapsed beneath him, and his leg dropped through the flooring. He nearly went down before he pulled his leg free and charged into the house.

In the parlor it appeared the water had partially doused most of the flames. His enemy was mostly the blinding, suffocating smoke. He made his way to the staircase which seemed intact, and he started the climb. The flames were worse as he moved higher. When he reached the upstairs hallway, he saw that part of the roof had caved and the starlit sky was visible, ordinarily a scene to savor. Flames danced about him, and he felt the sting of fire against his ear. Then he saw her on the floor in the hallway outside his room. Her escape must have been blocked by timbers when part of the roof and ceiling caved. Several charred timbers were crisscrossed over her form.

He kicked the smoldering boards out of his way, and nearly burned out, they crumbled, allowing him to pass through. When he reached her he pushed the boards off her with his foot. He knelt beside her. Most of her clothes had burned off or been left imbedded in blistered, swollen flesh. But she breathed. There was no time. Smoke and flames were engulfing the floor, rising as the fire finished its first-floor work. He found himself choking and coughing now.

Grant lifted Moon from the floor and commenced his retreat down the hallway. Flames were eating at the stairway now, and he feared their combined weight might send them crashing through the steps, but there was no other option. The floor held but when he reached the landing, he felt his lungs were exploding, and his head was spinning. He could not see the doorway, but his instincts sent him stumbling where he thought it should be. "Moon," he said. "Hang on. We're almost there."

His knees buckled. He felt Moon's weight escape his arms. He went to his knees, but something clasped his arms and lifted him back up. "Moon, Moon, where are you?"

Matt Gaines' voice: "I've got her, Grant. We're almost to the doorway. Let Gabe and Johnny help you."

He could not resist if he wished.

He would never forget the exhilaration of fresh mountain air hitting his lungs even as he felt he was coughing his guts out. He was aware that he was sitting on a blanket on the roadside. His first thought was Moon. "Moon," he called.

"She's beside you on the blanket, Grant. She asked for you." It was Hannah, her voice soft but cracking.

He turned and saw Hannah sitting beside Moon. He looked down at his friend and lover. The fire's flames provided enough light that he could see the horror of the once beautiful face, but all he cared about was that she lived. He would marry her, and they would still share a life together. "Is she...?"

"She is alive, Grant. She wants to speak with you. Put your face near hers, so you can hear."

He did, seeing then that her eyelids had been burned away and her eyes shriveled to nothingness. "Oh, Moon."

"Find Jasmine," she said, her voice no more than a whisper.

"I will. I promise."

"It was Colbert's man. Ryker. Saw him at the parlor window before the torch came through the glass. Tried to get the fire out. Got away from me. So went to wake the boarders." Her voice faded with each word. "Loved you, Grant. Made me happier than ever been. Afraid vulture came for you."

Vulture? "I love you, Moon. Always will. Now we've just got to get you better."

Silence.

"She's gone, Grant," Hannah said.

He bent over and softly kissed Moon's cracked and swollen lips. "I know."

They both stood, and Hannah began sobbing uncontrollably. He stepped over and took her in his arms, finally surrendering to his own grief and crying with her.

When they separated, a stocky man with a fireman's helmet came up and said, "Matt thought this might be yours, Sheriff." He handed Grant the canvas satchel that contained his manuscripts. "Found it on the ground outside."

"Yes. This is mine. Thank you." He turned to Hannah. "She must have tossed it out the window. They're just words on paper. I can always write more. She probably lost her life over this. For that matter, she would be alive if she had never met me."

"Grant. Don't do this to yourself."

Chapter 47

THE STABLE AT the destroyed boarding house had been left undamaged by the fire, and Hannah said that she would be certain the old drover who had looked after the horses when needed would do so until the boarders had opportunities to make new lodging arrangements. Since he had no belongings to move, Grant figured he would bunk at the jail until he found another place to live. For the first time since his arrival in Lockwood, he was having doubts about staying, fearing that the reminders of Moon Dupree would be too painful.

Moon would be buried on Hannah Locke's ranch according to Hannah, who would be executrix of Moon's will and Jasmine's legal guardian, assuming the girl was recovered alive. He did not like the thought of leaving Moon behind here. He was certain this valley would be where her spirit would always reside. He did not truly want to part with whatever of her remained. There would be time for decisions about his future. For now, his focus must be Jasmine. He had promised to find her, but he was increasingly concerned that the girl would not be alive.

He slept a few hours on one of the cell bunks, but his mind had been unable to shut down as he struggled to regroup and plot his next moves and shake the grief that threatened to overwhelm him. Sunrise was teasing with a few slivers of light from the east end of the valley when Grant began heating a pot of coffee on the woodstove. At The Tipi he would have enjoyed a hearty breakfast, but he had no appetite for anything this morning. Mostly, he was numb and felt like he was walking around in a drunken stupor.

Bushwa had shown up a few hours earlier and collapsed on a bunk in the adjacent cell, but Grant heard him stirring in back already, probably headed for the privy at the rear of the lot. Ozzie had stayed on to supervise the volunteer guards at the hospital, mostly cowhands from the nearby ranches that had been recruited by Hannah.

He was sitting at his desk, a mug of steaming coffee in his hands when the back door slammed, and he heard Bushwa's footsteps in the hallway. When his deputy appeared, Grant nodded a greeting and pointed to the coffee pot on the stove. Bushwa filled his mug and sat down at Ozzie's desk.

"Sorry about your lady friend," Bushwa said. "None better than Moon."

Bushwa's comment removed any doubt that word had spread that Moon was more than just a landlady to him. That was fine. He was proud that she thought him worthy of her love. "That's true enough. But now we've got to find her daughter."

"I ain't tossing in my cards yet. Tell me what you want."

"I'd like you riding with me if you can be spared from guard duty."

"One of the gunslingers died before I left. Another's on his way to hell. That leaves one we took down on the street and Jones."

"And how is he doing? I didn't get back to talk with Doc."

"Doc says he will make it but can't be moved for a week. We'll have to provide his protection at the hospital. Ozzie's got a schedule made out—says we've got the next two days covered. He's working on the next. You know, I'm thinking that old Ozzie's got what it takes to do the sheriff's job someday, maybe five years or so."

Grant said, "That won't be my worry. Jim Tolliver better get back to work soon. I've got to find Jasmine and shut down whatever Colbert's involved in at The Doll House at that prison above your place. After that, I'm leaving my badge on the desk. Unless you want it, Ozzie can pin it on till the sheriff gets back."

"Me? Hell, no. Not a chance. I'll stick around with you for now, but I'm about finished with my lawman career. No money. No glory. Nothing but a target on your back. Never seen a shootout like the one we was in last night, let alone been a party to it. Ain't looking for more of that."

"If you're staying on, it's likely not over. I'm visiting The Doll House in a few hours. After that, I'm heading up to that mountain compound."

Bushwa said, "Need more than us. Let me talk to Jeb Oaks and a few others and round up some backing before we make a visit."

"You do that. I would like some men who can give us a day. The Doll House is the first stop, and then we head for the compound. I don't know how many men they have there yet. We thinned out the bunch last night. I'll talk to the mayor and bring him up to date. I don't know if he will be at the bank yet. He was fighting the fire last night. Maybe he can help find guards for the hospital if we need them after the next few days."

"Don't worry about Matt Gaines. He ain't going to leave you holding an empty sack."

"I had already figured that, but I don't care what help I've got, I intend to find Jasmine Dupree."

Chapter 48

HANNAH HAD NOT had an opportunity to bathe and change clothes since the gunfight and fire, snatching only a few hours early morning sleep at her office desk before leaving Ham Fish a note to cancel her appointments unless the clients had problems he could help them with. She was confident Ham could handle an initial meeting with most on his own.

She had retrieved her mare at the livery, ridden the fifteen minutes to her ranch, completed chores that could not be delayed and returned to town. She stopped at Ty Brown's cabin on the edge of town and spoke to the old wrangler about looking after The Tipi stable. She also asked him to handle chores twice a day at her place until she told him otherwise. She sought his help often, and he knew the routine and liked the extra money.

A quick stop to check with Dayton Roberts, the post-master-telegrapher, turned up important messages. The first was transmitted in a letter from her Santa Fe friend, lawyer Jael Rivers. There were telegrams from Beadle's Dime Novels and Percival Garth. As sheriff, Grant must be informed immediately about the Rivers letter. She hated to burden him with the telegrams, but as her client he was entitled to know what had been added to his menu. She paid Roberts to arrange for immediate delivery of a message to her friend, Skye dePaul Ramsey, and headed for the sheriff's office.

She intercepted Grant just as he opened the door to depart his office. "Can you spare a few minutes?" she asked.

"Why not?" he said. "Come on in and sit down."

He offered her the chair in front of his desk, gentleman that he was, seating her before taking his own chair. His face was drawn and grim, his hazel eyes cold as ice, a man focused on a mission. She laid out the letter and telegrams on the desk for him to see.

"The letter first," she said. "You can read it."

"Just tell me."

"It's from my Santa Fe lawyer friend. Rayburn Cox, the owner of The Doll House real estate and the property above Bushwa Sparks' place is a prominent figure in the

Santa Fe ring. When they were young men, he and his brother Elmer became wealthy abducting Navajo children from eastern Arizona and selling them into slavery in New Mexico Territory and across the Rio Grande in Mexico. This was mostly during the 1850s and 60s but continued to a lesser extent in the decade after that when the government finally intervened to stop the trade."

"So they shifted their source to the northern tribes."

"It appears so. Jael explains that much of her letter is based upon undocumented information. Every time the Rayburns have been charged, the witnesses die or disappear before trial. They always keep intermediaries between themselves and the abductions and sales."

Grant said, "We might be able to take witnesses who would implicate the Rayburns. Regardless, we will choke off the supply line and put them out of business."

"You do remember this is a federal issue, don't you? That you should be waiting for the marshal service."

"If the damn government wants to raise a fit over it, I will assure them that I went against my legal counsel's advice. You will not be involved."

"That was not my concern. I am just nervous about the possible repercussions."

"The repercussions of doing the federal government's job? I don't much care. Waiting one day could cost Jasmine her life. She is either being held with the others at the compound, or they have already killed her. I am betting she is alive and was taken hostage because the sheriff was taking advantage of her mother."

Hannah said, "You might be right that Jasmine was taken hostage because of your relationship with Moon, but don't make my dearest friend out a helpless fool. Anyway, I can see you have made up your mind about this."

"Yes, I have."

"The telegrams are from Beadle and Garth. You will be having visitors next week."

He picked up the telegrams and letter and flipped them back to her. "Not interested. I may never write again. Tell them to stay away."

Hannah snapped, "I did not hear that. We will talk later. And you are behaving like a child." She picked up the papers and folded them. "So what is your plan?"

He told her. She thought he was being a bit reckless, but she did not know what else could be done. "Count me in as another gun," she said.

Grant opened his mouth to protest.

"Don't say a word. I will be Jasmine's legal guardian, and if we find her, I must be there to tell her about her mother. Under the circumstances you are the last person who should inform her. I have some errands, and I will get my weapons and horse. You said everyone is meeting out front at ten o'clock. I will be here."

Grant said, "But I assumed you would be here to make funeral arrangements for Moon."

"There will be no funeral. Moon will be buried at my ranch this afternoon. She left instructions. No funeral. No embalming. Her body is to be wrapped in a buffalo robe and buried. A Sioux holy man will be there to carry out the ritual. My partner's wife, Skye Ramsey, will take care of everything. I sent one of Dayton Roberts's boys out to the Ramsey ranch with a message explaining the situation. He is to wait for a reply, but I would be surprised if Skye does not arrive at the office before I meet you here. Regardless, she will do what must be done. Moon's body is at George Caldwell's, and he will not cheerfully surrender his potential embalming fees and a casket sale, but he will not resist Skye."

"We have already delivered a fortune to George Caldwell, but I can't believe you would just drop this in another woman's hands."

"You have not met Skye yet. If you knew her, you would believe. She is the founder of The Lame Buffalo Association and half Brule Sioux herself. Ham Fish will give Skye Moon's written instructions at my office and she will carry them out to the letter."

"I just feel we should be there."

"Would Moon want us to postpone the search for Jasmine? You may come to my ranch and visit Moon's grave when we return."

Chapter 49

G RANT SURVEYED THE group clustered with their mounts in front of the sheriff's office. Jeb Oaks and his wife, Carissa, also known as She-Bear, had signed on again. He had not seen them during the previous night's slaughter but had been told that the former buffalo soldier and the alleged warrior woman were in the middle of it. The Sioux woman had seemed gentle and refined when she helped him at the general store. Today, however, wearing a buckskin war shirt that left her arms bare, her hair tied back with a leather strip, and a sheathed knife on her hip, there was a fierce look about her.

He wasn't certain about Hannah. Her hat brim cast a shadow over her face, and he could not see her greenish-blue eyes that were always a challenge to read anyway. The hair that fell from beneath her hat to her shoulders gleamed like copper in the morning sunlight. He was surprised to see that Trouble Yates had joined the group along with banker Matt Gaines. The two stood side by side, and Grant was suddenly struck by the uncanny physical resemblance between the two. They might have been father and son.

"This is all you got?" Grant asked, speaking in a near whisper. "This is our posse?"

Bushwa shrugged, "Kind of sudden, boss. Most other men that could be rounded up on short notice are taking on guard duty at the hospital. Might want to put this off a spell."

Grant did not respond. He had already waited past his limit. He spoke to the little gathering. "My thanks to the volunteers that turned out this morning. We've got a busy day ahead. I don't know how much you've heard about this situation, and I'll try to explain more along the way. We're dealing with an organization that reaches as far as Santa Fe. They have been abducting Indian children, mostly girls, from the reservations to the north and bringing them through Lockwood and holding them at a compound in the mountains less than two hours from here. The headquarters has been The Doll House, and the manager of the operation is Winston Colbert. He hired the men who tried to end the investigation last night.

Thanks to most of you, it didn't work. Now we need to finish the job. Questions?"

Jeb Oaks spoke. "Are these the same folks that burned down The Tipi and killed Moon Dupree last night?"

"Yes. I spoke with Moon before she passed. She said she saw Colbert's man, Bart Ryker, start the fire. You may not be aware that Jasmine Dupree went missing earlier in the evening. If she is still alive, she is likely being held at the compound. Our first stop is The Doll House. I hope to arrest Colbert and Ryker there." He hoped for enough resistance to justify his killing of the two.

Matt Gaines said, "Just tell us where you want us, Sheriff. You're the boss."

"Jeb and Carissa, I'd like you to take up positions near the back door, cutting off access to the stable. If anybody comes out, take their weapons and keep them close by till I can talk to them. If they resist, take them down."

Jeb said, "We'll head back down the street and circle around." He nodded at his wife, and they reined their horses out of the cluster.

Grant said, "Bushwa will go in with me. The rest of you wait out front. If you hear gunfire, don't barge in. I'll holler if you are needed inside. Otherwise, wait and don't let anybody past you unless you know they are customers

Ron Schwab

getting out of the way. There shouldn't be but a few there this time of day."

The riders mounted, and Grant led the party east on Main Street to the dead end near the livery, where they turned left to their destination. They hitched the horses on rails some distance from the doorway to protect the animals from stray gunfire. Then Grant and Bushwa pushed back the batwing doors and entered the huge barroom and found the area deserted. They walked slowly toward the bar, where they found no bartender.

Strange, Grant thought. The place appeared closed save for the open entrance. A trap, of course. He saw movement on the second-floor stairway landing overlooking the big room, and his ears rang from the echo of gunshots. Bushwa stumbled against him, falling on the floor, his Colt clattering on the hard wood. Grant had his own pistol in hand, searching out his target when he saw the upstairs gunman tumbling down the steps. A quick glance behind him revealed Hannah just inside the doors with her rifle lowered. Another man burst through the doorway at the far end of the bar. Grant swung around and placed two slugs in the gunslinger's chest after the attacker got off one wild shot, dropping him like a rock behind the bar.

Alert now, he waited for another assault before he heard gunfire to the rear of the building, likely someone attempting escape. He doubted they had been successful. Seeing that Hannah and the others were in the building and covering him now, he turned to Bushwa, noting that his deputy was sitting up now, collecting his gun and the hat that had fallen off when he went down.

Bushwa stretched his arm toward Grant. "Don't stand their gawking like I'm a shot duck. Help me up."

Grant took Bushwa's hand, planted his feet and pulled the husky man to his feet. "Are you hurt?"

"My pride and my ass. I saw that feller up there and stepped back when I went for my Colt and caught my boot heel on something. Glad there wasn't no picture of that."

Grant said, "Keep your eyes open and wait here. I'll see what happened out back." He headed down the long hallway he had followed only days earlier, feeling like he was revisiting an earlier chapter of a book. He opened the door a crack and yelled out, "Don't shoot. It's Grant."

"Come on out, Grant," Jeb Oaks's voice replied. "Got a live one here."

He pushed the door open and stepped out, noting an obviously dead man sprawled on the ground. She-Bear held a younger man at the point of her rifle. As he neared, he guessed that the captive was more boy than man, not more than a year or two older than Trouble.

Jeb said, "The dead man came out shooting. She-Bear and I both let loose on him. This young man had the good sense to toss out his gun and walk out with his hands raised."

Grant walked over to the prisoner who looked at him with wide, fearful eyes. He was a short kid, no more than five and half feet tall, Grant guessed, with no more than a few dozen wild blond hairs spread over cheeks and chin, which apparently represented a beard. "I'm Sheriff Coolidge. What's your name, young man?"

He answered with a quavering, high-pitched voice. "Willie Wilder. You going to hang me?"

"I don't know. Your best chance is to answer my questions truthfully and help me out. You get points in your favor for that."

"I'll give you the truth. I swear. I got in too deep with this outfit. Didn't know how to get out."

"Well, you're out now, and be glad you are alive to know it. Where's Winston Colbert?"

"Ain't here. He took off last night after all them killings. Waited for Bart Ryker to get back from doing something, and then they left together."

"Do you know where they went?"

"Not for sure but likely up to the 'relay station.' That's what Colbert called it. Said it was where he kept all his little princesses."

"I assume you have been to the relay station?"

"Oh sure. Live there lots between trips from up north with the guys that bring the girls in."

"And where is the relay station?"

"Just up the mountain a ways. Don't look nothing like no relay station. Just some sleeping buildings and a stable. They hold the girls there till they got two wagons full and then they move them south someplace, pass them on to somebody else, I guess, and bring the wagons back for the next loads. My work stopped at the relay station. I was supposed to head back north with some others tomorrow to collect more cargo."

"Okay, I'll have more questions later." He turned to Jeb. "Jeb, would you and Carissa take this guy down to the jail? If Ozzie isn't there yet, cell keys are in my top desk drawer. Lock this guy in a cell and leave a note for Ozzie. We will swing by the sheriff's office on the way out of town if you just wait there."

"We'll take care of it."

When he returned to the barroom, he found Hannah engaged in conversation with two of the prostitutes while Bushwa, Trouble and Gaines waited near the entryway. Grant did not interrupt, deciding that Hannah must have gained the women's confidence, and he joined the other males at the doorway.

When Hannah left the women, they all went outside and stood on the boardwalk and talked. Hannah said, "Jane and Marta said the place is closed, and they're locking the doors. They were told they could stay here if they could hold on. I told them that somebody in Santa Fe owns the place, so I doubted if they would be evicted anytime soon. There are four women left here. Marta said she thought Ginger and Sugar could be at a place called the relay station, where they were taken sometimes for short stays. It sounded like the compound you and Brady checked out, Grant."

"Did they know anything about the men who were waiting for us?"

"Not much. They said that the two killed here were Luke and Tabor. You were expected, and they and two more were ordered here to set up an ambush. The gunman in charge and meanest of the bunch headed out the back way with a kid named Willie when he saw things were not going to go well. His name was Tom Avery. He's the one who shot Sheriff Tolliver."

"He won't be shooting anybody else. Jeb and Carissa took him down. Willie is alive and talking, and they escorted him to the jail. I should talk to him before we head for the relay station and see if I can get an estimate of how many men we might encounter there. They have left a lot of them for the undertaker here in Lockwood, which reminds me that I need to alert George Caldwell there is more business over here."

"I'll take care of it," Gaines said. "He will want a guarantee that the county or town will pay him. I will meet you at your office." Gaines mounted his horse and rode away to tend to his task.

Hannah said, "Jane and Marta had no idea how many men might be at the relay station. Jane said they came and went all the time. She doubted there would be more than ten not counting Colbert and Ryker. They knew something illegal was probably going on, but they didn't understand it all. You stay alive in their business by not asking too many questions. It is dangerous sometimes to know too much, which was apparently Ruby's undoing. Ginger and Sugar may have made the same mistake."

Grant said, "I hope we can help them before it is too late."

Chapter 50

G RANT CALLED THE posse to a halt when they reached Bushwa's cabin a short distance beyond the foothills. Bushwa tended to a few chores while the others watered their horses at the stream. The pump near the cabin also offered a chance to fill canteens. The two women took advantage of the privy while the men slipped into the surrounding woods and watered the trees.

When they were ready to move on, Grant spoke. "If Willie Wilder can be believed, there could be as many as fourteen men at the relay station unless they have already moved the wagons out. Then we might have to trail them till we catch up. I'd like for Trouble to go on ahead and scout the situation." He nodded at Trouble. "Go ahead, Trouble, we'll meet you farther up the trail."

"Won't take long," Trouble said, mounting his sorrel gelding. "I know a place where I can get a good look."

Grant continued. "We'll go up the trail slow-like and wait for his report before we ride in. My thought is that we will spread out around the place and avoid any close-in gunfighting if possible. Find a spot with cover. If there is nobody at the stable, I'd like to have somebody take cover there and cut the devils off from escape."

Jeb said, "Me and She-Bear will claim the stable. Won't be anybody leaving the place."

"What about the children?" Hannah said.

Grant said, "When Trouble and I scouted the so-called relay station before, it appeared the captives were confined to a single building. That doesn't mean they would all be gathered there when we arrive. We don't know if Jasmine is there or where she might be. We'll be improvising today, but we aren't going to let them leave with those kids, no matter what happens. What those girls would face ahead of them is worse than anything that might happen to them today. Now let's saddle up."

A half hour later, Trouble intercepted the posse on the trail. "Ten minutes away," he said. "One wagon is gone. The other is hitched to two mule teams next to the stable. They must be planning to pull out soon. I'm guessing the skinner is in the stable, maybe with another man or two. He wouldn't be straying far from the teams."

"Where's the stable?" Jeb Oaks asked.

Trouble said, "Peel off to the left when we get there. It's not far off the wagon trail east of the lodging site."

Jeb said, "Me and She-Bear will try to take care of those folks quiet-like."

Grant saw She-Bear fingering her knife hilt and did not want to think about what Jeb had in mind. "Okay, tie your horses off the trail first chance you get. Then find a spot that gives you a decent view of the buildings. Trouble will show you where the men bunk, but if they are getting ready to pull out, the gunmen could be anyplace. Some would have left with the other wagon, so I wouldn't expect more than eight to ten here. Improves our odds nicely, I'd say."

When the party drew nearer the house, Trouble pointed out a little clearing off the trail where they could leave the horses. "You'll need to tie them to saplings or tree limbs. Won't get a stake in the ground. It's an inch of dirt and a mile of rock."

Grant did not dismount. Hannah asked, "Aren't you going to tie Blue?"

"Nope. I'll be riding in to announce their arrest."

She led her horse nearer to him and tried unsuccessfully to speak softly. "Are you insane? They'll shoot you down in a minute."

"I'm the law. They need to know they are up against the law and that I expect them to surrender."

"You are crazy. You're playing Marshal Buck Tyree. He's invincible; you're not. He's fiction. This is real life."

He shrugged. "You'd better be taking a position. We'll be needing your gun. By the way, thanks for your good shooting this morning. Bushwa and I owe you."

"Then pay me by getting off the horse."

He shook his head. "Sorry."

"You can get a new lawyer if Blue gets killed." She turned away and led her horse through the trees and into the clearing.

Jeb and She-Bear had already disappeared. Hannah glared at him as she walked past, trailing Bushwa and the others. Giving his posse another ten minutes to get positioned, Grant kneed Blue ahead and soon rode into the yard and reined his horse in at the open end of the 'U.' He heard Jeb's voice behind him. "Two down."

Grant yelled his loudest in the direction of the buildings. "Attention all. I am Sheriff Grant Coolidge here to make arrests and procure release of any children or others who are being held without consent." He heard the crash of breaking glass from the building he and Trouble had identified as holding the abducted children. A rifle barrel poked through the empty frame. Grant rode nearer to the building. "Hello there. Did you hear what I said?"

He heard a gunshot from inside the adjacent building. Silence.

Two more shots from behind him. Silence.

None of the fire seemed to be directed at himself. He waited a bit, watching the rifle barrel that seemed to be frozen in the empty window frame.

Finally, a gruff voice responded, "I heard you, Sheriff. And a squeeze of the trigger will drop you with a single shot."

"Before you squeeze that trigger, you had better listen. I have a posse of over twenty men surrounding this place. If I go down, my deputies are instructed to give no quarter. They are to hang any man who is not killed by gunfire. You cannot reach the stable to escape. The two men there have been incapacitated. You heard the other gunshots. My men were not squirrel hunting. Unless you have an army, I suggest you put down your weapons and walk out into the open with your hands raised."

"Sheriff," a woman's voice called.

He turned his head and saw Sugar waving from just outside the door of the adjacent building. "One dead here.

Me and Ginger got him. It was him or us. You're talking to Moose Collyer. He's not smart, but he can count. He can't have more than two or three men with him. They were going to load the girls into the wagon."

Grant yelled at Collyer. "Well, Moose. You've got two minutes." He pulled out his timepiece. "Then, I signal my posse to attack." He slipped his Colt from its holster.

A tall, lanky man charged from the doorway, getting off two wild shots at Grant, while Blue stood his ground and Grant aimed carefully and squeezed the trigger, driving a slug high into the shooter's chest, dropping him instantly. Two pistols and a rifle flew through the open doorway and landed in the dust. "We're coming out, Sheriff. Hands held high," yelled the man called Moose.

Two men, one a huge, hulking figure with black beard that draped to mid-chest, stumbled out, hands reaching for sky. The other man was a mustachioed, small, fine-boned soul, who could not be Moose.

Grant hollered at his posse. "Move in with caution."

Sugar and Ginger were walking his way now, Sugar seemingly unfazed by what had taken place. Ginger veered off and hurried into the building where Moose and his companions had been holed up. As she approached, Sugar said, "Welcome, Sheriff. We held out hopes the law would finally get to this place. Ginger and

I had our tickets for hell. Colbert ordered us killed, but he chose the wrong man. Bobek didn't know I'd figured out his plans and asked Ginger for a quick poke. She said, 'Why sure, darling' and when his britches dropped to his knees, I snatched his Colt and placed a slug in the back of his neck. I learned a long time ago to make your move when a man's thinking with his pizzle. Brain in the head shuts down then."

Grant dismounted. "Where is Colbert?"

"He's with the other wagon. He and Ryker took off with a load of girls this morning, eight of them, I think. Headed for wherever they go, near Laramie, I've heard."

"Any other men?"

"Should be four more counting Tex Garber, the mule skinner. The other three are new gunslingers that showed up here a few days ago. I think they were sent by the big boss out of Santa Fe."

"You seem to know a lot about this outfit."

"More than was good for me."

"Will you talk to the law?"

"I'm talking to you, aren't I?"

"I think we're clear, boss. Four from back here are meeting the devil this minute."

Grant turned and saw that Bushwa had come up be-hind him, and the rest of his crew was not far behind.

"Just a minute, and we will make some decisions." He asked Sugar, "Is Ginger with the other girls?"

"Yeah, she's sort of a mother hen, loves kids. Hope she can find a man to give her a few someday. She's a sweet gal. She didn't run out on you that night at The Doll House. Avery made her go with him, and he drug her out here. Colbert had Ryker bring me here, too. If we wanted to live, we carried on our work at the relay station."

"We're looking for a town girl. Her name is Jasmine Dupree. Do you know anything about her?"

"She must be the one Mickey Lavender brought up here yesterday afternoon. Dropped her off and left. She's with the wagonload that rode out with Colbert and Bart Ryker."

Grant was swept by a surge of hope. Jasmine was alive, not out of danger, but still living just hours earlier. "Did Lavender ride a buckskin stallion?"

"That's the one. Charmer. Handsome. Young. Never used the girls here. Bragged he never had to pay for poon-tang. Colbert wanted Mickey to go after the girl after he ran into you the night the sheriff was shot, and Ruby was killed. I don't know why."

Bushwa interrupted. "Grant, look." He pointed to the building doorway. Frightened dark-eyed girls, some wearing little more than rags, were being led by Ginger onto the rocky, dusty yard. Most of the girls were rail thin, all obviously of Indian lineage. When they were all collected on the grounds, he counted nine in all, ranging from ten to fifteen years of age, he estimated. She-Bear was already moving among the girls, reassuring them and smiling, bringing comfort that likely only one of their culture could bring at this moment.

Hannah stood silently at his side now, and Gaines and Trouble joined them. Gaines said, "Jeb's gathering up tethers for the stabled horses. He says there are ten we should take back with us for now. Those in the pasture have grass and water. He said somebody could be sent out tomorrow to round those up. Brady suggests they be stabled at The Doll House barn for now. He and Enos can look after them and hire on some extra help for a spell— for a price of course."

"With that many horses, we should be able to find a way to pay the stablemen."

Gaines said, "By my count, we have at least six bodies out here. Bushwa took down a man that was working his way up the slope to get a shot at you. Trouble got another. Two in the barn, Miss Sugar claims one, and there is one in front of the building."

"We'll just tie them to the horses and haul them to the undertaker."

"The two in the barn had their throats cut. George Caldwell will be taking photographs and likely post them, but I guess it will give folks something to gossip about. He'll probably charge admission."

"We've got to do something with these Indian girls."

Sugar, who had been listening to the conversation said, "The Doll House."

Grant said, "What about The Doll House?"

"We can lodge them there. We have plenty of rooms. There is nobody around to claim the place. If she will take me as a client, I would like to have Miss Locke help me buy the property. I've got money saved up, and I've always wanted my own house. I just don't know the legal things I've got to do."

"I consider myself hired," Hannah said. "I've got a hunch you can buy the property cheap, and I know a lawyer in Santa Fe who can likely help us. My partner's wife, Skye Ramsey, is president of the Lame Buffalo Association, and I am sure she will help with returning the girls to their people or finding homes for those who can't."

Grant said, "Matt, can you take charge of organizing an exodus to town? Hopefully, you can make it into the foothills before it gets too dark."

"You're going after the other wagon, aren't you?"

"Damn right. And Bushwa and Hannah, too, if they are willing."

Hannah said, "Try and stop me."

"That's what I figured. This way it's my idea."

"How soon are we leaving?" Bushwa said.

"As soon as we put together bedrolls with some blankets from this place and round up something edible to take with us."

"I can help with that," Sugar said. "Anything to take down that bastard Colbert."

Chapter 51

AS THE THREE riders followed the wagon road deeper into the mountains, Grant found himself taking on a new burst of energy at the prospect of rescuing Jasmine. Aside from keeping a promise to a woman he would never forget, this would be like recovering a part of Moon Dupree, and he swore this girl would have his help for a lifetime if she wanted it.

Bushwa led a packhorse now, carrying food supplies and cooking gear. The sorrel gelding had resisted some at first, a saddle horse that likely considered the new job beneath its dignity. Grant had decided they should be prepared for a trek that could last some days before they returned to Lockwood. The riders had newly improvised bedrolls tied behind their saddles.

Hannah had been uncharacteristically quiet since they separated from the others over two hours earlier, seemingly engaged in thought. He did not envy her the task of telling Jasmine about her mother's death. Apparently, Hannah had also committed to taking the girl into the lawyer's home, a responsibility that could be formidable.

Still, Hannah Locke seemed to thrive on challenges, and he had no doubt she would find ways to handle whatever faced her in the days ahead. Of course, first they must recover the girl alive, and there was no guarantee that any of them would see another sunrise.

The road was taking them higher with each step, and the late afternoon sun was hidden by the curtain of tall pines and aspens that threatened to invade the road. Grant figured that they had little more than an hour of daylight remaining, and with little starlight sifting through the trees, it would be near pitch black by full nightfall.

He spoke to Bushwa. "How far ahead do you think the wagon is?"

"By the time we got packed up, they'd been on the trail a good eight hours as near as I can figure. They got that big wagon full of girls, so they ain't going to be moving none too fast, and till they reach the pass that takes them between the peaks, it's all uphill. How long we been out?"

"I just checked my timepiece. Maybe two hours."

"I'm guessing we're six hours behind. They'll stop for the night. I ain't been up this way for a few years, but there's a cleared camping place near one of the streams that travelers used for years before the railroad come. Only an hour or so before you hit the pass from there. When they stop, we can close any gap in four hours, but dark's going to stop us now," Bushwa said.

"I wonder."

"What do you mean?"

"Does dark have to stop us? Our horses need a few hours' rest, and we didn't get much sleep last night. But let's say we took a three-hour break, even four. That would get us out of here before midnight. We could catch them before sunrise while it's still dark. If we could surprise them, that would help even the numbers."

"I don't know. I suppose that's possible. We're taking a broken trail. It's rough some places but not what I'd call dangerous underfoot."

"I don't think they will expect anybody coming on this fast," Grant said. "They're likely assuming the gunmen they left at The Doll House did us enough damage that any pursuit would be delayed or that nobody would come after them. They might even think that nobody knows about the relay station or the captured Indian girls. They could be taking their time to give the other wagon a

Ron Schwab

chance to catch up. Colbert headed out because he wasn't taking any chances. I am guessing he saw Jasmine as a potential hostage given my—uh, friendship with her mother but plans to put her on the market with the others when they eventually reach Santa Fe."

"Do you think that's where he's headed?"

"Well, that's where the girls are supposed to end up. There is somebody farther down the line waiting to take over—maybe Laramie—but Colbert's days in Lockwood are done. He may have in mind making the entire trip to visit his bosses. Of course, it is our intention to cut his trip short."

Hannah finally broke her silence. "Let's take them at sunrise."

Grant looked at Bushwa. "What do you say?"

"Hell, why not?"

Chapter 52

S LEEP ELUDED GRANT as he tossed and turned in
his bedroll, trying to wedge his hip and shoulder
between the rocks that covered the ground. They
had found a campsite of sorts along the roadside that af-
forded no more than a hundred square feet for the three
campers. There was just enough space to lay out bedrolls
and build a small fire to brew some coffee and savor a bit
of warmth. Sugar had rounded up beef jerky and hard-
tack for the journey, so the fire had been luxury rather
than necessity. Grant had learned early after his arrival
in Lockwood that warm mountain days tended to turn
downright chilly after sunset, and tonight was no excep-
tion.

He would not find warmth tonight, and supper had
been joyless. He would rather write about this life than
live it, he decided. When his lawman days were finished,

he would leave this existence to Marshal Tyree and his kind.

His thoughts bounced from the challenge that faced him in a few hours to his sorrow and emptiness at the loss of Moon. The comfort and amenities of The Tipi and the joy of all his moments with Moon. In a few hours' time, his new life had gone up in flames. But he had a life to salvage, and Moon Dupree did not. The anger churned in him, and his mind switched again to the upcoming confrontation with Colbert and Ryker.

"Grant," came Hannah's soft voice from less than five feet to his right.

"Yes?"

"You're not sleeping either, are you?"

"No. Pretty much hopeless, I think, even without Bushwa's snoring. At least, he should keep the mountain lions or other unwelcome creatures away." He looked over and saw that Hannah was sitting up, swallowed by her blankets and leaning against a tree. He crawled out of his bedroll and scooted over beside her, dragging his blankets with him. Then, facing her, he wrapped himself in his own blankets.

"Have you thought about just how we're going to do this when we catch up to Colbert and the wagon?" she asked.

"Not much but that. Unfortunately, whatever I come up with will probably be worthless because we can't control where guns or children will be."

"That's what the troubles me—Jasmine and the other children."

"And that should be your focus. Jasmine will know and trust you. Maybe it can't be done, but if you can find a way to separate the children from Colbert and his gunmen, that's what you should be looking to do. Get the kids out of any crossfire and into the timber if it's possible. I am going to see if I can find a way to draw the men away from the girls. They wouldn't necessarily be hanging too close with them. Where would anybody run away to up in this isolated country? Think about how you might do this. We've got a freer hand if we don't have to worry about hurting the kids."

"I will do that. Grant, I'm so sorry about Moon. She was my dearest friend, and I will miss her forever, but I know you brought a joy to her life she had never known. I am grateful for that. I suspect she did much the same for you."

He sighed. "I can't quote verbatim, but I think it was John Hobbes who wrote that there are events that happen in our lives that become a part of our personal calendar, so to speak. These events change us and our destiny for better or worse or both, and we find ourselves measuring time with them. In my case, the first event was the war. Life before the war, life after. There are likely other such events, if I thought about it, but Moon will always have a permanent place on my calendar. Life before Moon, life after. It's so damned unfair to Moon. I think we could have shared much happiness."

"I think so, too."

"But she changed me somehow, and I haven't sorted it all out. But meeting her and her death will alter the course of my life. I'm sorry, blubbering on like this. Normally, I would just write down those thoughts."

"Don't be sorry. Thank you for sharing. I must think about what you said."

She leaned back against the tree, and they sat there silently until her chin dropped to her chest, and Grant saw she was asleep. He curled up in a fetal position, burying his head in the blankets before sleep captured him and took him away.

He did not know how long he had slept before a boot nudged his buttocks and Bushwa spoke. "Hey, you two, I got to do this job by my own self?"

Grant struggled out of his tangled blankets and was surprised to find Hannah curled up beside him in her own blankets, probably having toppled over from her spot against the tree. She was rolling away now and working at her own exit.

"Got to find my boots and step into the trees a spell," Grant said.

"Me, too," Hannah said with a sleepy voice. "You go south. I'll go north."

"You was sleeping like babies. Hated to wake you up. You ought to be rested and ready for fun. I got the horses saddled and packed. Let them drink from that little stream that trickles across the wagon road downslope."

"You're a good man, Bushwa. I owe you supper."

"You? A man that don't got a place to sleep. More likely, I'll be feeding you."

"I didn't have a lot of money in the house," Grant said. "You have heard of banks, haven't you?"

"Yep. Never use one except to cash a check. My business is generally in gold and silver coin, and I turn paper to one or the other as quick as I can."

"And what if somebody steals your coins?"

"It's buried where it can't be found."

"And what if you drop dead?"

"Don't plan on dying till I'm ready. But I told somebody."

"That's good."

"Of course, it was Moon Dupree, God bless her soul."

Chapter 53

BUSHWA WAS THE only one who had traveled the fading wagon road before, so he led the riders. Grant felt they were moving like a cluster of snails, realizing now why Bushwa had been skeptical about night travel. He worried most about the safety of the horses, so he did not press his deputy to move faster. If Colbert and his captives were gone before the pursuers arrived at the assumed location, they would just be forced to replot a strategy, and their plans were rather vague anyhow.

Hannah followed Bushwa, and Grant trailed her, leading the packhorse. All he could see in front of him were shadowy forms that appeared more ghostlike than human. Again, he was seeing the potential folly of launching a night attack. Targets would need to be carefully chosen if he chose that course. He almost pushed Blue into Hannah's mount before he realized Bushwa must have signaled a halt.

Shortly, the deputy led his horse past Hannah's and came up to Grant, who had dismounted now. "The trail takes a sharp bend up ahead," Bushwa said. "Maybe a half mile or so. Then it heads straight for the pass for about the same distance. That's where I figure they should be camped. It wouldn't make no sense at all to take that big wagon through that pass in the dark. It's rougher than a gator's back. Good way to bust a wheel or a critter's leg. Got to do some fancy dancing through them rocks that have caved off the mountain bluffs above the pass over the years."

"Assuming they are camped where you expect them to be, how much cover would we have if we tied our horses at the bend and walked in?"

"Plenty, if we stayed off the road proper."

"Which side of the road is the campsite on?"

"Right. That would be west, downslope."

"So if we work our way into the trees on the east side, we would claim the high ground and the sun at our back if we waited till sunrise to hit."

"Yeah. True enough. You ain't so dumb about this strategizing stuff."

Hannah joined them now and had been listening to the conversation. "I should get positioned as near as I can to the girls."

Grant said, "Yes, but we must locate them first. Let's try to get in place while it's still dark. Then we'll figure out what you do as soon as we get the lay of the camp."

A half hour later, they came to the turn in the trail, dismounted and led their horses into the trees. The horses secured, they moved to the side of the trail and walked as quietly as possible in the direction of the presumed camp.

Grant signaled a halt and turned to the others. "Smell it?"

"Don't smell nothing," Bushwa said.

Hannah shrugged. "What?"

"Smoke. They're camped ahead."

Bushwa said, "You must have some hunting hound in you. I'll take your word for it."

Grant said, "We'd better slip into the trees. They've probably got a lookout posted."

The others smelled smoke as they inched southward through the timber. Grant calculated they had a bit less than an hour before sunrise when they

reached a stone outcropping that gave them a view of
the camp below. Grant was uneasy about the setup.
The campfire was in the center of the clearing as
might be expected, and he could make out a shadowy
form hunkered down by smoldering coals that spat
out occasional low flames. He surmised this was the
lookout.

The wagon was at the westernmost end of the
clearing near the edge of the woods. Dark lumps on
the ground beneath the wagon were possibly some of
the captors, but he could not yet locate all the men.
That would have to wait for a sliver of daylight to be
certain.

Bushwa nudged him. "Horses are staked out on
down the road not far from the opening of the pass. I
could get down there and turn them loose—leave the
mules tied since we couldn't chance losing one. Fire
a few shots, and they'd scatter fast and send those
bastards into panic. Some would run for the horses."

"I want to head for the wagon," Hannah said.
"I need to be there when the sun comes up."

"Too dangerous," Grant said. "You would have
to cross the wagon road and then you'd be trapped
down there on your own."

"I'm going, so you'd best tell me what's going to start the party."

Damn her. Buck Tyree would not tolerate this insubordination. He would likely hogtie the female.

"I'll stay here with my rifle for now. This is a perfect sniper's spot. I will fire the first shot. Then Bushwa spooks the horses. That's when you make your move. If you can't get to the girls, just stay put. Use your rifle if you get the chance. I do wonder if I should work my way down the slope and declare these men under arrest, give them a chance to surrender."

Hannah snapped, "And you will get your fool head blown off. Declare the arrest. That's a big deal for your fictional friend Tyree, isn't it? I always thought that was nonsense. I say shoot the bastards, every one of them."

She whirled and headed back into the forest, angling away from the camp and toward the wagon road. Grant thought her attitude regarding arrest did not seem very lawyerlike, but he conceded that he might be pressing his luck to try the arrest business again. With his posse down to three and the stakes high, it was not a time to gamble with the niceties of formal arrest.

Chapter 54

HANNAH FOUND THE path on the west side of the road easy to negotiate. The land was more level for some distance before it dropped again, probably one reason travelers over the years had chosen a portion of the ground as a natural campsite. She circled around the camp and eased her way up to within twenty feet of the covered wagon.

She could see a row of wrapped bundles under the far side of the wagon, obviously sleeping girls, but she could not get a count. Some probably slept in the wagon. If only she could communicate with them before the chaos. She went nearer the wagon, almost to the edge of the clearing, but it left her a dozen feet short of the wagon. She could reach it unseen, she thought, but if she startled one of the girls and she screamed, it could throw off the attack's timing.

She could not just stand there, she decided, so she gambled and dropped to her knees and belly down, rifle clutched in her left hand, she commenced crawling toward the wagon. When she reached the sleeping girls, she decided to start at the end of the row of what seemed to be five girls. That would leave four in the wagon. Luck favored her with the girls' heads resting on her side of the wagon.

Hannah set the rifle down, carefully traced her fingers over the blanket and clasped her hand across the girl's lips. The girl's head jerked up, but Hannah used her other hand to hold it in place as she whispered, "I am a friend. I have come to help you. Do you understand?"

The girl gave an affirmative nod, and Hannah released her. The girl turned her head to view the visitor, and Hannah could make out a tentative smile. "Now," she said, "tell the girl beside you and tell her to pass the word on. When they hear a gunshot just before sunrise, they are to run into the forest behind me and wait there. Hide behind the trees. I am Hannah. What is your name?"

"Primrose."

"A good name. Can you do this?"

She nodded and woke her companion, conveying the instructions.

Hannah, remaining pressed to the ground, then asked Primrose, "Can you climb into the wagon and tell the other girls?"

"Yes," Primrose said. "The guard would think nothing of it if he saw me."

She guessed Primrose to be one of the older girls, perhaps fourteen or fifteen. "Are all the girls here?"

"All but Jasmine."

Oh, God, please, no. "Where is she?"

"Bart took her to his blankets."

A wave of nausea swept over her. Ryker. The son-of-a-bitch who was responsible for Moon's death. If he lived when this night was done, she would kill him herself.

Chapter 55

GRANT REMAINED PERCHED on the outcropping as the glow of first light preceded the sun over the mountaintop. His rifle was poised to fire. The distance to the camp was less than he had thought in the darkness, no more than a hundred feet, insignificant for a marksman. He figured he would just fire a wild shot to ignite the attack, but he was prepared to find a target if it seemed more prudent when the critical time arrived.

Then he saw a man crawl out of his bedroll, kick at a form still lying within it. Another struggled up. A girl. The light still hampered his sight, but he thought it could be Jasmine, though it did not matter. Rage consumed him. The man gave the girl a shove toward the wagon, and she ran. Grant aimed, squeezed the trigger, the Winchester cracked and the man dropped with a lead slug in his brain. His death should not have been so easy, Grant thought.

Gunfire commenced in the direction of the horses. The lookout was on his feet, swinging his rifle around, seeking a target. Grant dropped him for good measure.

Two men raced for the horses, pistols ready, obviously panic-stricken. Grant started down the slope. Gunfire continued near the horses, but he figured Bushwa would handle that fine without him. He was looking for two men: Ryker and Colbert.

Grant heard two shots in the direction of the wagon and when his feet struck level ground he raced toward the gunfire, passing the man who had kicked Jasmine from his bedroll, recognizing him instantly. A hefty man stood at the edge of the camp, empty hands raised skyward.

When he reached the wagon, he saw Hannah holding a sobbing Jasmine in her arms, her Winchester lying at her feet. Next to the rear wagon wheel lay Winston Colbert with sightless eyes seeming to stare in disbelief at the sheriff, two bloody holes burrowed in his chest.

It appeared Grant and his alter ego, Buck Tyree, would have a single prisoner for this day's work.

Chapter 56

"WE GOING TO load up them corpses and haul them down the mountain?" Bushwa asked.

"Nope. We'll get Tex the muleskinner to help us lay out the bodies in the campsite here. I'll tell the U.S. Marshal's office where to find them if they finally get up to Lockwood."

"Ain't even going to bury them?"

"I'm not. You can if you feel a need to."

"All we got is near solid rock up here. No shovels. I suppose we could pile a few rocks on them."

Bushwa walked away, shaking his head. "I'll get Tex over here."

"Marshall Tyree would have buried these men."

Grant turned and saw Hannah facing him, her mouth set serious but her eyes twinkling like emeralds in the late morning sun. "I'm not Marshal Tyree. I haven't been since the shooting started. Tyree took a long nap. Besides, I always furnish Tyree with soft dirt for burying the outlaws he kills."

"I guess Tyree was sleeping when you didn't declare arrests this morning."

"You could say so. That was Private Coolidge living in a world his imagination did not create. Now, tell me about Jasmine. Does she know about Moon?"

"I told her before breakfast. That's why we didn't appear. It was considerate of you to send the plates of flapjacks and syrup over to the wagon. And the coffee. I ate more than my share, but I coaxed Jazzie to eat a bit."

"Well, we have ample food supplies in the wagon to get us off this mountain. But Jasmine will require more than food—probably most of these girls will."

"She's devastated, of course. She's been through so much. It will take time and a lot of understanding by those close to her."

"I feel I should speak to her, but don't know what to say. I'm not sure how she feels about me. If I had never come into their lives, Moon would be alive today. She may not want to talk to me, and I would not blame her."

"I think you should say something. Just tell her that you are sorry for her loss and that you loved her mother, too, and will never forget her, and that you will be there to help any way you can. That would be a start. Her response will tell you what to do from there. Possibly nothing more for now."

"Where is she?"

"She is with the Arapaho girl, Primrose. They seem to be kindred spirits and started to strike a friendship in the brief time they have known each other. She is an orphan, too, so she can relate to Jazzie's grief."

"I will try to speak with her before we leave. I don't want to anticipate it any longer than necessary."

"I think that's wise. And Grant, I may tease you about Marshal Tyree, but he is nothing compared to the man you have been these past days. Don't be hard on yourself. Now, I had better see if I can get these girls prepared to travel back to Lockwood." She turned away and hurried toward the wagon.

It occurred to Grant that Moon frequently chided him about being too hard on himself. He spent the next hour helping the other men lay out the bodies near a big boulder. After salvaging the weapons and any valuables from the corpses, Grant relented some, and they covered the dead men with a layer of stones that might discourage the coyotes and buzzards and other creatures of prey. A bear, however, could dig up a meal or two with several swipes of big paws.

Ron Schwab

While they finished that unpleasant task, Grant asked Bushwa, "How long to get back to Lockwood?"

Bushwa said, "It's downslope all the way. We'll set up camp tonight someplace, but we should be in Lockwood by late afternoon tomorrow. Can't have the mules trying to race down the mountain. They'll tip the wagon over for damn sure." He nodded at the muleskinner. "That right, Tex?"

"Yessir," Tex answered with a deep, Southern drawl. "Got to handle them critters careful like. But I'd sure like to know what happens to me when I get there. I ain't going to hang, am I? I ain't killed nobody. Just skinned my mules and done some cooking."

Grant said, "But you had to know that you were hauling illegal cargo. We've got a cell for you and will hold you for the U.S. Marshal. If you cooperate with the law, you should escape the noose and get by with some prison time."

While the mules were being hitched and the horses saddled, Grant sought out Jasmine who was with Primrose and saddling one of the outlaw horses, a black mare. When he approached, he said, "You girls planning to go horseback?"

Jasmine looked at him and then turned her head away. Primrose smiled and said, "Yes, this one is Jasmine's. I have claimed that sorrel. He is a gentle thing." She gestured toward the gelding that was still staked to a tether line nearby. Another saddle and bridle lay near the black mare.

Grant noted that Jasmine was struggling with the saddle cinches. He said, "Could I help you finish saddling your critters?"

Jasmine did not reply but did not resist when he stepped up and finished cinching the saddle. Primrose retrieved her mount, and he saddled the gelding. He suspected that she was comfortable on the back of a horse but had not had that much experience with the traditional western saddle. She was also a tiny girl and hoisting the saddle onto the horse's back would have been no small battle.

"Thank you," Primrose said. "I do appreciate it."

"You are welcome. Now if you will hold the horses a bit, I would like to have Jasmine come with me. I need to speak with her." He looked at Jasmine. "Would you step off with me, Jasmine? It won't be long."

She hesitated, and a look of panic crossed her face before she stepped away from the horse and followed him to the far end of the camp clearing. When they were away from any other persons' hearing, Grant stopped and faced her. She waited but her eyes refused to meet his.

"I have tried to give you some room, Jasmine, but no matter what you think of me, I cannot let this silence exist between us. You must understand how sorry I am that you lost your mother. You have had to deal with more the past several days than many people must face during a lifetime. I loved your mother, too, not for as many years as you did, but I have never known anyone so special. I would never have done anything to intentionally hurt her."

She spoke so softly he could barely hear her. "She loved you. I know she did. I liked you, but I guess I was jealous. For as long as I can remember, I was the only one mama loved."

"I can understand. You will have to sort things out for yourself, but Hannah will be there to help, and I will not be far away if there is anything I can do."

She nodded slowly, turned aside and walked back toward Primrose and the horses. Grant decided that they had made a start at least.

Chapter 57

G RANT DECIDED HE had put off his visit to Moon's grave long enough, and he had a personal matter to discuss with his lawyer, so he embarked on a late afternoon ride out to Hannah Locke's Box L ranch. This was Grant's first visit to the place located not more than two miles west on the main county road leading from Lockwood. He supposed the thousand-acre spread would not qualify as a ranch to some in a territory where ten thousand acres, not counting government grazing lands, would ordinarily be considered a small operation.

It was a winding road with branches that veered off in all directions like a giant spiderweb. Obviously, the roads and trails paid no attention to section lines like those near perfect squares plotted in his native Ohio. He suspected that many of the roads crossed private property and were considered public only if you had the owner's permission or legitimate business there. Possibly some crossed federal government lands.

As he approached the Box L, he found himself in awe of the breathtaking setting. Majestic, still snow-capped, mountain peaks loomed north and west on the horizon, probably miles in the distance. In the foreground rose the lower mountain country and the foothills. A clear, rapid-flowing creek snaked through seemingly endless, lush green grasslands.

When he arrived at the Box L, Grant encountered a small sign nailed to a single post. The sign exhibited a burned, engraved image of a square box enclosing the letter 'L.' Grant suspected it might have been made with a branding iron. The county road split here and formed a 'T' with arms heading north and south.

Grant saw the log house set back more than a hundred feet from the road, and he continued down a wagon trail that was fenced on both sides until he reached the ranch yard. The first thing that struck him was how few buildings there were: a log house, a large stable-barn and a chicken coop. The second was that the structures were relatively new.

The house was rectangular in shape, but it was long and wide, and there appeared to be ample room to accommodate the new occupants. The roof was covered with cedarwood shingles not yet weathered and extended over a railed veranda that ran the length of the house. A porch swing was suspended at one end of the veranda, one of the few Grant had ever seen. A rocking chair sat not far from the door, and a long bench rested against the structure's front.

Hannah came out the front door to greet him, dressed in faded denims and ranch work garments. He dismounted, and she stepped off the veranda to greet him, shaking his hand with a firm, businesslike grip. "Welcome to the Box L," she said. "I was hoping you would come. I have some business we need to discuss. Why don't we put Blue up in the stable and treat him with a bit of corn? I have his favorite stall available. Then we can visit Moon's grave."

Blue nickered and tossed his head when she came near, obviously recognizing his former owner. Hannah took the reins and rubbed his nose and muzzle, pressing her cheek to the gelding's. "I love this guy," she said. "I hated to let him go. I gelded him before I realized what a magnificent creature he would become. But a gelding isn't too helpful if you are in the horse breeding business. I could not have kept him anyway. Inbreeding issues. I wasn't sure at first, but I am glad now that you bought him."

"You didn't like me much at our first meeting, did you?" Grant asked.

"I told you that I tend to be wary of strangers, but when Moon indicated her approval, I softened. She was a solid judge of people. Then I came to know you better, and you didn't seem so bad after all. Besides, when lawyers have prospects of finding a profitable client, there is a tendency to find new virtues in people who have the potential of enhancing their bank accounts."

She did not smile, but he assumed she was directing some sarcasm at her profession and teasing him a bit. He never quite knew what to think of the lady. One minute, warm and joking, and the next ice cold with words slicing like a razor blade. Hannah Locke was a complex person.

After Blue was settled in his stall, Grant followed Hannah to the south end of the building site where a corner had been fenced off for a cemetery. There appeared to be only two small plots in the cemetery. The first they came to had two gravesites marked with small, engraved stones. Grant glanced at the gravestones. They were for John and David Hathaway, same dates of birth, deaths slightly more than four years later, six days apart. They were obviously twins.

"Diphtheria," Hanna said. "About six years ago. I bought the place from the Hathaways a year later. The

mother lost her mind over the deaths of her only children. Her husband thought if they returned east to be
near her family, she might recover. I promised to fence
off an acre around the area where they had buried the
boys for a cemetery and care for the graves. I assured
them they would always be welcome here. That was five
years ago, and I haven't heard from them."

"Terribly sad," Grant said. "So many families have
shared these tragedies."

The other gravesite was identifiable by a mound of
fresh dirt on the opposite side of the tract. Grant walked
over to it and noticed Hannah remained behind, apparently allowing him some time to be alone with Moon. He
was surprised to find a second grave there. A small stone
read "Gabriel Pierre Dupree, May 10, 1866 - December
25,1879." The son Moon never spoke of. He stood there,
looking down at the place where the woman he loved now
lay. Tears did not come, but the melancholy of his memories of their brief time together threatened to consume
him, and he turned away and rejoined Hannah.

They strolled in silence toward the stable until Grant
spoke. "The boy—Gabriel—I had heard of, but Moon never mentioned him."

"Same epidemic as the Hathaway twins. She was never one to seek sympathy, but she would have mentioned it

eventually. She asked if he could be buried here but never said why. Just said she had a feeling this was where he should be. Her husband died a few months later, but she arranged his burial in the town cemetery." She abruptly changed the subject. "Join me in my study for coffee. Jasmine and Primrose are out riding, and we should talk."

"I have a few items on my agenda, too. Is Primrose staying with you?"

"For now. The girls are becoming fast friends and Primrose is a godsend for Jasmine right now. They are sharing my guest room, and I hope the girl will choose to stay. She has no real home among the Arapahoe, but I know her people would find a place for her. She has had some schooling and seems quite intelligent. She would finish school here before the Bureau of Indian Affairs sorts it all out."

"I understand that the Lame Buffalo Association will help financially with the girls living at The Doll House, and that Sugar and Ginger will supervise their care with the help of the women who choose to remain. A strange turn of events."

"Yes, the arrangement will provide a different sort of work for those ladies for at least a few years and give them time to make other choices if they wish."

Grant said, "I'm just glad my sheriff's job is about finished."

They stepped onto the veranda and Hannah said, "Jim Tolliver's coming back to work?"

"I don't know how soon that will be, but I got a telegram yesterday morning that a U. S. Marshal and a deputy will be arriving on the train tomorrow to take over the case."

"What case? There is nothing left for them to do."

"They can take custody of our prisoner, I guess, and interview Jones, the bartender, and other witnesses at The Doll House. I've already warned Matt Gaines that after I've told my story to the marshal, I will be tossing my badge on the desk. Bushwa will, too. Ozzie will take charge until the elected sheriff returns. From here on I intend to be sheriff only with my imagination and pencil and paper."

"Are you still sleeping at the jail? Where are you going to stay?"

"The answer to your first question is 'yes' for a few days. The second question is what I want to talk to you about."

Chapter 58

GRANT AND HANNAH sat in stuffed leather chairs on each side of a lamp table in one corner of Hannah's study. Steaming mugs of coffee sat on cowhide pads next to the unlit oil lamp. It was a spacious room, probably fifteen by fifteen feet, he guessed, with a desk and book-lined walls. A west window furnished ample afternoon light.

The house appeared to be post and beam construction encased by the log exterior and all the interior walls and ceilings he had seen were sheathed with pine or other woods he could not identify. A small woodstove sat in another corner of this room, and he had noted another woodstove for cooking in the kitchen area. A massive stone fireplace dominated the sitting room.

Hannah took a sip of her coffee and placed her cup back on the pad. "You wanted to talk about your living arrangements. I gather your recent unhappy experiences are not going to turn you back east just yet."

"To the contrary, I'm here to stay. I expect to die in Lockwood, although I hope that won't be for a spell yet. Moon is here. With a few exceptions, I love the people. I've made more friends here in a month's time than I did in a lifetime back in my old hometown—of course, I was something of a recluse. The setting in this valley is like nothing I've ever experienced. If I am going to write about the west, this is where I must be."

"I'm glad to hear this." She hesitated. "I didn't want to lose a good client."

It seemed to Grant that Hannah could show a bit more enthusiasm about his decision. Her speech was always laced with sarcasm, though, and he was far from figuring this woman out, likely never would. "Bushwa said you might have a house for sale."

"Unofficially. It is more shack than house. Two rooms: an open area that I suppose you could call a parlor, kitchen and sleeping area wrapped in one, and a bedroom. There is a decent fireplace there. The other room would be a separate bedroom, but there is no fireplace or stove. You get some heat in it from the main room if you leave the door open."

"Any outbuildings?"

"A decent stable. Out here, people tend to house their animals better than themselves. I moved the chicken house over here."

Grant said, "Bushwa said there is some land with it."

"The house and stable sit on a twenty-acre tract across the road from the rest of my land. It's a half mile south of here. It was the original homeplace for Albert and Minnie Hathaway. They had just started the foundation for this house when they lost the twins. This was going to be their new home. Albert was a carpenter and planned to build most of the house himself over a period of several years. He made his living as a craftsman, not a rancher. He planned to build a large workshop where I put the stable."

"Death rearranges life."

She looked at him quizzically like she expected him to say more. "And . . ?"

"Nothing. Just thinking out loud, I guess. What's the price for this place?"

"You haven't even seen it."

"Hathaway was a carpenter. I assume the roof won't leak."

"Not the last I knew."

"What's the price?"

"One thousand dollars."

"Okay. Just take care of the paperwork."

"You are not going to make a counter-offer?"

"No. You are my lawyer. I trust you."

"It will be eight hundred dollars then. Matt at the Gaines Bank would want to see that much applied against my loans, since he will have to release the mortgage against that portion of my real estate. You really do need a lawyer. John Rich could help you with the property purchase. No wonder you have given your books away. You do understand that I cannot represent you on this transaction?"

"I refuse to pay another lawyer. Make up a waiver or something for me to sign."

She sighed. "We will ride over, and I will show you the place before you go back to town. I will not have you buying something you have not even seen."

"That's good. I might want to move in tomorrow or at least the day after."

"I guess there is no reason why you can't. You might have to kick some critters out that have beat you there."

"Like what kind of critters?"

"Mice, packrats, raccoons, possums. Hard to say. Hopefully not any bears."

"Snakes?"

"Rattlesnakes generally stay up in the foothills or mountain timber this time of year. There could be some bull snakes or other harmless reptiles."

Harmless was not his concern when it came to snakes. A snake was a snake. He got a glimpse of a smile that was trying to break across her lips and suspected she might be joshing him. "Well, I'll just have to boot out any uninvited tenants, I guess. Now, you had some other business to discuss."

"Percival Garth will be in town Wednesday. You should be at my office at one o'clock to prepare for a meeting with Mister Garth at two o'clock. We need to decide if you are going sign on with him before we speak with the Beadle lawyer. His name is Samuel Towne. He will be at my office the next day, same time."

"Can't you just take care of this?"

"No. You will be there or find another lawyer. Are you prepared to do a longer novel for Garth under your own name? He is going to want something within a year."

"Books would sell better if I wrote under West or Bowie."

"Forget about it. Towne sent me the contract you had with Beadle. The publisher owns the pen names. Another writer can be West or Bowie if you don't do some more books. The good news is that they must think your work is special because they are pressing for you to do the novels, especially the Marshal Tyree stories."

"I came up with the ideas for the pen names."

"It doesn't matter."

"Let's go look at my new home."

Chapter 59

G RANT ROLLED OUT of the blankets that were spread out on the hard cedarwood floor of his cabin. The sun would rise soon, and he had scheduled a tub at the local barbershop for a bath after a haircut and shave. After that, he would change into the new suit he had purchased at the Oaks General Store two days earlier and was undergoing emergency alterations by Samantha Morris or one of her assistants at the town's newest business. The fire at The Tipi had forced purchase of an entire new wardrobe. Fortunately, a single suit, which his lawyer had mandated, should satisfy his 'dress-up' needs for a long time. When he got back to writing at his hideaway, he could work naked if he chose.

Of course, if he could not negotiate book contracts, he might be required to seek other work, for his bank balance was sinking fast. The brief duration of the sheriff's

Ron Schwab

job would probably not yield much more than one hundred dollars. Hannah Locke made him a bit nervous. He knew she was planning to press the publishers for more money than he would settle for. He feared she might kill the opportunities with her aggressiveness. Well, at least he had a roof over his head now, and a better roof than he had anticipated.

The cabin was clean and seemingly well-constructed and had not been occupied by creatures. Hannah warned, though, that the presence of food on the property could bring on uninvited guests. He went outside into the brisk mountain air to piss but did not make the trip to the privy some distance from the rear of the residence. Afterward, half-frozen, he got dressed in the clothes he had been wearing for a good number of days but put fresh underwear and socks in his saddlebags to don after his bath. The other garments would be changed at the general store when he retrieved the new suit.

He hoped to enjoy breakfast at The Chowdown since he had neither food nor cooking implements and utensils in the house or, for that matter, a dining table and chairs. There were some nice cupboards in the kitchen area, but they were currently bare. He doubted he would find time to remedy these deficiencies today. It occurred to him that the mere daily living tasks had become more complicated than chasing down outlaws.

Later, dressed in the new blue suit, white shirt and string bowtie, Grant appeared at the Ramsey and Locke office, where he encountered Samantha Morris and Hannah looking at some papers on the reception area counter. Samantha had measured him for the suit and supervised alterations. She turned and smiled at him when he entered. "The suit looks splendid on you, Grant." She looked at Hannah, who seemed to be appraising him with undue scrutiny, Grant thought. "Don't you agree, Hannah?" she said.

With a trace of a smile, Hannah said. "You did a nice job on the suit, Samantha, and he doesn't clean up too badly. Now, as to your task. I don't want to get involved unless there is no other choice. I would like to see you take over the banking matters, make the deposits and pay the bills. Try to sell him on the notion."

Sammy gathered up the papers from the counter and put them in a leather satchel. "I'll see what I can do and try to report back in another week if that would be all right."

"That would be fine. I do appreciate what you are trying to do. I have no doubt you will be successful."

Sammy tossed him a look and another smile as she departed the office.

"Come in," Hannah said, and Grant followed the lawyer to her office. Hannah immediately turned her attention to papers spread out on her desktop, nodding and gesturing for him to claim a chair.

Finally, she looked up and spoke. "Mister Garth has shown up prepared. He came in on the morning train and first thing left a contract for our review. I think he hopes to depart Lockwood with your signature tomorrow. I assume he will bring another set with him." She collected the half dozen sheets of paper, sorting as she placed them in order and slid them across the desktop to Grant.

Grant said, "I will glance at them. Why don't you summarize?"

"He wants you to contract for a 90,000-word western novel. It is to be historically and geographically accurate."

"That's three or four times the length of a dime novel."

"The contract provides that you must furnish the completed book within one year, subject to edits or revisions required by the publisher. The book will be published under the name of Grant Coolidge, no pseudonym. Your previous works as a dime novelist will not be noted in any promotions or publicity. Garth seems quite astute in the matter of publishing issues or has a lawyer who is. He evidently anticipated that Beadle owns the right to your other names."

"Seems like he is taking quite a chance on an unknown," Grant said.

"He obviously sees something in your work that suggests he can sell it. He may look to a tie-in with a larger publishing house. You don't care if you get your money. Look at page three."

Grant flipped the pages and looked at a sheet that set forth compensation terms. His eyes blinked in disbelief when he saw the figures. "Three-thousand-dollar advance when I sign the contract. I don't believe it."

"That would be applied to your share of royalties of fifteen per cent of all sales. If your royalties are less than the advance, you still keep your advance."

"I don't need royalties at that figure."

"Yes, you do. But you must refund all but $1000 of the advance if you fail to meet the deadline. Can you produce a novel within a year, especially if you are still doing the West and Bowie books?"

"I've already thought about a novel for Garth with a working title, 'Accidental Sheriff.'"

Hannah surrendered a rare smile. "I wonder what inspired that?"

"Dedicated to Bright Moon Dupree."

"That would be a wonderful tribute."

"With Garth's money, I could forgo any other projects, but if the book doesn't sell, I would have cut ties with Beadle. And I could easily produce six dime novels for Beadle. I didn't tell you, I guess. Three are finished with just a little editing."

"Are you serious?"

"Two Marshal Tyree books by Bowie, and one featuring Wild Bill Hickok by West. They were in the satchel that Moon tossed out my bedroom window the night of the fire. I haven't talked about it; I suppose because I worried that she had lost her life over those damned manuscripts."

"I truly doubt that, but it was something she wanted to do for you."

Hannah returned to the contract's first page and reviewed the document paragraph by paragraph with Grant, who was not that interested in the details. When she was finished, she asked, "What do you think?"

"What do you think?"

"I am quite satisfied with it. Very fair and thin on legal jargon. I would just like to hear how Mister Garth proposes to market this book."

In answer to her question, there was a rap on the door and Fish brought Percival Garth into the room wearing the same green suit he had worn on the train at their first meeting. He doffed his hat and grinned broadly as he stepped forward to accept Hannah's handshake. "A pleasure to meet you in person, ma'am."

Then he turned to Grant, "And so wonderful to see my guardian angel again. I hired a young man with a carriage near the station to take me and my bags to the hotel. I mentioned that I was here to visit with you. My heavens, you picked up right where you left off with me. You are already a legend, it appears."

They sat down, and Hannah looked at Grant, who could feel the heat on his cheeks that were likely flushed. She said, "Guardian angel? You never told me."

Garth said, "He saved my life." He laughed. "Or Marshal Tyree did." He told her the story of the altercation on the train, while Grant wished he could just creep out the door and disappear.

"He is a modest man," Hannah said, as they spoke about Grant as if he were not present in the room, "but now I suggest we turn to business. I want to thank you for leaving the contract at my office for review."

"I hope you found it satisfactory."

"Frankly, it addressed any legal concerns and was well-drafted."

"A young lawyer in Lincoln just setting up shop there did the work. William Jennings Bryan is his name. He is hungry, bright and hard-working. I intend to have him do the work for all my enterprises. But I sense you have a reservation."

"Curiosity more than anything. As far as the reading public is concerned, Grant is a new writer. You are paying him a generous advance, and you would certainly expect to earn it back. My client, of course, is interested in potential royalties beyond the advance. How do you expect to market the book?"

"The contract permits me to work with another publisher, even publish under its umbrella, so to speak."

"Yes."

"I sent three of Grant's dime novels to a publisher friend of mine before I decided to offer this contract. He saw the same talent I did and agreed to partner with me if he liked a full-length book. He is one of the most successful publishers in America. You may have heard of him. Samuel Clemens."

"Also known as Mark Twain?"

"That Samuel Clemens."

Grant said, "I am ready to sign."

Chapter 60

S AMANTHA MORRIS SCOLDED Trouble as they stood outside the livery. "I have gone over the bank statements from the bank. They don't come close to reconciling with the figures you have been giving me. I am not going to keep books if you don't give me the information I need."

"I know what I got in my head."

"I can't prepare reports for the bank and Hannah from what is in your head. On second thought, maybe there would be nothing to report."

"Well, I write down the drafts when I think of it, deposits, too."

"I need all of them, and you are writing drafts for the other businesses off the livery account and vice versa. Your wages to me will take all your profits if I am forced to spend the time to straighten this out every month."

That grabbed his attention. "What do you want me to do?"

"Set things up at the bank, so I can handle your banking, write drafts and the like."

"I don't know."

"Give the bills, cash and drafts to me every week. I will pay everything and make deposits. I will give you a copy of the reports I give the bank and lawyer, so you know where every penny goes. It will save you loads of time, and you can use that time to make more money."

He had never thought of it that way. It seemed that Adam Smith had said something about that. He sighed. "We will try that for three months and see how it works."

"That seems fair, and I know it will please Hannah. She has authority to take over all the accounts, you know."

"You been talking to her, ain't you?"

"I won't deny it. She is my boss, too, you know. By the way, I saw the sheriff in her office today looking like something of a dandy."

"If you're talking about Grant, he ain't sheriff anymore."

"He's not?"

"Nope. Dropped his badge on the desk yesterday and said he was done. Jim told me. Bushwa's out, too. Works out all right. Jim will have to use the buggy for a spell—

can't ride a horse yet—but he can come into the office to tend to things there. He wants to get back to work, and Ma wants him out of the house."

"Well, your friend can get back to writing his books now. I think Hannah likes him more than a little."

"What makes you think that?"

"Just stuff a female notices. She wasn't looking at him like he was just a client this morning."

"He's still hurting terrible from losing Moon."

"I didn't say anything was going on. I just spied a spark there. Maybe it starts a fire, and maybe it doesn't."

"I think we ought to stoke our own sparks and not concern ourselves about somebody else's. This courting needs to liven up some."

"Is that an invitation to next week's barn dance?"

He shrugged. She had him cornered now. "I guess we got to start someplace."

Chapter 61

AFTER DEPOSITING GARTH'S draft in the Gaines Bank the previous afternoon, Grant wondered why he even cared to meet the Beadle lawyer. Today, though, reality returned, and he was prepared to make a commitment. If the Garth novel dropped dead heading out the gate, his career as a top dollar novelist would die with it. The dime novels would support him indefinitely with steady income.

Today, he sat in Hannah Locke's office with his lawyer and Samuel Towne, the lawyer Beadle had assigned to negotiate the new contract. Towne, a skinny, pale-complected young man, seemed a bit intimidated by Hannah. Certainly, his shaky, high-pitched voice did little to diminish Hannah's authoritarian tone. Grant was almost insulted that the publisher had sent an errand boy on this mission.

He found himself dozing as the lawyers discussed possible contract terms, but his mind was alerted when he sensed negotiations were concluding.

Towne said, "My clients will not agree to royalties and will not consent to anything other than outright copyright ownership by Beadle. You can see from the prior contracts that Mister Coolidge's dime novels are works for hire. I am sorry, but my instructions were that I could not concede those points."

Hannah said, "My client will not do the novels for the paltry sums he has been paid in the past. If five hundred dollars is the best you can do, we had just as well pack up and call it a day."

"Well, my client recognizes there is some advantage to the consistency of using the same author for the series books." He plucked two sets of fastened sheets out of the leather bag on the floor next to his chair and placed them on the desk. "For a three-year contract for six novels annually, I am authorized to fill in the sum of seven hundred dollars per book."

Hannah opened a desk drawer and produced two sheets of parchment. She passed one to Towne. "Two copies of a two-year contract. The agreement provides for six novels annually for the sum of one thousand dollars per book. No royalty rights for the author. Beadle retains the copyrights and exclusive use of pen names. Note, however, that my client is entitled to contract with other publishers for works under his own name or such other pen names he might select."

"Dime novels that might compete with those he does for Beadle?"

"He has no current plans for other dime novels, but you may assure your client that Beadle is not his only opportunity. The agreements are already signed by Mister Coolidge. Take them with you, have them signed by the company president and return one to my office. If I do not receive confirmation of acceptance by telegram within two weeks, I will telegraph withdrawal of this offer."

A flustered Samuel Towne said, "I will discuss this with my client immediately upon my return to New York. I can make no commitment, however."

After Towne departed, Hannah said, "Well, I feel badly for poor Mister Towne. He was no doubt the courier for a large law firm and will take a scolding from his superiors. But the fact that Beadle would send any lawyer this far signals the value they place on your services. They will sign."

"If I didn't have the Garth contract and advance in the bank, I likely would have settled for five hundred dollars.

That young man certainly did not fit my image of a lawyer."

"Do I fit your image of a lawyer?"

He chuckled. "Well, no. Before you, I had never seen or heard of a female lawyer."

"But there are others. Not many now, but they are on the way. I won't live to see it, but someday there will be as many or more women in the law as men. Many will be judges."

He shrugged. "Could be, but it is hard for me to envision."

"Your picture of a lawyer is a stoop-shouldered man with a potbelly, a thin, black moustache and dark, beady eyes."

He gave her a perturbed look. "Why do you say that?"

"Four of your books include lawyers, and they are all described roughly in that way. I notice such things. I suggest a woman lawyer in your next novel—perhaps one with auburn hair and green eyes."

He convinced himself to take her jibe with a sense of humor. "You are cast."

She smiled. "I want to read it before publication. Now, tell me how your move into the cabin is coming. We should be ready to make the property transfer next week."

"It's not. I expect to go over to the furniture store and select a few things after we are finished here. The extra room will be an office, and I will get a desk and chair, some bookcases maybe. The other stuff I will put off, I guess."

"What do you sleep on?"

"The floor. I will purchase a bed and kitchen table and a few chairs as soon as I get around to it. I don't even own any oil lamps. Nothing for the kitchen—pots, dishes, utensils. I should get some food basics in the house."

"I have an idea. Jasmine asked if we might have you over for dinner Saturday."

"Jasmine?"

"Absolutely. She is coming around. She realizes now that your action likely saved her life. You are not a hero yet, but you are working your way there. Primrose is a blessing, and together they seem to be finding their ways back from their terrible experiences. Anyway, you would not wish to eat my cooking, but Jazzie has been cooking in the boarding house since her chin reached the table-top. She and Primrose will prepare the meal."

"I am honored. Of course, I will be there."

"Moon would be delighted. I know she would want you to be an important part of her daughter's life. That is something you can do for Moon—and yourself. School is out for the summer on Friday, and the girls could use a project. If things go well on Saturday, why don't you ask them to take charge of choosing the things for your cabin? I know you are dreading it."

"An excellent idea. Do you really think they would do that?"

"I will prepare them for the possibility."

"I guess I can consider it done. Maybe we can get past this tragic chapter and still have a happy ending . . . all of us. Somehow, I don't think this story is over yet."

About the Author

Ron Schwab is the author of the popular Western series, *The Blood Hounds, The Law Wranglers*, *The Coyote Saga*, and *The Lockes*. His novels *Grit* and *Old Dogs* were both awarded the Western Fictioneers Peacemaker Award for Best Western Novel, and *Cut Nose* was a finalist for the Western Writers of America Best Western Historical Novel.

Ron and his wife, Bev, divide their time between their home in Fairbury, Nebraska and their cabin in the Kansas Flint Hills.

For more information about Ron Schwab and his books, you may visit the author's website at www.RonSchwabBooks.com.